Also by Tony Strong

THE POISON TREE
THE DEATH PIT

and published by Bantam Books

THE DECOY
TONY STRONG

BANTAM BOOKS

London • New York • Toronto • Sydney • Auckland

THE DECOY
A BANTAM BOOK : 0 553 81365 X

Originally published in Great Britain by Doubleday
a division of Transworld Publishers

PRINTING HISTORY
Doubleday edition published 2001
Bantam edition published 2002

1 3 5 7 9 10 8 6 4 2

Set in 11/12pt Sabon by
Falcon Oast Graphic Art Ltd.

Bantam Books are published by Transworld Publishers,
61–63 Uxbridge Road, London W5 5SA,
a division of The Random House Group Ltd,
in Australia by Random House Australia (Pty) Ltd,
20 Alfred Street, Milsons Point, Sydney, NSW 2061, Australia,
in New Zealand by Random House New Zealand Ltd,
18 Poland Road, Glenfield, Auckland 10, New Zealand
and in South Africa by Random House (Pty) Ltd,
Endulini, 5a Jubilee Road, Parktown 2193, South Africa.

Printed and bound in Great Britain by
Cox & Wyman Ltd, Reading, Berkshire.

THE DECOY

PROLOGUE

On the day of departure, guests are requested to vacate their rooms by noon.

By eleven o'clock the fifth floor of the Lexington Hotel has nearly emptied. This is midtown Manhattan, where even the tourists are on busy schedules of galleries and department stores and sights. Any late sleepers have been woken by the noise of the maids, chattering to each other in Spanish as they come and go from the big laundry cupboard behind the lift, preparing the rooms for another influx of guests that afternoon.

Dotted down the hallway, discarded breakfast trays show which rooms still have to be cleaned.

There's no tray outside room 507.

Each morning, a folded copy of the *New York Times* is delivered to every room, with the hotel's compliments.

In the case of room 507, the compliment has been refused. The paper lies on the mat, untouched.

Consuela Alvarez leaves 507 till last. Eventually, when all the other rooms are done, she can leave it no longer. She taps on the door with her pass key, calls 'Maid', and listens for a reply.

None comes.

The first thing Consuela notices, as she lets herself in, is the cold. An icy draught is blowing through the drapes. She clucks disapprovingly as she goes to the window and hauls on the cord. Grey light floods the room. She bangs the window closed ostentatiously.

The person in the bed doesn't stir.

'You have to wake up now, please.'

The bed clothes are pulled right up over the face, smoothing the body's contours, like something buried under layers of snow.

Consuela has a sudden sense of foreboding. Last year there was a suicide on the second floor. A bad business – a boy hanged himself in the bathroom. And the hotel had been fully booked; they'd had to clean the room and get it ready for the next occupant at five o'clock.

Consuela crosses herself. Nervously, she puts her hand on the bed covers, where a shoulder should be, and shakes it.

After a moment, a red flower blossoms on the white linen, where her hand has pressed.

Consuela knows there's something wrong now, something very bad. She touches the bed again, pressing with just a finger this time. Again, like ink spreading through blotting paper, a red anemone blossoms on the white covers.

Consuela summons all her courage and yanks the bed clothes back.

For a long moment she doesn't move. Then, instinctively, she lifts her right hand to cross herself again. But this time the hand that touches her forehead never completes the gesture: comes down, trembling, to her mouth, to stifle a scream instead.

PART ONE

'We are all hanged, or should be.'
Les Fleurs du Mal, Baudelaire

CHAPTER ONE

Her friend hasn't showed.

That's what you'd think if you saw her, waiting on her own in the bar of the Royalton Hotel, trying to make her Virgin Mary last all evening: just another young professional waiting for her date. Perhaps a little prettier than most. A little more confident. A little more daringly dressed. She hasn't come straight from the office, that's for sure.

The bar is packed, and when a table finally becomes free she goes and sits at it. Across the room a young man wearing too much jewellery catches her eye and smiles. She looks away. He says something to his drinking buddies, who laugh briefly before returning to their beers.

'Excuse me?'

She looks up. A man is standing in front of her. He's wearing a suit, but one of an expensive, casual cut that suggests he's something more than the usual corporate drone, its collar lapped by hair that's just a little too long for Wall Street.

'Yes?' she says.

'I'm sorry, but . . . this is my table. I just went to the restroom.' He points at the glass on the table. 'I left my drink to keep my place.'

Around them, one or two heads have turned

curiously in their direction. But there's going to be no confrontation, no overspill of New York stress. The woman is already standing up. She pulls her bag onto her shoulder. 'I'm sorry,' she says. 'I didn't realize—'

The heads turn away again, back to their conversations.

There's a brief shuffle as the man stands aside to let her pass and she moves in the same direction, a fleeting *pas de deux*.

Of course, he asks her to stay. Who wouldn't?

'Unless you don't mind sharing,' he says, gesturing at the table.

For a moment, she seems to hesitate – but after all, the bar is crowded, and there's nowhere else to sit now. She shrugs. 'Why not?'

They both sit down again. Surreptitiously, out of the corners of their eyes, they examine each other more closely. She's wearing Donna Karan; a soft black woollen jacket which clings to her slight frame, sets off her dark hair and her pale skin, makes her eyes look more startlingly blue than they really are.

'Are you waiting on someone?' he asks, and his voice has changed subtly: a thickening of interest, of sexual attention. 'Maybe he's been held up by the snow. It's chaos out at LaGuardia. That's why I'm staying an extra night.'

And she smiles to herself, because it's really pretty neat, the way he tries to find out if this person she's waiting for is a man or a woman, while at the same time letting her know he's on his own.

'Looks like I could be here a while,' she says. 'Hey ho.'

'Hey ho,' he repeats. He isn't quite sure what she means by that. 'Let me buy you another one of those, anyway.' He beckons to the waitress. 'What are you drinking?'

'Thanks. A Bloody Mary.'

'And where are you from? I'm trying to place that accent.'

'From Idaho, originally.'

'Really? I never met a girl from Idaho before.'

Something about the way he says 'met' makes it sound provocative, almost sexual, and she smiles. 'But you *meet* a lot of girls, right?'

He grins back at her. 'A few.'

Somewhat to his surprise he finds that they're flirting now, their bodies carrying on conversations of their own as he tells her he's a lawyer, and she says no, surely he's not ugly enough to be a lawyer. In the music industry, he says, and she asks, here on business or pleasure?

Well, he says, hopefully both. He leans back and crosses his legs, smiles an expansive, confident smile. He has time for a little fun, after all.

'Before you fly back tomorrow to your wife and kids.'

For an instant the smile flickers uncertainly. 'What makes you think I'm married?'

'The good-looking ones always are,' she says.

The waitress finally brings their drinks. She's been gone five minutes, and the lawyer gives her a hard time. He's showing off, and the waitress apologizes sulkily, blaming the crowds. She turns away with a little tug at her right ear, almost as if she can pull his words out of it and flick them to the floor. Without breaking her conversation or taking her eyes off the lawyer, the girl who says she's from Idaho thinks, *I could use that*.

It's put away somewhere deep, somewhere in the filing system.

The lawyer's name is Alan. He hands her a business card on which his name is written in embossed, silvery letters. She tells him her name is Claire. She apologizes for not having a card. She doesn't carry business cards, she murmurs, in her line of work. An amused smile twitches at the corners of her mouth.

He asks her what she does. 'As little as possible,' she says. She nods at the waitress, who's being harassed by another table now, and tells him she used to do that, before.

'Before what?'

'Before I realized there were easier ways to make a buck.'

Understanding appears in his eyes like a lightbulb.

He doesn't rush it, though. He tells her about some of his clients, back in Atlanta – the famous teenage idol he names who likes underage girls, and the macho heavy-metal star who's gay but doesn't dare to admit it. He tells her, with a hint of emphasis, how much money there is to be made, doing what he does, drawing up contracts for those who are temperamentally unlikely to abide by them, necessitating the services of people like him at both ends, both the commission of the contract and its eventual dissolution. And finally he suggests that, since her friend clearly isn't going to show, they could move on someplace else, to a restaurant or a club, whichever she'd prefer.

'Somewhere . . . expensive,' he adds, with just a hint of emphasis.

Encouraged by her silence, he says quietly, 'Or we could just get some room service. I'm staying right upstairs.'

'Well,' she says, 'room service can be pretty expensive, too.' She leaves the briefest of pauses. 'If *I'm* in the room.'

He exhales. 'I'm not the only one who's here on business, right?'

Again, that smile pulls at the corners of her mouth. 'You sure worked that one out fast, Alan.'

'I'm a lawyer, after all. It's my job to know when a witness isn't telling the truth.'

'Am I a witness?' she murmurs, and he shakes his head.

'Hopefully more of a participant.'

She watches the waitress pull a pen out of her hair so a customer can sign. Another one for the filing system.

'That trick with the table was pretty neat,' he says admiringly. 'Picking me up right under the noses of the bar staff.'

She shrugs. 'You get to learn these things.'

'So,' he says, leaning forward conspiratorially. 'Just how expensive does room service get around here?' His grin has widened. He is a lawyer, after all. The negotiations are part of the fun.

'How much is it usually?'

He frowns. 'You think I make a habit of this?'

She touches his arm. 'Let's just say you seem to know what you're doing.'

Mollified, he says, 'How does two hundred sound?'

'That's what they charge in Atlanta, is it?'

'For that', he assures her, 'you get a lot in Atlanta.'

'What's the most you've ever paid?'

'Five hundred,' he admits.

'Double it,' she says softly.

'Seven hundred?'

'For a lawyer, Alan, your math is frankly terrible.' She shakes her head in mock sorrow. 'Nice meeting you.'

'OK, OK,' he says quickly. 'We have a deal.'

'What's your room number?'

'Fourteen oh nine.'

'We'll go up in separate elevators. You can catch me up in the corridor. And I'll need half the money in advance.'

He blinks.

'I'll be right ahead of you,' she points out.

'Sure. It's just . . . isn't this a little public?'

'Which is why I feel safer doing it here. Just put the money on the table, like you're paying the waitress.'

He lays six bills on the table. As they get up to leave, she casually picks up five of them and drops them in her bag.

The tiny elevators leading from the lobby are packed with guests going up to their rooms. 'Fourteen, please,' she says, unable to reach. Someone presses it for her. Alan waits for the next one. He looks impatient.

The elevator stops on the third to let out some guests. She gets out with them and, immediately the doors have closed behind her, turns and presses Down. While the second elevator is coming she gets the Minicam out of her bag and hits Rewind, Play, Rewind, until she hears her own voice say, 'You can catch me up in the corridor.' Then she

16

puts her palm over the lens and presses Record again.

She's in the next elevator now, travelling back down. A couple of models, dressed for a night of clubbing, look at her curiously as she puts the camera back in her bag. She ignores them.

By the time she steps back into the foyer Alan is going up thirteen floors in the slowest elevator in NYC.

Outside it's still snowing. The fire hydrants along the sidewalk are all wearing lopsided white toupees of snow. Claire crosses the street quickly and walks to where a stretch limo is waiting with its engine running. She pulls open the door.

She's about forty-five, Alan's wife, with the kind of jaded but expensive looks that suggest she was part of the music business herself before she started having his children and hosting his corporate dinners. She's sitting very close to Henry on the back seat, shivering despite the warm air blowing from the heaters. She looks terrified.

'Everything OK?' Henry asks.

'Fine,' Claire says. She's dropped the accent now. In her real voice, which is British, she asks the client, as she always asks, 'Are you sure you want to hear this? Sure you wouldn't rather go home and make it work?'

And the woman says, as they always say, 'I want to know.'

Claire hands her the machine. 'The bottom line is, he's a regular user of prostitutes. Not just when he's away, either. He talked about paying up to five hundred dollars a time back in Atlanta.'

The wife's eyes fill with tears. Henry puts his arm around her.

'I'm sorry,' Claire says awkwardly. She slides out of the limo. Henry passes her an envelope with his free hand. Four hundred dollars. Not bad for an hour's gig.

As he hands it to her he whispers, 'Did he give you any?'

'Uh-uh. I left him in the lobby. It's all on the disc. I swear.'

'You know I'd know if you were lying.'

'I know you would.'

He nods, satisfied, and she puts her hand in the air for a cab.

Claire Rodenburg. Almost twenty-five years old, and almost beautiful. Eye colour, blue; hair colour, flexible; occupation – well, if you looked in her passport you'd read *actress*, but in truth that was a little flexible as well.

She hadn't realized, when she'd boarded her cut-price flight from Gatwick six months earlier, how difficult it would be to get work – any work – in the States. Used to the relaxed attitude of British employers to casual workers, she had instead discovered a labour market where enthusiastic students were two a penny – or rather, a dime a dozen – where you couldn't open a bank account without a social security number, or rent a room without a reference from your bank.

She'd managed to cobble together a patchwork of part-time jobs, sprinting from her rush-hour cover in a Midtown deli to a bar on the Lower East Side, where the owner cared more about the way his staff looked than their paperwork. But he had an inexhaustible supply of pretty girls to choose from, and it didn't make sense to let any of them stay too long. That way, if the IRS or Immigration came checking, he could claim the new girl's forms were in the post. After three months he told Claire, not unkindly, that it was time to move on.

She was blowing everything she earned on seeing shows, not the dumbed-down blockbusters or endless Euro-musicals that played to packed houses on Broadway, but the smaller, performance-orientated pieces at Circle in the Square and the Pyramid Club, getting to know the names of the best directors and casting agents.

The auditions advertised in *Variety* were only for chorus parts and extras, of course, but she had to start somewhere.

At her first audition the casting director asked her to stay behind. When everyone else had gone, she'd approached Claire thoughtfully. In her hand was the form every hopeful had to fill in before the session, giving their name, height, previous experience and agent.

'It says here you don't have an agent, honey,' the woman had purred.

'Not in this country. I had one back home.'

'I'd like you to meet a friend of mine. I think she might be interested in representing you.'

The agent, Marcie Matthews, had indeed been delighted to meet Claire. She'd taken her to lunch at Orso, an Italian restaurant in the middle of the theatre district, and thrown around the names of shows for which she could get Claire auditions, directors she must meet, film producers she would be perfect for.

Until she discovered Claire didn't have a work permit.

'Get out of here. No green card?'

'Does it really matter?'

'It does if you want to work,' Marcie had said bluntly.

'Isn't there anything I could do? Just to earn some money?'

'Sure. Table dancing, stripograms, nude modelling. What they call the glamour industry, though personally I don't imagine it's all that glamorous.' Marcie had waved a ringed hand dismissively. 'I don't get involved in that stuff, but I can give you the names of some people who do.'

'There's really nothing else?'

Marcie sighed. 'I shouldn't say this, but I've got a lot of friends in this business. Maybe I can slip you into a few things.' She held up her hand to forestall Claire's thanks. 'And voice-overs. The advertising people always want British accents. But it's going to be tough. If I was you, and if I really wanted to work in the States, I'd go right back home and apply for a card.'

Claire had shrugged.

'You want to stay in New York? Well, I don't blame you. But don't expect it to welcome you with open arms. The days when we embraced the huddled masses yearning to be free are long gone.'

Claire found herself another bar job and waited.

And waited.

There was a single voice-over, and an audition for a non-speaking part in a pop video. In the casting session she'd had to strip down to her underwear and mime riding on horseback. She didn't get the part.

Another month passed.

She'd met some other young aspiring actors by now, and was rooming with one of them, a friendly

Texan called Bessie. Claire paid her in cash, which took care of the bank-account problem. Unfortunately, it didn't take care of the fact that she never had any cash in the first place.

Then she got a phone call from Marcie, asking her if she'd have a chat with an old friend of hers called Henry Mallory.

'I'll be honest with you,' the other woman had said on the phone. 'It's something you might not want to do. But the money is amazing and, well, I know you'd be good at it.'

CHAPTER TWO

Detective Frank Durban rides up in the elevator with the Lexington's manager, a pile of equipment in metal flight cases, a major crime scene search officer and a couple of tourists with subway maps tucked into their money belts, wet with snow.

It's the fourth load of equipment to go up, and the hotel manager is developing a twitch.

The silence is broken by one of the tourists, who wants to know what's going on. Are they shooting a movie?

And, in fact, it's not such a stupid notion, the logistics of a modern crime scene demanding much the same equipment as a film shoot: lights, cameras – both stills and video – playback monitors, finger-print people with their little make-up cases tucked under their arms and a small army of technicians with walkie-talkies strapped to their belts.

'That's right,' the manager says nervously. 'A movie.'

Frank Durban lifts his eyes to the elevator's roof.

'Who's in it?' the man's wife asks. 'Anyone famous?'

The manager looks at Frank desperately, but Frank's inspecting the ceiling tiles.

'River Phoenix,' the manager blurts at last. The man's wife nods, impressed.

'He's dead,' Durban says under his breath.

'I mean, it's about River Phoenix,' the manager corrects himself. 'They're using a double.'

The lift stops at four and the couple get out. 'Need any extras?' the man asks, holding the door.

'He's really good,' the woman agrees. 'Go on, honey, do your Clint Eastwood.'

Durban sighs and looks at his watch ostentatiously.

Rattled, the manager flaps the tourist's fingers away from the elevator door. 'Have a good evening. I hope you enjoy your stay,' he snaps.

They ride up to the fifth in silence.

After she leaves the lawyer's wife, Claire tells the cab to take her to a theatre on 53rd and Broadway. Bessie, her roommate, has just opened in a musical, and Claire promised to drop by the cast party.

It isn't actually a first night, just a change of cast in a show that's already been running for two years. Since it's a sell-out, opportunities for self-expression are somewhat limited; even more limited than they usually would be, playing a singing, dancing sheep.

When Claire gets there the actors are standing around backstage, flushed with applause, and the place smells of make-up and scenery paint and spotlights, the peculiar addictive smell of a theatre. She pauses and breathes it all in.

For a brief moment a pang of longing stabs at her guts. This is the forbidden kingdom.

She pushes the feeling away. It's unfair to Bessie to get jealous on her big night. She finds her friend and gives her a hug of congratulation.

Bessie returns the hug a little absent-mindedly. She's still working, Claire sees, one of a group of young actors shamelessly flattering the director, a fat toad of a man whose jokes, surely, can't be half as funny as their laughter suggests. Claire leaves her to it. Bessie loves her like a sister, but when all's said and done, Claire's part of the competition.

She looks at her watch. The lawyer, pacing up and down in his suite at the Royalton, will just be getting a phone call to say his wife's downstairs.

'Hey, Claire,' a voice says.

It's Raoul Walsh, a guy she went out with a few times when she first came to New York. 'How's tricks?' he asks.

Is it her imagination, or does he give the word 'tricks' a subtle emphasis, a hint at its other meaning?

'Not bad,' she says. 'My agent's got me some voice-overs. And I'm auditioning for *Vanya* next week.'

'Really? I heard they gave the last part to Carol. Carol Reuben,' he says, looking over her shoulder and nodding at a passing acquaintance.

'Oh,' she says. 'I hadn't heard that.'

'Still, voice-overs, that's great. Really great.' He smiles at her, a plastic New York smile.

She thinks, He's a good enough actor to fake that better, if he wanted to.

'And how about your investigator friend,' he drawls. 'Still working for him?'

'Henry Mallory,' she says. 'Yes, sometimes.'

'Henry Mallory,' he says. His lips twitch. 'My God, Henry *Mallory*. I loved that guy when I was a kid. When he was in *Gumshoe*. Is he, you know, OK?' He mimes the gesture of drinking from a glass.

'Henry's fine,' she says wearily.

'Oh, well,' Raoul says, drifting away from her. 'I'll see you around, OK?'

It's true, Henry isn't even a real private detective. Once upon a time he played the part of an investigator in a television mini-series, from which his character was abruptly dropped. People said he'd been too drunk to read the cue cards.

Whatever the reason, he'd decided to change careers but not roles. He'd started a detective agency, a real one. There had been a court case once, long before her time, when the network had sued to stop him using the name of his character from the show.

Not surprisingly, matrimonial work is pretty much all he gets. That and missing pets.

All Marcie had told her on the phone was, 'Treat it as a go-see. If you get along with him, we'll talk some more. If you don't, it's just another wasted afternoon.'

Claire had taken the subway to the Lower East Side, and struggled with the grille of an ancient lift in a dilapidated office block. On the fourth floor there was a row of doors with company names in brown lettering, like something from an Edward Hopper painting. 'Sahid Import', 'Nutreen Clothing', 'Downey Insurance' and, finally, 'The Mallory Private Investigation Bureau'.

'I'm looking for Mr Mallory,' she'd said to the gaunt old man behind the desk.

'That's me,' he replied, swinging his feet stiffly onto the floor. His craggy face was still handsome, but his eyes were rheumy, the whites as yellow as his nicotine-stained fingers. 'And you must be the dame.'

'The dame?' Where she came from, dames were a part in pantomime.

'The dame who made the bishop kick a hole in a stained-glass window.'

She must have looked puzzled, because he'd laughed, a short, chesty bark. 'Don't they teach young actors anything these days? *Farewell My Lovely*, starring Dick Powell and Claire Trevor. All the best detective stories start with a dame.'

Suddenly she realized why the little room seemed so familiar. Henry Mallory had dressed his office like something out of a 1950s film noir. A heavy steel fan scythed smoke-filled air over a hat-stand, a pre-war filing cabinet, a bentwood chair and a brown deal desk. The only things missing were a Bakelite phone and a fifth of bourbon, and, as she soon discovered, the latter was missing only because Henry generally kept his fifths in the wastebasket.

One thing she never discovered, though, was whether the props were for the benefit of the customers or the proprietor.

'Marcie said you were auditioning—' she began.

Henry shook his head. 'Uh-uh. Not auditioning. Auditioning means a hundred talented people made to feel like stale meat on a rack. This is more like . . . executive recruitment. You've been head-hunted, Claire.'

'To do what?'

'To work for me.'

'As a *detective*? Listen, there must have been—'

'As an actress,' he interrupted. 'Marcie said you can act.'

26

She shrugged.

'But can you really?' he wondered aloud. His shoes swung up onto the desk again as he slouched back in the chair, looking at her with eyes that, despite being rheumy, were, she saw now, also bright with intelligence. 'Perhaps you can walk on a stage and do the things other actors do, all the little mannerisms and affectations that people call acting. But can you do it for real?' He gestured with his thumb in the direction of the street. 'Can you do it out there?'

'I've been acting professionally since I was fourteen.'

'Aha. A stage-school brat.'

'We weren't brats.'

'Takes one to know one.' This time the thumb jerked at his own chest. 'When *I* was fourteen I was being directed by Orson Welles.'

'You were in an *Orson Welles* movie?'

Henry winked and pushed the second chair at her with one of his feet. 'Take a seat,' he suggested, 'and I'll tell you about the time I was seduced by Audrey Hepburn.'

A week later, Claire sat in a quiet bar just off Central Park and allowed a businessman to tell her that his wife no longer attracted him. Afterwards, in a limo waiting just across the street, Henry handed her an envelope containing $500, and she handed the man's wife a Minidisc of their conversation.

Even in hindsight it seemed like a better deal than riding a horse in her underwear.

CHAPTER THREE

Frank Durban stares intently at the video monitor as the camera plays over the body. It tracks down, past the wrists, which have been handcuffed to the bedframe, past the grisly mess between the legs, towards the feet.

'There,' he says into his headset. 'Go in on that.'

The camera closes in on a two-inch square of white card at the foot of the bed.

'Take a look.'

The crime search officer takes the white square in surgically gloved hands and flips it over. It's a Polaroid, a close-up of what the video camera has just tracked past.

'Any sign of the camera?' Frank asks.

'No. There's a wallet, though,' the voice in his earpiece says. Frank, along with a small army of waiting technicians, is in the room next door to the murder scene, temporarily banished to prevent pristine evidence getting trampled before it's put on tape.

'Let's take a look.'

The camera focuses on the nightstand beside the bed. A gloved hand enters the frame, flips open the wallet and pulls out the driver's licence.

Even through the grain of the video monitor,

Frank can see from the photo that she had been an attractive woman.

'Stella Vogler. *Mrs* Stella Vogler. An apartment on Mercer,' the search officer says.

'Mercer?' Frank thinks hard. A SoHo address, and not a cheap one. 'But the room was booked in her name, right?'

'That's correct, sir,' says the manager, who's still hovering around.

Why book a hotel just a mile or so from her own apartment? Frank wonders.

The disembodied voice of the search officer breaks into his thoughts. 'So she comes here to meet her lover, he brings a few toys, some cuffs, a Polaroid to take some dirty snaps. Meanwhile her husband finds out, follows her, and – wham.'

'And after he's killed her in a jealous rage, he stops and takes a couple of photos himself,' Frank says drily. 'As you do.'

Stung, the crime search officer goes through the contents of the wallet.

'Six hundred bucks. It wasn't a robbery.'

'Well done, Sherlock,' Frank mutters under his breath.

'And what's this?' A note of malicious pleasure has crept into the other officer's voice. He holds a business card up to the camera lens. 'Looks like you've got some competition, detective.'

'What's that?'

' "The Mallory Private Investigation Bureau." Want me to give you the phone number?'

'Wait. What's that on the back?'

The officer turns the card over.

'Here,' he says, holding the card so it fills the monitor's screen.

On the back, someone has written in pencil,

Claire Rodenburg = the decoy.

'Yeah,' Frank says. 'Yeah, give me that number.'

Claire and a group of actors from the show go on to the Harley Bar. Even though it's gone midnight the place is packed. Springsteen blasts from the jukebox.

Claire orders a Martini. The barman fills a shot glass to the brim with Jack Daniels and slams it down on the counter.

'I asked for a *Martini*,' she shouts at him over the music and the crowd, pushing it back.

He pushes the glass back at her again. 'That's the way we make Martinis round here,' he yells cheerfully. He's Australian. He grins at her, daring her to complain. The men at the bar whoop and cheer.

He's young and muscular, wearing just a T-shirt despite the cold that surges in every time someone opens the door from the street, and she's already noticed the way his dishcloth, tucked into his belt, whisks round his muscular butt like a tail whenever he turns to the row of bottles behind the bar.

She picks up the glass, drains it and says, 'In that case, give me an Ocean Breeze.'

He pours another measure of Jack Daniels into a glass, then adds another measure of Jack Daniels, then finishes it off with another measure of Jack Daniels.

She tips it down her throat, and some of the guys at the bar break into a spontaneous round of applause.

Applause. Now there's a sound she hasn't heard in a while.

'And line me up a Long Island Iced Tea,' she says. 'With plenty of tea.'

She was never the most beautiful of Henry's women. In her opinion that would be Alana.

Alana has the hair of an urchin, the voice of a little girl and the figure of the model she used to be before she hit twenty-seven and the magazine bookings began to dry up. Alana is neurotic as a thoroughbred, and her habitually bare midriff is as taut as a tennis racquet.

Sometimes, though, there are men oblivious to Alana's cover-girl charms, and these men usually go for Lizzie. Or, more specifically, they go for Lizzie's breasts. Lizzie's breasts are big and creamy, and they undulate like a waterbed when she moves, which isn't very often. Claire especially covets the left one, the one with the scorpion tattoo on its upper slope.

And then there's Lola. While pretty isn't exactly a word you would use to describe Lola, she definitely has her fans. Half-Japanese, half-Jewish, with the unfathomable eyes of a geisha and the filthy mouth of a Brooklyn pimp, Lola used to be a stripper at a table-dancing club. Where her speciality, for an extra fifty bucks, was to lean over the punter's lap and, underneath the curtain of her long black hair, violate the club's no-touching rule for about ten seconds or so. She didn't even bother to undo their zippers, she told Claire once. She didn't need to.

Claire never liked to ask how Henry found Lola. But though she might not be the prettiest, or the sexiest, or the sassiest, Claire has one quality that, as far as Henry's concerned, makes her unique.

She gets results.

Henry maintains it's because there's something about her that makes her seem more approachable than his other girls. Claire knows that isn't true. It's because, alone amongst his decoys, she can *act*.

Paul, who runs the drama class she's joined, likes to say acting is called that because it's all about action. It's not who you pretend to be but who you become, not what you say but what you do.

Claire isn't sure. Maybe this Method stuff she's learning is just Hollywood bullshit.

But she's seen actors go on stage with a streaming cold and have it dry up for three hours, only to start sneezing again when the make-up comes off in the green room.

And she's seen men who would throw away everything they have – wives, fiancées, families, careers – just for the chance of a few minutes with a figment of their imaginations.

With her.

Claire isn't proud of what she does for a living. But she's proud as hell of the way she does it.

CHAPTER FOUR

Dr Susan Ling carefully slides a long steel thermometer out of the dead woman's rectum and holds it up to the light. Involuntarily, Frank averts his eyes.

'Forty-eight hours,' the medical examiner pronounces. 'Give or take a few.'

'You sound pretty confident of that,' Frank says.

'Sure.' Dr Ling reaches out to the buttocks and shakes one dispassionately, as one might shake a jelly. 'Rigor has been and gone. It might be forty-four if she put up a struggle.'

The crime scene has been filmed from every angle now. The handcuffs securing the corpse's wrists to the bedframe have been removed so the pathologist can make her examination. The room smells of meat.

Stella Vogler's buttocks and shoulder blades are a dark, angry purple, as if all the blood in her body has slowly pooled and solidified in the lowest part of her. Which, Frank knows, is pretty much what happens.

The bite marks and belt weals patterning her thighs, buttocks and lower back are a less familiar sight.

Dr Ling steps back to the body and signals to her

assistant, who helps her turn the corpse back over. The corpse's head shakes from side to side, groggily. The mess between its legs slithers and twists. Frank clears his throat. 'What killed her?'

Like all the other people in the room, apart from the pathologist, he's standing with his hands in his pockets. It gives the scene a deceptively casual air. Only when all the technical people are done will they be allowed to take them out.

'Well, I can't give you a definite answer until we cut her up, but I don't think there's much doubt. See this line around the neck?' Frank had, but he'd known better than to comment before the pathologist. 'It's a ligature mark. Possibly a belt or a strong necklace, but more likely rope or wire. Here.' Dr Ling produces a tiny Maglite from her pen pocket and thumbs open the eyes. The corneas are cloudy now, opaque as cataracts. Frank has been around enough corpses to know they all do that after a while. He also sees that the eye and its lid are dotted with tiny red specks.

'Petechiae,' the doctor says. 'Tiny haemorrhages in the blood vessels. She was strangled, for sure. When we open her up we'll find bloody froth in the lungs.' She makes it sound like getting under the hood of a car.

'What about the other wounds?'

'Approximately twenty-seven superficial haematomas – it's hard to be exact because some are overlaid – consistent with blows from a belt or a stick. All pre-mortem. Eighteen bite marks, some puncturing the skin, possibly post-mortem. Dental identification unlikely, but we'll see what we can do.'

'The whipping, was it sex play? Or an assault?'

The doctor bends down and starts to comb the corpse's hair with a fine metal comb. 'Well, motivation isn't my department. As far as the medical evidence is concerned, it could be either.' Stella Vogler's hair is blond and fine, and the metal teeth of the comb make a rasping sound as the pathologist drags it hard against the scalp. 'I can tell you she was gagged at some point. There are specks of dried blood in the corners of her mouth.'

Frank indicates the pile of guts between her legs. 'And this? What happened here?'

The doctor transfers her combings to an evidence envelope, seals it carefully and writes something on the front. 'I'm not sure. You'll have to wait for the autopsy.' She moves on to the corpse's hands, scraping delicately underneath each nail with a short wooden pick from the evidence box. The fingertips, drained of blood, are as white as candles.

'Sure. But if you've got any initial thoughts . . . Did he penetrate her with something? A knife, maybe?'

'I can't tell yet,' she repeats. She opens the last envelope in her box and takes out another comb, which she uses to comb the corpse's downy pubic hair. 'I can tell you there's bruising here,' she says. 'Post-mortem, from the look of it.' She parts the hair with the comb to show him. 'After circulation has stopped you don't get the vivid colours you get with pre-mortem bruises. But a tender spot will putrefy quicker than the flesh around it. Like the bruising on an apple.'

'Meaning what, in your opinion?'

'Meaning that whatever he did to her, he did after she was dead.' Dr Ling puts the comb back in the envelope, seals it and annotates the front. 'OK,' she says, 'I'm done here.' She pulls off her gloves and tosses them into a bag. The flaccid, milky balls of latex remind Frank of used rubbers.

'Thanks,' he says.

'I'll see you at the autopsy then, detective.'

Frank nods. He takes his hands out of his pockets. His fingers are stiff where they've been clenched into fists.

CHAPTER FIVE

Frank Durban sits alone in a bar, nursing a beer. Occasionally the bartender says something to him, to see if he needs company, or conversation, or just another drink, but each time Frank shakes his head.

Even small talk is too much, tonight. Tonight he simply wants to watch the people come and go. The pretty girls, reflected in the mirror above the bar. The ones who are still alive.

Something strange happens at a murder scene. It's not that you are disgusted or repelled by what you see. The strange thing is that it seems perfectly normal. Like the killer himself, you look on the naked, dismembered body of the victim simply as raw material, an opportunity to practise your professional skills.

But occasionally there's something else as well, something more disturbing than dispassion. Something instinctive and uncontrollable and almost savage. Not anger or revulsion, but a kind of fleeting bloodlust.

Like a wild dog chasing another one from its meal, you find yourself standing over the kill with your teeth bared and your hackles raised, while something deep along the blood says, *This is mine, not yours.*

Just for a moment, as the doctor held one of Stella Vogler's limp hands in hers and ran her pick under the white, bloodless nail, Frank had felt that tonight.

He puts down his beer and gets to his feet.

He knows he shouldn't take the job home. But the job comes anyway, uninvited.

When he gets to Brooklyn Heights, the mutilated body of Stella Vogler will be there already. Sitting in the unkempt kitchen amidst a mountain of dirty take-out cartons. Propped in front of the flickering TV. Laid out on the pillowless side of the bed.

To tell the truth, he'll be glad of the company.

Two a.m. comes and goes. Bessie has long gone home, and the barman is trying to persuade Claire to come back with him. When the house lights are turned on she waits at the bar for the last customers to stumble out into the snow, some of them still dancing, like an audience exiting from a show. The barman, whose name is Brian, puts a roach bomb in the middle of the floor and sets the security system. He's still only wearing his T-shirt, but he says he isn't cold. They walk through the snow to his apartment, a little drunk. Wet flakes drift down through the murky sky, as if they're underwater and the snow is plankton drifting down towards the sea's bed. Trees have become reefs of fuzzy grey coral. Their breath bubbles up and is lost, like divers', a stream of silver wriggling up to the distant darkness of the surface.

When they reach his apartment it's even more of a dump than he'd said it would be, hardly more than a mattress surrounded by piles of laundry. But suddenly she wants nothing more than to get into his bed, still fully clothed, to be warmed up by that big heat-engine of a body and be undressed piece by piece under the covers until she's warm enough to make love.

She does things like this after a job for Henry. Why, she couldn't have said.

Just as she couldn't have told you whether the sounds she's making now, as she pulls the barman into her, are real or fake or a little bit of both.

CHAPTER SIX

Next morning the sidewalks are covered in a filo crust of wet snow, towering crazily on the parked cars and the trash cans. Here and there, steam vents in the road have made melt holes, smoking lazily in the winter sunshine.

Claire buys a newspaper from the subway vendor to see if Bessie gets a mention in the theatre reviews. She does. 'Among the other cast members, Bessie Heron's energetic Sheep, Raoul Walsh's Mouse and Victoria Kolans' lithe and sexy Piglet all stand out.' She clips it to take home.

There's something on the second page about a body found in a hotel. The police haven't released any details.

When she gets to the tiny brownstone she shares with Bessie the other girl is still asleep, a shape huddled under the bedclothes. Claire wakes her anyway, hanging the Donna Karan dress back in Bessie's closet. She empties the pockets first. A sliver of card falls to the floor. The lawyer's business card.

'I'm worried about you,' Bessie's voice says from under her comforter.

'Why? It was fun.'

'Bullshit. It was meaningless sex with a total stranger.'

Claire grins. 'That, too.'

'It's not safe.'

'He used a rubber.'

Bessie's head emerges from the bedclothes. 'Not safe sex, stupid. Safe *life*.'

'Bessie,' Claire says evenly, 'do you ever think you might just be a tiny bit paranoid? I mean, what the fuck is *this*?'

She's holding up the thing she's just found in Bessie's underwear drawer – gingerly, in case it's loaded.

'What do you think? It's a pistol, Claire.'

'OK, I can see that. What's it doing next to your panties?'

'It was a present from my dad.'

'But you really wanted a doll's house that Christmas, right?'

'A *leaving* present. In case I ever need to protect myself in the big bad city.'

Claire puts the gun back carefully in its hiding place. She takes out a jersey, a shirt and some black Alaia leggings and tosses them onto the bed.

'Then again,' Bessie says thoughtfully, 'I might need to shoot the person who steals all my clothes.'

Claire jumps onto the bed. 'Who needs fashion labels when you're a star?'

'What's that supposed to mean?'

Claire hits her with the paper. 'Review. The management summary is, you're brilliant. An energetic and outstanding contribution to the history of the musical. And here, three months' rent. Sorry it's so late.'

41

Offered both the paper and the money, Bessie grabs the paper first.

Frank has back-up now, three good detectives who'll be working the case with him: Forster, Weeks, Positano. Their supervisors are crawling all over the four of them already, all the way to the top. All wanting to review the paperwork and offer an opinion.

The paperwork. Frank's been in since dawn, tapping the initial crime scene report into the computer on his desk.

These days, he's heard, they teach touch-typing in police college.

But he'll bet they don't teach you how to tell a man his wife has been found dead and violated in a hotel room.

And they certainly can't teach you how to tell if he already knows.

'Sir, can you think of any reason, any reason at all, why your wife should book a hotel just a short distance from your apartment?'

Christian Vogler shakes his head. 'She told me she was going to her sister's,' he mutters.

He's a tall, dark-skinned man, his hair cropped so short he might as well be bald, with the kind of physique that makes Frank think of turn-of-the-century prizefighters: a barrel chest on narrow hips, the body shape contrasting oddly with an immaculate three-piece suit, lace-up shoes and cufflinks. Frank estimates him at around forty, forty-one. A fair bit older than his wife.

Vogler's voice is soft, almost a whisper, as he answers their questions, though that might be from shock. He has just come from the mortuary, where he has identified the blotchy, marbled remains of his wife. The pathologist, or one of her assistants, had wrapped a cloth round the neck, covering the ligature mark, like a napkin folded round a bottle of wine. Even so, Stella Vogler hadn't been a pleasant sight.

Frank had deliberately scheduled this interview for immediately afterwards, the moment of maximum distress.

'And you?' Mike Positano prompts. 'Where were *you* three nights ago?'

'I was working late. At the library.' He shrugs. 'Stella was away. There was no reason to go home.'

'She called you,' Frank says. He shows Vogler the printout from the hotel computer. 'She called you from her room. This *is* your home number?'

'Yes. But I wasn't there.'

'Well, that's another thing we're having trouble understanding, sir,' Positano says gently. 'You see, according to this record, she was on the phone for nearly three minutes.'

There's a silence, then Christian Vogler says, 'She must have been checking to see if there were any messages. You can access our machine from an external phone.'

'Did you notice any messages when you got back?'

'We had separate voicemail.'

Frank notes the use of the past tense. In his experience, relatives generally took about a week to start speaking of the deceased that way.

'Or she could have been *leaving* a message,' Positano suggests. 'For you. Telling you where she was.'

43

Vogler blinks slowly. Now that Frank has had a little time to study him, he notices the almost arrogant way the tall man holds their gaze, the hint of disdain in his cold green eyes. 'There was no message.'

'We may want to take your machine in so our technical people can take a look,' Positano says. Vogler shrugs his assent and crosses his legs. The shoes are immaculately polished. Frank wonders if they're handmade.

'Mr Vogler, did anyone see you at the library? Anyone who could vouch for you?'

'There were people there, sure, but I don't know any of them.' He stares at Frank. 'You can't possibly think . . . Do I need a lawyer?'

Frank sighs ostentatiously.

While Vogler is phoning his attorney, Positano says, 'There's one born every minute.'

'There's one finds out every minute, too,' Frank says.

'Think he's the perp?'

'Too early to say. But he's got a lot of composure for someone who's just been bereaved.'

Positano nods. 'What about VICAP?'

VICAP – the Violent Criminal Apprehension Program – is a database set up by the FBI to track serial offenders as they move around the country. Thirty pages of computerized forms to fill in, just to tell you whether or not your crime resembles another one that hasn't been solved yet, either.

'Even if we get a match, VICAP won't tell us why Stella was in that hotel room. That's the first nut we've got to crack.' Frank gets to his feet and drops the Starbucks cup of cold latte into the trash, carefully, so the liquid won't splatter his trousers. 'We're done for now, anyway. Vogler's lawyer will tell him to shut up until he gets here.'

'And afterwards, if I know lawyers,' Positano says morosely.

The medical examiner places her scalpel on Stella's right shoulder and carefully cuts down towards the centre of the chest. She has to hold the breast out of the way to make the cut straight. Then she cuts again, from the other shoulder, so the two lines meet just below the ribs. From there the scalpel goes in a straight line, down Stella Vogler's stomach.

A gym-toned body, Durban thinks. The stomach lightly muscled. All those hours on the Stairmaster for this.

Her navel is complex and intricate, like the knotted mouth of a balloon. The pathologist's scalpel slices it in two, continuing all the way to her pudenda.

Which has been shaved, roughly, to reveal the bruising Dr Ling spoke of at the crime scene, a faint chromatograph of decay under the straw-coloured stubble. Dr Ling has also performed an internal examination, with the corpse's feet held up in stirrups in a grotesque parody of a gynae-cological exam as the pathologist's gloved hand probed inside her.

'The vaginal rupture is about three inches by three-quarters of an inch,' she'd reported. 'It's a tear, not an incision.'

'What sort of implement are we talking about?'

'Well, it might not have been an implement. The tear is about the size of a human fist.'

Frank felt his mouth go dry. 'Could that have happened accidentally? During sex play?'

'I doubt it. Nature designed this part of the body for childbirth. It takes a lot to damage it.' The doctor met his eye. 'The reports came back from the lab. There were traces of glycol stearate on the vaginal swab.'

'What's that?'

'It's a compound used in moisturizing creams. At a guess, the killer used some on his hand as a lubricant. You might want to check the complimentary toiletries in the hotel room to see if one's missing.'

'We'll do that.' Frank made a note.

Now that the body has been cleaned up, a small round scar is visible on the inner thigh, no bigger than a dime. There appears to be some kind of pattern or relief within the hard, white tissue, like the brass rubbing of a coin.

'What's that?' Frank asks. 'Did the killer do this?'

'No. That scar's years old.'

'Any idea what might have caused it?'

'Maybe she got off a motorbike the wrong way in a pair of cut-offs and burned herself on the engine casing. Or she could have dropped something in her lap at a barbecue; it's just below the bikini line.' Dr Ling shrugs and turns back to her work.

The shears with which she cuts through the ribcage are as big as hedgecutters, and she grunts with the effort of forcing them closed.

Frank stands back. There's no smell in here, yet. Icy air roars from huge air-conditioning vents above their heads.

The pathologist puts on a mask and hauls guts

out of the cavity, endless handfuls of grey intestine in which the other, more brightly coloured organs nestle. Occasionally she removes one, with deft movements of her scalpel, and hands it carefully to her assistant.

After a few minutes she stops and goes over to the bench where the organs have been placed in a line, awaiting further dissection.

'That's strange,' she says, pushing back her floater mask. 'We haven't got a full set here.'

'Sorry? I don't follow you.'

'The spleen is missing. Not one of the most spectacular organs – all it does is store red blood cells – but you wouldn't want to be without it.'

'Was it . . . taken?'

'I think we can assume so. There's no medical procedure which would account for it not being here.'

The pathologist and the policeman look at each other for a moment. Whatever either of them wants to say, whatever they are thinking, this is not the time or the place. Dr Ling returns to the body and busies herself with the chest cavity, cutting and slicing. When she straightens up, Frank can see all the way down through the opening to the white of the spine.

Stay professional, he tells himself.

Dr Ling moves up to the head and makes an incision across the temples. She folds down a flap of skin, exposing ivory-coloured bone, as neatly as a chambermaid turning down a bed.

'You need to go outside now,' she says, pulling her mask back on. 'You can watch through the glass.'

Next to her, on a trolley, is an array of power tools.

She selects one with a fine-toothed circular blade and thumbs the button. An electric motor begins to screech, making speech impossible.

A few moments later the air is a blizzard of bonemeal.

CHAPTER SEVEN

Claire says, 'I'm in a box.'

'Who put you in the box?'

'My father.'

'What else is in there?' The young man asking the questions is sitting opposite her, very close, his legs almost entwined with hers.

'A rat,' she says.

'What's the rat wearing?'

She thinks, but only for a second. 'A diamond ring.'

'Where does the ring come from?'

'A beautiful woman.'

'What else has the rat got?'

'A knife.'

'It sticks the knife where?'

'Into my stomach.'

'What comes out of the hole?'

'Snow.'

'What happens to the snow?'

'My father drinks it.'

Across the rehearsal space, Paul claps once to stop them and says, 'Not bad. But, Claire, you're still thinking too much. How many times do I have to tell you? Don't think, just say the very first thing that comes into your head.'

'Could they have done more with the ring idea?' another student suggests. 'The exercise seemed to kind of fizzle out at that point.'

'I agree,' Paul says. 'Claire, turn it around now. You ask Keith the questions.'

The acting class takes place in a large, pale rehearsal room near the university. There are just a dozen or so students, and Paul.

She remembers her audition with him four months ago. The NYU/Tisch courses were the best of the best, and many times oversubscribed. Even if she could pay the exorbitant fees, she'd known that getting into the class would be tough.

She'd prepared a monologue – Brecht, or Tennessee Williams: something worthy and literary – and sat nervously outside the audition room off Lafayette, waiting her turn with all the glamorous New York beauties, confident, willowy creatures who'd dismissed her with a glance. When at last it was her turn, she'd gone into the rehearsal room to find it empty, apart from a tiny, pixielike man in a plain black T-shirt. He was sitting on the only furniture in the room, a white table, playing with a plastic coffee spoon.

She told him her name, and he pretended to write it down on a clipboard with the spoon. Then he looked at the spoon, puzzled, as if surprised it wouldn't write. Dipping it in an imaginary pot of ink, he flicked it at her.

Immediately she put her fingers up to her eye and wiped the imaginary ink away. He nodded.

'OK,' he said, 'you've passed.' He pulled out a real pen and wrote something down.

'Just like that?'

This seemed to amuse him. 'Why? Do you want

to go on and see if I can find a reason to fail you?'

She'd shrugged, and he'd said, 'Good. Classes begin when full semester starts. I'll see you then.'

She took a deep breath. 'There's something I should tell you. I'm not actually a resident here. I mean, I don't have a green card or anything. I'm not even a student at the university.'

'You can act, can't you?' Paul had said.

She shrugged. 'I hope so.'

'Then act like a student. If I'm right about you, it's the least you're capable of.'

On their first day, Paul had got them to perform a scene from *Hamlet*. Claire had thought her fellow students were pretty good. Then he made them do it again while balancing broom handles on their fingertips. In the effort to keep the handles upright the scene fell apart, the actors tripping and stumbling over the unfamiliar language.

Afterwards, Paul had gathered them around him. 'Let me tell you something. What you were doing just now, the first time, wasn't acting. It was *pretending*. You were copying what you've seen other actors do, but it wasn't real to you. That's why you couldn't do it the second time, when you had to concentrate on something else.

'I am going to tell you only one thing today, but it's the most important thing I'll ever say to you: Don't think. Acting isn't faking or impersonating. Acting is *doing*.'

'Is this a Method class?' one of the students asked.

An expression of mild annoyance crossed Paul's face. 'Don't ever let me hear you use that word. It implies that there's a set of rules or a formula of some kind. The phrase Stanislavski himself used was "inhabiting the moment". That's our goal.'

Today they end up improvising a story in which two washroom attendants have been mistaken for brain surgeons and are operating on the president's mistress. Claire, lying on the floor, plays the mistress. The surgeons have just decided they will replace her brain, which they have accidentally mutilated, with one of their own, when someone walks forward into the circle.

She sees a man in a long brown raincoat, snow all over his Hush Puppies. He stops and says, 'Claire Rodenburg?' to no-one in particular, and somehow he says it in a way that instantly, brilliantly, wearily, conveys that he's a cop.

'You can't take her!' one of the surgeons yells. 'She hasn't got her brain in!'

An expression of distaste flits momentarily across the policeman's face. He looks down, directly at Claire. 'Miss Rodenburg?'

'She's a very good friend of the president's,' the other surgeon says. 'Be careful what you do with her.'

She notices that he isn't fazed by any of this surreal nonsense. He just holds out his ID, down low where she can see it, and says, 'Detective Frank Durban. Why don't you people take a break?'

There's an empty room next door. A few plastic chairs are scattered around. She sits, though the detective remains standing.

'Forgive me for interrupting your afternoon,' he says.

She has already realized what this is all about. The lawyer she ripped off has made a complaint. 'Look, I'd better explain—'

'Am I correct in thinking you sometimes work with Henry Mallory?' he says abruptly.

'Yes.'

'What do you do for him, exactly?'

'I see if men . . . you know, if they're going to be unfaithful,' she says nervously. She touches her hair, embarrassed. 'His clients pay me to make a pass at their husbands.'

The detective pulls out a photograph in a clear plastic sleeve and shows it to her. 'Do you recognize this lady?'

'Yes, I do,' she says. And she has to keep the surprise out of her voice, because it's not the lawyer's wife but another client entirely, one from nearly a week ago.

'Do you know her name?'

'I think it's Vogler,' she says hesitantly. 'Stella Vogler.'

'According to Mr Mallory, she was a client of yours.'

'That's right, yes.'

'Why had she come to your agency?'

Claire tells him what she can remember. It isn't much.

Stella had been worried about her husband, Christian. They'd been married for two years, and in that time he had changed, she'd said. Always secretive about his movements, he had taken to going out at strange times with no explanation. On other occasions he was evasive and resisted being questioned. And, although as possessive as ever about Stella, he had started to regard her with a coldness that at times appeared close to hatred.

Same old familiar story. Claire has only been working for Henry for a short while, but already she feels like she's heard it a thousand times before.

The detective scribbles rapidly in his notebook now. 'So you were asked to, uh, meet with Mr Vogler. How did that meeting go?'

'Well, that's what was odd.'

'In what way?'

'In that he wasn't interested in me.'

Frank taps his pencil on his teeth. 'That happen often?'

'No. That was the first time, in fact. Usually I'm . . . well, usually I'm pretty successful.'

'I can imagine,' he says.

There's an awkward silence. She looks at the floor. The policeman clears his throat.

'Tell me', he says, '*exactly* what occurred.'

The bar was a big, quiet place, the front room of an old chop house. The kind of place she never usually saw the inside of, on her budget.

His wife had told them that Vogler went there often. He sometimes did research at the public library, and the bar was near his route home. Invariably he sat on his own, drinking a single glass of red wine and reading a book.

They had arranged for Stella to tell him she'd be out of town for a couple of nights, so that if he wanted to play around behind her back he had the perfect opportunity. In fact, she'd booked herself into a hotel uptown.

'The Lexington?'

'That's right.'

Frank, writing all this down, nods thoughtfully.

Claire had ordered a drink and sat at the bar, near where Christian Vogler was sitting. After a few moments she noticed him raising his head to look at her. She sipped her drink and waited.

She was on her third Virgin Mary before she realized that, this time, waiting wasn't going to work.

At one point he got up from his table and came to the bar, striding impatiently across the room towards her. But he was only getting change from the bartender for the phone.

'How long was he on the phone?'

'Not long. A minute, maybe more.'

'OK. Go on.'

While he was gone, she casually went over to his table and picked up the book he'd been reading. It was a volume of poetry in French.

He returned, and she'd started guiltily. 'Oh, I'm sorry. Is this yours?'

'Yes,' he'd said curtly. There might as well have been a sign over his head saying, Do Not Disturb.

She looked at the book's title. *Les Fleurs du Mal*. 'That means "The Flowers of Evil", right?'

'That's right.' He held out his hand to take the book back, and just for a second she glanced into his eyes. Christian Vogler had striking eyes – gooseberry-green, with a secondary ring of black, as if the iris had been edged in charcoal. She had to make herself look down again at the book. ' "*J'ai plus de souvenirs que si j'avais mille ans*," ' she read aloud.

And he'd blinked, surprised. 'You have a good accent.'

'I did some French at school. But this is hard . . .
a grave of pyramids . . . no . . .'

'There's a translation over the page. If you're
really interested.'

She turned the page. 'So there is.' She started to
read it aloud, taking her time, her trained voice
milking the pauses and line breaks.

> I have more memories than if I had lived a
>   thousand years.
> An old cabinet stuffed with dead ideas –
> bundles of abandoned verses, old receipts
>   and bills,
> dusty locks of hair, and long-forgotten
>   wills –
> is not more full of secrets than my aching
>   head.
>
> It's a sarcophagus, an immense grave where
>   the dead,
> those bodies I have loved, are tumbled
>   willy-nilly,
> prodded and nudged incessantly
> by morbid reveries, like worms:
> It's a house of shuttered, closed-up rooms
> where closets full of wedding clothes
> are slowly pulled to lace by moths.

She paused, glancing at Vogler. He was looking
at her intently. 'Please, go on.'

She shrugged and continued:

> The days go on forever. Boredom and ennui
> are in themselves a kind of immortality.
> Slowly, I become the opposite of flesh:

antimatter, darkness, life's antithesis;
like some old statue of a half-forgotten god,
abandoned in the desert, starved of blood,
whose enigmatic, weatherbeaten frown
lights up, for one moment, as the sun goes
    down.

A beat of silence lengthened into two. While she was reading Christian Vogler had closed his eyes. Now he opened them again, regarding her without expression. 'It's kind of weird,' she said into the silence. 'What does it mean?' Then she noticed the photograph on the back cover. 'Oh, that's you. "Translated and with an introduction by Christian Vogler." You're a poet.'

He shook his head. 'A translator. And only in my spare time.'

'What's it about?' she asked, to keep him talking.

Again, the blank, indifferent stare. 'It's not about anything. It's about itself.'

'Sure, but why did he write that particular poem?'

'Ah.' Vogler thought for a moment. 'He had a complicated love life.'

'Sounds like my kind of guy.' *Careful, girl. Take it slowly.*

'He was involved with two women.' Vogler looked off across the bar, as if marshalling his thoughts. 'Though perhaps "involved" isn't quite the word. One was a prostitute, a negress whom he called his *Vénus noire,* his Black Venus. The other was a sophisticated society beauty, the wife of a friend. She was called Apollonie Sabatier, but biographers call her the *Vénus blanche*, the White Venus. The prostitute was in love with him, and he

57

was her lover, but he was also in love with the *Vénus blanche*.'

'A love triangle.'

'Of a sort.'

'What happened?'

'He wrote an extraordinary series of erotic poems. He said he wanted to do something completely new, to create beauty out of evil. The poems touch on every kind of perversion, but their effect is strangely gentle. He sent them to the *Vénus blanche* anonymously. Eventually she guessed who it was. She offered to sleep with him; it was no big deal, she had slept with many of her husband's friends. They spent a single night together.'

'She ditched him?'

'No. Nobody knows what happened. The only clue is a letter of rejection that *he* sent to *her* the next day. He said he preferred to remember her as a goddess rather than as a woman.'

'I guess some people don't like to be tied down,' she said. 'What about you?'

It was a mistake, too obvious, too crass. She knew that the moment the words had left her mouth. Christian Vogler got to his feet. 'I have to go,' he muttered, looking around.

'Oh, please, I wanted to ask you something. About, uh' – she glanced at the page – 'Baudelaire. Where can I find a translation like this? It sounds so interesting, and—'

'Keep it.' He pulled money from his pocket for the waitress.

'Keep it? Look, why don't I give you my number, and—'

'My address is written inside. Send it back when you're done.'

'Are you sure? It won't take a moment to—'

'It's no problem,' he said, pulling on his jacket.

'Can't I even buy you a drink?' she asked desperately.

He paused. For a moment he ran his eyes over her with a kind of curious reluctance. 'I enjoyed talking with you,' he said. And then he was gone, and she'd found herself addressing some last-ditch question to the empty air.

'Think he worked out what was going on?' Frank asks sceptically.

Claire shrugs. 'I don't see how.'

'What about Mrs Vogler? How did she react when you told her?'

'Pleased, obviously. Reassured. Happy.'

'She pay you?'

'Of course. Why wouldn't she?'

'We found a large amount of cash on her person,' he says flatly, and Claire's eyes widen.

'You mean . . . she's dead?'

Durban nods, watching her reaction.

'Oh God,' she says, appalled. Then, 'How?'

'We're treating it as homicide.'

'That's *terrible*.'

He takes her over it again, and then a third time, until eventually he puts his notebook away. 'Last question. What happened to the book?'

'The book?'

'The book of poetry. You ever send it back?'

'I guess it's still lying around my apartment somewhere.'

'Well, it's probably not important,' he says, getting to his feet. 'Just don't throw it out, OK?'

CHAPTER EIGHT

Frank Durban sighs and leans forward on the orthopaedic stool he's installed in front of his computer. The stool forces him into a half-kneeling position, as if he's on his knees before the great god Paperwork.

He's almost finished page twenty of the VICAP submission form. Despite the stool, his lower back is killing him.

At last he clicks on Send. In just a few moments, a computer at the FBI's headquarters in Virginia scans the report and compares it with over 30,000 other reports of unsolved crimes from all over the USA.

Statistically, you were more likely to find your killer by sticking a pin in the phone book.

The pin was quicker, too.

A message flashes on the screen.

Thank you for your submission.
According to our records, <one>
previous submission indicates a
possible match.

Intrigued despite himself, Frank clicks on Next. But instead of showing him the details, the computer says:

Claire gets home just as Bessie is getting ready to go out to the theatre. Bessie's channel-hopping, her head turbaned in a towel.

'Good day?' she asks as Claire dumps her groceries on the counter.

'Weird day.' Claire explains about the policeman and the murdered client. 'I feel a bit strange,' she concludes. 'Apart from the hotel staff, I guess Henry and I were just about the last people to see Mrs Vogler alive.'

'Did you say Vogler?'

'Yes. Why?'

'He was on the news just now.' She thumbs the remote. 'There.'

The screen shows a tall, bald man, his face dark with tiredness, speaking to a battery of microphones. Flashguns strobe his face.

'That's him,' Claire says. 'Turn it up, will you?'

As the volume increases they hear him say in a soft voice that's barely more than a whisper, '. . . grateful for any assistance, any assistance at all, that can be given to the New York Police Department.' He stops, blinking owlishly in the renewed barrage of flashes. A uniformed policeman sitting next to him reaches for the microphone.

'Press conference,' Bessie says significantly. 'You know what *that* means.'

'They're having a conference for the press?'

'No, stupid. They think he did it.' She sighs, exasperated at the incomprehension on Claire's face. 'God, you are so *innocent* sometimes. When the police think the husband did it, but his lawyer's stopping them from asking any really tough questions, they get him to do a press conference so the journalists can ask the questions for them. Next time you see him on TV he'll have a blanket over his head.'

Claire shakes her head. 'Not him. He was a happily married man, remember?'

'Don't give me that crap,' Bessie says lightly, towelling her hair. 'There's no such thing.'

The next day Claire goes to see Henry.

He's given up on the fifths of bourbon now. Instead, his liver-spotted hand is curled round a full-size bottle of Wild Turkey.

Seeing her, he puts it in a drawer. 'Claire,' he says. 'What can I do for you?' His words aren't slurred, but she knows that's just the old actor's voice training. Henry would fall over before he'd misplace his diction.

'The police came to see me, Henry.'

He pulls the drawer open again. 'Want a drink?'

'Yes,' she admits.

While he's finding glasses he says, 'There won't be any more work for a while, Claire. The police paid me a visit, too. They weren't impressed. Apparently recording people without their permission requires a warrant or a licence or some such thing. I'm to stick to missing pets in future.' He pours the first shot and immediately swallows half of it himself. 'Not much call for acting in pet work, I'm afraid.'

'Are you firing me, Henry?'

'Of course not.' He makes a gesture with the glass. 'Intermission. Curtain down. Ice creams in the stalls. We'll be back, Claire.'

She knows he doesn't believe it, either.

PART TWO

'My wife is dead: I am free.'
The Murderer's Wine, Baudelaire

CHAPTER NINE

Time passes.

For a while the Lexington murder is a *cause célèbre*. As details leak out, they are pored over by newspapers, pontificated on by columnists, speculated about in bars and offices all over New York.

Then a major soap star is photographed in a bondage club, the Lincoln Tunnel is closed for repairs and the president sends American troops into Antigua.

People move on.

Bessie, whose dad turns out to be something big in oil, gives Claire a little leeway on the rent. She waits tables, sometimes, in bars where they need help over the summer holiday season. Marcie gives her the number of someone who manages exotic dancers. Somehow Claire has managed not to call it yet.

She's scraping by – just. But soon the acting classes will have to go.

The room is filled with sunshine. They're lying on the floor in a starfish pattern. The whole group, their heads touching, staring up at the ceiling.

From somewhere near by she hears Paul's voice.

'This is a very old game. A ritual, almost. It's called The Story Tells Itself.

'The way it works is, we're going to start a rhythm with our hands on the floor, and every time we make a beat, we're going to take it in turn to add one word to the story.'

Someone says, 'What's the story about?'

Paul says, 'I don't know. That's the point. The story's there already. All we have to do is let it out.'

Over the last few months the exercises have become progressively harder. Paul has made them spend whole days calling everything by the wrong name, just to see how it feels. He has made them improvise bizarre, extravagant characters – a sales-man with a suitcase full of sweaters knitted from hippopotamus wool; a soldier armed with an in-visible machine gun – then sent them out into the street, still in character, to accost passers-by and tell them about it. Rather to her surprise, Claire found that the passers-by were generally happy to listen. Either she's becoming better at what she does, or the passers-by are getting crazier as summer kicks in.

'Let's go,' Paul says, and starts to slap his palms on the floor. First one, then the other. A slow, loping rhythm. Gradually they all pick it up.

'Once,' he says.

A fraction off the beat, the person to Paul's left says, 'Upon.'

'A'

'Time'

'There'

'Was'

'A'

It's her turn. *Don't think, act.* Though in truth

68

there's no time to think, the implacable rhythm of the hands forcing her to say the first thing that comes into her head. 'Princess,' she says.

And the story passes on, gathering momentum as it goes round and round the group. A fairy tale, something about a prince who falls in love with a statue in his garden.

The next time Paul makes it harder. If you hesitate you have to drop out. And the rhythm gets a little faster each time it goes round.

This time he doesn't start with anything so obvious as 'Once'.

It's a strange, glittering story that emerges this time, a dark fantasy about a little girl who lives in a graveyard among ravens and crows.

One by one they stumble, curse and get to their feet.

But not her.

And in the end it's just the two of them, Claire and Paul, lying at right angles on the rehearsal space floor, their hands clapping in triple-time, the words flowing so thick and fast it's as if she's memorized them.

She feels possessed, exhilarated, captured. As if she's simply the mouthpiece of another personality, a host to some voodoo spirit.

She understands now. Don't think, act.

At last Paul stops, and she lies there, coming back to her senses. Propping himself up, he sees the look on her face and smiles.

The group stands silently. She raises her head and looks around. Usually, at the end of an exercise, they applaud.

Detective Durban is there, watching her. He looks exhausted.

'Miss Rodenburg,' he says. 'Can we talk?'

She takes him to the little refectory bar. Around them, students sit in groups of two or three, chatting or reading.

It's too hot for coffee, so he gets them each a Diet Coke from the machine.

'America,' she murmurs. 'Land of the calorie-free.'

He doesn't smile. Again she notices how tired he looks.

'Miss Rodenburg,' he says brusquely, 'I'd like you to do something for me.'

She shrugs. 'What?'

'We're backtracking over some old ground here. Re-checking statements, seeing if there's anything we missed the first time around.'

'You haven't made an arrest, have you? I've been following it in the papers.'

'We've eliminated a lot of people from our investigation. There was a media appeal for other guests at the hotel to come forward. Eventually all four hundred and twenty-six were accounted for. We haven't been idle.'

'I'm sorry. I didn't mean—'

'Most of our work has been centred on one individual,' he says.

'Can I ask who?'

Now it's his turn to shrug.

'The husband,' she guesses, remembering what Bessie had said about press conferences.

He looks at her, as if unsure how much he should be telling her, then leans in close. 'After the television appeal we were contacted by a young woman who dated Christian Vogler before he met Stella. They were engaged, in fact. She broke it off.'

'Why'd she do that?'

'She didn't like the things he was asking her to go along with. Violent stuff. Then she started waking up in the mornings with headaches and unexplained bruises on her body. This went on until she woke once in the middle of the night to find herself naked. Vogler had stripped her of her nightclothes, laid her across the bed and surrounded her with candles. That's all she recalls before she became unconscious again. She believes he drugged her with Rohypnol and was using her in some kind of passive sex ritual.'

Claire makes a face. 'Why don't you arrest him?'

'The girl made no complaint at the time. And if he did drug her, what she saw might have been a hallucination. A good defence attorney would make mincemeat of her in court.' He pushes his fingers into the thin metal of the Coke can, denting it.

She makes a helpless gesture. 'What can I do?'

'Can you still recall your conversation with him? The poem and so forth?'

'Of course.' She's been over it in her mind many times since then.

'We've got someone who's looking at Vogler's background, his personality, all that kind of stuff. A psychiatrist. Come and talk to her.'

'When?'

'Now would be good.'

'Well . . .' she hesitates, glances back at the rehearsal room.

When he speaks again his voice has hardened.

'This is important, Claire.'

She notes the use of her first name. 'It's just that
. . . what use can I be? He wasn't even interested.
The man had nothing to say to me.'

'Why did he leave?'

'What?'

'Vogler. When you had that conversation you
said he seemed in a hurry to get away. That's what
I keep wondering about. Since he was only going
home, and his wife was away, why the hurry? Why
break off a conversation with a pretty girl in a bar
who's prepared to discuss French poetry like she
really gives a shit?'

'I think I bored him,' she says.

'Well, maybe. That's one possibility.'

'What's the other?'

'Maybe he broke it off because he thought he'd
said too much.'

They take a yellow cab. Frank gives an address in
Queens. The Puerto Rican driver tells him he'll
need directions once they're over the river.

'Illegal immigrants,' Frank mutters under his
breath.

She feels him glancing at her.

'Here,' he says, taking a piece of paper out of his
pocket and passing it to her.

She unfolds it. It's a photocopy of her immigration card, dated nearly a year ago. Purpose of
visit: tourism. Duration of visit: sixty days.

'I've got better things to worry about,' he
says.

'If I hadn't agreed to come with you, would you
still have had better things?'

He shrugs.

The cab driver has turned off the air-conditioning, to save fuel. They sit and sweat on the vinyl seats all the way to their destination.

CHAPTER TEN

It's a long, low building, just another ugly office in a street full of ugly offices and half-empty parking lots. Though she notices that it's the only one in the block with no company logo outside.

He signs her in at reception and walks her down a long, humid corridor. There's a faint smell she can't identify for a moment, before she realizes.

It smells like a hospital.

At the end of the corridor they're met by a large black woman, who whispers something to Frank. 'In here,' he says, opening a door.

The room is tiny, as bare as a cell. On the metal table is what looks like a portable TV.

Frank turns it on. It's not a TV, she realizes, but a closed-circuit monitor. The image is grainy. At first she thinks she's watching something recorded earlier, in this same office. The furniture is identical. Then she sees that the room on the screen is larger than this one.

Frank manipulates a joystick and the image moves.

'The camera's just on the other side of this wall,' he says, fiddling with the sound.

She understands now: this is an observation room.

There are two people in the other room. An

elegantly dressed woman in her forties, with her hair pulled back in a tie, and a man in his twenties, with a thin weasel face. They sit facing each other.

'What am I wearing?' the woman asks. Her voice is deep and husky. A smoker's voice.

'Panties,' the man mumbles. 'White panties. And a skirt. A short skirt. A blouse that buttons.'

That doesn't make sense. The woman is wearing a suit. Claire looks at Frank for an explanation, but he indicates for her to go on watching the screen.

'Where am I?' the woman is asking.

The man says, 'In a playground.'

'Can you see my white panties under my skirt?'

He nods abruptly.

'And how does that make you feel?' she asks softly.

He licks his lips. 'Aroused.'

'That's good, isn't it?'

'Yes,' he whispers.

'I turn around. I see how aroused you are. Then what?'

'You smile.'

She nods. 'Of course I do. I smile.'

'You know how you make me feel. You want it as much as I do.'

'And . . . ?'

'You take my hand and lead me behind the bushes.' He swallows. 'You're wearing white socks. I can see they're dirty. They've got mud on them. I tell you they'll have to come off.'

'Do I agree?'

'Oh yes.' He smiles weakly. 'You agree because you want it.'

'Of course.'

'I lift up your legs, one by one, to take off your shoes and your little white socks. Your legs are bare and very smooth. I can see your little white panties at the top of your legs.'

'Then what?'

He snorts. 'Then you get scared. You think you've had enough. You're not sure what you're getting into.'

'Do I struggle?'

'Yes. You struggle deliciously. I put my hands around your neck to stop you struggling. Your neck's so small it only takes one hand to go all the way around. With my other hand I take off your panties.'

'Am I still struggling?'

'Oh yes. It's good. It makes me feel powerful. And when you stop struggling, when you go limp . . .'

'Yes?'

'You lie there with your legs apart and I get my cock out.'

'Yes,' she breathes. 'Your cock.'

'And I pull you onto it, but it's tight and I push and your little face is twisted with pleasure.'

'Go on,' she says.

'And I put my hands around your throat again and it's like I'm holding my own cock, my own huge cock. And I'm twisting and pushing and you're loving it.'

'More,' she murmurs. 'More.'

'And I twist and pull and it feels so—' His hands grip the arms of his chair. His body seems to shudder and convulse, so that for a moment Claire wonders if the chair is somehow electrified.

Then she realizes he's come in his pants.

His head sags. 'Listen to me,' the woman says. Her voice has changed. No longer seductive, but crisper, more authoritative. 'I'm going to count backwards from five. When I reach two, you will wake up.'

The man's head moves. He groans.

'When you wake up, you will remember everything you have told me.' She counts from five to one. 'Have some water,' she says dismissively.

The man reaches for his glass. He's shaking. Another man, an orderly of some sort, who has been sitting quietly in the shadows beyond the camera's reach, comes forward and gently helps him to his feet.

'I'll come and see him in a while,' the woman says. 'Put him on suicide watch.'

Frank presses a button and the monitor goes blank, the grainy image sucked abruptly into a white supernova in the middle of the screen.

'That's Dr Constance Leichtman. It's her I want you to meet.'

In the flesh she's both slighter and more poised than she had seemed on the monitor. She shakes Claire's hand, and nods at Frank with the easy familiarity of a colleague.

'That man,' Claire says, still shocked. 'Did he really murder that girl?'

Dr Leichtman shakes her head. 'No. It was a fantasy.'

'Thank God.'

'But he will,' she says matter-of-factly. 'When he finishes the prison sentence he's already serving for sexual assault on a child, he'll go out and kill someone. Unless he either accepts treatment or kills himself first. Now then' – Dr Leichtman sits at her desk, closes one file and reaches for another – 'Christian Vogler.'

She starts to read the file. While she reads she taps a cigarette from a pack of Merit and lights it. Eventually the file is closed. 'Right,' she says. 'Tell me about Vogler.'

Claire recounts the story of her meeting with Vogler yet again, while Dr Leichtman looks at her thoughtfully over a plume of smoke.

'Thank you,' she says when Claire's finished. 'You've been very helpful. You can go now.'

'Connie,' Frank says entreatingly.

'She isn't right,' the psychiatrist says quietly.

'Would you excuse us for a minute, Claire?' Frank asks.

Claire goes and waits in the anteroom, where Dr Leichtman's assistant glances at her incuriously, then turns her attention back to her keyboard.

She waits and waits. And after a while the assistant waddles off with a pile of papers.

Claire slips into the observation room and turns on the monitor. She doesn't use the joystick because the moving camera might alert them. So she can't see them, but she can hear what they're saying.

'. . . she has no records, no bank account, no social security number. We can invent a past for her. She can be whoever we need her to be.'

It's Frank. He sounds insistent. 'And she can act, Connie. I mean, she can *really* act. I've watched her.'

Dr Leichtman's voice cuts across his. 'Give me a break, Frank. They can all *act*. MAWs, they're called. "Model, Actress, Whatever." New York's full of them.'

'I think this one's different. She's—'

'She's also a civilian. There's the issue of control.'

'She's used to being directed. If she agreed—'

Abruptly, Claire switches off the monitor.

Don't think. Act.

The assistant is still out of the anteroom. Claire picks up a pile of letters from the printer. The assistant is black, fifty and overweight. And the voice . . . let's see.

Claire lets her posture sag and waddles into the doctor's office. Frank is looking out of the window. Dr Leichtman is blowing smoke rings and tapping one elegant shoe.

'Would you sign these, Doctor?' Claire, or rather, now, the assistant, asks.

Leichtman makes a little gesture of irritation. 'I already did today's post,' she says, reaching out her hand to take them. Then she looks more closely at the hand holding the letters and glances up at Claire's face.

'That diet's doing you good, Joyce,' she murmurs. 'Well, well.'

Frank turns round from the window. When he sees that it's Claire his eyes light up.

'All right,' Dr Leichtman says at last. 'Tell her. That can't do any harm.'

'About a month ago,' Frank says, 'I asked Dr Leichtman if it was possible to design an operation' – he pauses, searching for words – 'a covert operation, in which a suspect would reveal whether they had the correct psychological make-up to be our killer. Dr Leichtman thought that it might be, if the killer had sufficient trust in the person he was revealing himself to.'

'*Theoretically*,' Dr Leichtman murmurs from the desk. 'I said it was *theoretically* possible.'

'You mean like entrapment?' Claire asks incredulously.

'Not the sort of entrapment *you* do,' Dr Leichtman says. 'This would be a rather more sophisticated process. I think of it as being like a series of snakes and ladders. The suspect would have to actively climb successive ladders of self-incrimination – without any inducement from the decoy, of course – while at the same time avoiding various snakes, or actions which would eliminate them from suspicion. Do you see?'

'I think I can just about follow that,' Claire says sweetly. Something about the way the doctor talks down to her is pissing her off, just a little.

'We've looked at some candidates,' Frank says. 'Mostly women, for obvious reasons. Undercover police operatives. Connie hasn't ... We don't think we've found the right person yet.'

'It won't be easy. The decoy will have to make up the script as they go along,' Dr Leichtman says.

Frank says to Claire, 'Where are you?'

Immediately she answers, 'In a street.'

'Where does the street lead?'

'To a jeweller's shop.'

'Why are you going there?'

'To sell my crown.'

'Why do you want to sell your crown?'

'To buy a canoe.'

'What's the canoe for?'

'To get back to China.'

'Yes, yes,' the psychiatrist says impatiently, breaking across them. 'She's fluent, granted, but it's fluent *nonsense*. Our decoy needs to know what she's doing.'

'You could teach her that part,' Frank says.

Claire breaks the silence first. 'Whoa,' she says, 'wait a minute. Why would *I* want to get involved with something like this?'

'Civic duty?' he growls. When she doesn't respond, he says, 'Money, then. We'd pay you a detective's salary for as long as it takes.'

'I want a green card,' she says slowly.

'That's Immigration's—'

'A green card and a salary. That's my price.'

'If I might interrupt your negotiations for just *one* moment,' Dr Leichtman says behind them. 'There isn't going to be any green card, because there isn't going to be any operation.'

They turn to look at her, and she stares back at them across the desk. 'It's completely out of the question,' she says.

CHAPTER ELEVEN

Connie Leichtman stares at Claire for a long time. A very long time. She busies herself lighting a cigarette. 'Tell me about your family,' she says through a mouthful of smoke.

It's nine o'clock the next morning. Reluctantly, Dr Leichtman has cleared her diary. Her purpose, she's told Claire, is to get inside the girl's head and have a poke around, to see just how tough she really is.

'Unless, of course, you'd agree to be hypno-tized,' she said a little wistfully. 'We could do this really quickly if you'd agree to be hypnotized.'

'No,' Claire had said. She isn't sure yet how much she trusts this doctor.

'Your family,' Dr Leichtman says again.

'My parents separated when I was four,' Claire says evenly. 'My mother tried to look after me, but she couldn't cope. So I went to stay with my dad in London.'

'But that didn't work out?'

'We've been through this,' Claire mutters.

The psychiatrist waits.

'It didn't work out, no. I didn't . . . My step-mother found me difficult to live with.'

'A personality clash.'

'It would have been.' For the first time there's a note of anger in Claire's voice. 'If she'd had a personality.'

Dr Leichtman makes a note. 'So you were put into care,' she says. 'You had foster parents.'

'I had people who looked after me for money. Like a hotel guest, except I couldn't check out.'

'I see.'

'*What* do you see?'

Dr Leichtman ignores her. 'And that's when you discovered acting?'

Claire laughs bitterly. 'That's where all this is leading, is it? I couldn't cope with my own life, so I started to pretend I was living someone else's. Case closed.'

'Well? *Is* that the way it was?'

'No. I'd discovered something I was good at, that's all.'

'A talent which your foster parents no doubt encouraged.'

'Did they fuck. They called me a liar, mostly.'

Dr Leichtman makes another note. 'But you managed to get a scholarship to a Performing Arts School.'

'Yes. When I was twelve.'

'Tell me about that.'

'I got a stage school scholarship when I was twelve,' Claire parrots. 'There. Now I've told you.'

'No, you haven't,' Dr Leichtman says mildly.

She waits out Claire's silence.

'I loved it,' Claire says eventually. 'More than I'd ever loved any of my foster families. Is that the sort of crap you want to hear? It was like an ordinary school, but with acting as well. Speech, movement, dance, even how to choreograph a fight. It had a good reputation in the business. Casting agents used us whenever they needed young actors.'

'And you were a star pupil.'

'Was I?'

The psychiatrist reaches into a folder and pulls out a sheaf of faxes. They're covered in Day-Glo stripes of yellow highlighter. Claire recognizes the headline on the topmost one.

Her reviews. Dr Leichtman must have moved fast to get these sent overnight.

' "Claire Rodenburg. A wonderful début as Alice in Wonderland,"' Dr Leichtman reads aloud. 'Here's another: "This production was greatly enlivened by the mesmerizing performance of Claire Rodenburg, a star in the making if ever I saw one." "Claire Rodenburg's ravishing presence." "A daring and sexually charged Desdemona, brilliantly brought to life by Claire Rodenburg, lights up the stage." "In a cameo role Bertolucci has cast young English actress Claire Rodenburg, of whom film insiders say we will be hearing much more shortly." Why didn't we, Claire?'

'Why didn't we what?'

'Why didn't we hear much more of you?' She drops the pile of faxes onto the desk. 'You'd almost made it. You were on the brink of major success. Yet you gave it up and came here, where nobody knows who you are. Why?'

'I'm not the first actress to come to America.'

'Oh, if you'd taken yourself off to Hollywood and had your tits fixed I could understand it. But you didn't come here in search of fame, did you? It's something else.'

'I'd been at stage school for nearly ten years. When other kids were going off to Europe and

Australia for their vacations, I was trekking round auditions and go-sees. Why shouldn't I want to travel? Maybe in a few months time I'll be in Mexico or Sydney.'

'Maybe.'

There's another silence.

'Are you accusing me of running away from something?'

'Is that what happened?' the psychiatrist bounces back at her.

The silence lengthens. When Claire speaks, her voice is low, her eyes focused on something over Connie's shoulder. 'I know what you're getting at. This decoy work. You . . . well, you don't have to be a shrink to work out what that's all about. I'm re-enacting the story of my childhood, aren't I? Finding men who betray their wives, just as my father betrayed my mother, and punishing them for it. Punishing them for the fact that no-one ever loved Claire Rodenburg.' A single tear rolls, glistening, down her left cheek. She dabs at it quickly with the back of her hand.

Dr Leichtman says calmly, 'Very good, Claire. But if it's a shrink you're after, look in *Yellow Pages*. I spent seven years studying forensic psychiatry, and I've got better things to do with my qualifications than listen to bullshit.'

Claire frowns.

'And spare me the tears,' the psychiatrist says, taking a box of tissues out of a drawer and tossing them across the desk. 'You learned *that* trick before you learned how to ride a bicycle.'

Claire takes a tissue and blows her nose.

'Come on.' Dr Leichtman gets up. 'Let's go for a walk. I need some air.'

*   *   *

By air, she'd evidently meant nicotine.

They walk slowly. Although it's early, the heat is already oppressive.

'Is what you do *fair*?' Dr Leichtman asks.

Claire shrugs. 'Life isn't fair. Men sleep around. If I get paid money to help their wives find that out, what's the big deal?'

The psychiatrist stops and grinds out her cigarette stub. Absent-mindedly she puts another cigarette in her mouth, then taps her pockets. 'Damn. I've left my lighter behind. Do you . . . ?'

'Sure.' Claire holds out a book of matches from the Royalton. When the other woman makes no move to take it, she opens it herself and strikes one. Dr Leichtman takes hold of her wrist to steady the flame. Her thumb, sliding beneath the wide watch strap Claire wears, touches harder flesh and tightens.

'May I?' she says around the cigarette, twisting Claire's hand so that she can peer at her wrist with sharp eyes. After a moment she looks up. 'And *this*?' she says. 'Was *this* fair?'

Claire pulls away. 'I fell on some glass.'

'With *both* wrists?'

Angrily, Claire pushes the matches back into her pocket. Dr Leichtman, unfazed, gets out a lighter and lights her cigarette herself. 'I do actually need to know this stuff,' she says apologetically.

Claire sighs. 'It was when we were filming the movie. The one you had the clipping about. He was – well, you'd know his name if I said it. He was the star, and the money: without him the film would never have got backing. He's famous and good-looking and everyone knows he has one of the happiest marriages in showbusiness. So when he fell in love with me I knew it was the real thing.' She laughs bitterly. 'That was before I heard the phrase they use on movie sets. DCOL, darling. Doesn't Count On Location.'

'And?'

'After seven weeks his wife . . . well, I guess she'd heard the rumours. Or maybe she was just used to his little ways. She turned up on set with his four kids in tow. Suddenly I was needed for new wardrobe fittings, second unit reshoots, technical rehearsals with the grip and focus puller. The word had gone out to keep me away from him.'

'So you decided to show him that, for you, it hadn't been just acting.'

'Something like that.' Despite the heat, Claire shivers. 'It was pretty messy. I was in hospital for a month. They had to write me out of the script. Afterwards, I found I was unemployable. I'd committed the cardinal sin, you see. I'd been unprofessional.'

'Thank you, Claire,' Dr Leichtman says quietly. 'That's all I needed to know.'

When they get back, Frank is waiting in Reception. 'How's it going?' he asks.

Claire's expecting the psychiatrist to take him off somewhere to talk in private. But Dr Leichtman just says matter-of-factly, 'Well, she's insecure, she's impulsive, she's desperately searching for some authority in her life and, though she tries very hard to hide it, she craves approval like a junkie craving a fix. What can I say, Frank? She's an actress.' She sighs. 'None of that matters, of course. If you want to know whether I think she could do it, then yes, I think she probably could. She's a quick learner, she's tough and she's smart. Somewhat against my better judgement, I think this might just be worth a try.'

CHAPTER TWELVE

Claire sits at a table in the office block. She holds a pen in one hand and a sheaf of papers in the other.

Consent forms. Dozens of them.

Personal-injury waivers, surveillance permissions, confidentiality agreements. And forms about the forms. Forms that say she understands what she's doing when she signs the other forms. Forms that say she gives her agreement freely and in the certain knowledge that it will fuck up her life. Forms that say she should really have a lawyer to explain the other forms.

She works through them, initialling each page and signing where requested.

'Welcome to boot camp, soldier. Now your ass is mine,' Dr Leichtman growls, gathering them up.

It's the worst Denzel Washington impression Claire's ever heard.

Training begins in a big, empty auditorium somewhere in the bowels of the building.

'First, a history lesson,' Connie says. 'Let's take a look at some monsters.'

The house lights dim. The psychiatrist clicks a remote control in her palm. Smoke from her cigarette pours across a projector beam, clouding the face on the screen.

'This is Peter Kürten, otherwise known as "The Beast of Düsseldorf". His wife told the police psychologist, a man called Dr Berg, that their sex life had been completely normal. Kürten, on the other hand, told Dr Berg that he fantasized about throttling her every single time they made love. These next slides are some of Kürten's victims, just as he left them.'

When Claire can bear to look again, there's a different face on the screen.

'Bela Kiss, who preserved his victims' bodies in empty petrol drums. Joachim Kroll, "the Ruhr Hunter". Hans van Zon; his turf was Holland in the 1960s. Among others, he killed his own girlfriend in order to have sex with her corpse.'

Somewhere behind Claire, the carousel of slides whirrs and clicks, slotting another face and another grainy image of a crime scene into Connie's litany. A jumble of names and atrocities, from which occasional details stand out.

'Patrick Byrne. He left a note by the violated body of one young woman that read simply, "This is the thing I thought would never come." Jack the Stripper – not his real name. The British tabloids called him that because flecks from a paint gun were found in his victims' hair. Your countrymen's famous sense of humour, I suppose. Jack literally asphyxiated his victims by pushing his penis down their throats. Albert Fish. Earle Nelson. Donald Fearn, who was obsessed with Pueblo Indians. He tied seventeen-year-old Alice Porter to an altar in an abandoned church, tortured her all night, smashed her skull with a hammer and raped her as she died.'

The list goes on and on, like a roll-call of evil.

'. . . kept the bodies of his victims in his apartment because, he said, "It was nice to have someone to come home to." These are some of the sketches Nilsen made of his victims. Good, aren't they? Jeffrey Dahmer. George Russell. And last, but certainly not least, Andrei Chikatilo, the Rostov Ripper, executed in 1994 for the torture and post-mortem violation of over fifty-two victims.'

Dr Leichtman stands up and walks to the front. Andrei Chikatilo's projected eyes swim briefly across her forehead. Then the house lights come up and the illusion is broken. 'I'm not showing you all this stuff just to spook you, Claire. As a result of studying these people, we know a considerable amount about the way a killer's mind works. We can look at the way he leaves a crime scene and make predictions about his personality, his intelligence, his relationships, even what kind of car he drives.' She holds up a bulging folder secured with a rubber band. 'This is everything we think we know about Stella Vogler's killer.' She places it on the desk in front of Claire. 'I warn you, it doesn't make easy reading.'

'Is this what they call a psychological profile?' Claire asks, picking it up.

'That's part of it, yes. And there are also photographs, case histories and some excerpts from textbooks. Our job is a bit like bomb disposal. Before you start pulling at the wires, you'd better know which one leads to the explosive.'

Christian Vogler knocks on the door of room 507 on the fifth floor of the Lexington Hotel.

Stella Vogler says cautiously, 'Who is it?'

'Room service.'

'I didn't order anything.'

There's no reply. With a gesture of impatience she goes to the door and pulls it all the way open. 'You've got the wrong—'

But Vogler has already pushed his way in. When she sees who it is, she takes a step back.

'Christian. What are you doing here? I thought—'

'Hello, Stella.'

'Christian, please. This isn't what it seems.'

Vogler throws a bag onto the bed. It makes an ominous, heavy noise. He looks over at Dr Leichtman. 'Do I hit her now?'

'Probably. The first thing you'd want to do is establish control of the situation. You'd need to get the gag on first, then the cuffs. That would happen now, while she's still disorientated.'

Frank nods. Back in character, he empties the bag onto the bed – a tangled snake coil of metal chains, handcuffs and strips of cloth for gags.

'I'd scream,' Claire objects.

'Not necessarily. However much people tell themselves they'd resist in these situations, the reality is that they're paralysed by a combination of indecision and disbelief. Plus, if Christian has hit you, you'll be in shock. He'll use that interval to get the restraints in place.'

Frank mimes hitting Claire across the face, then twists her round and snaps a cuff onto her wrist. His hand on her arm is heavy and implacable, twisting it back. She feels the masculine strength of him and yelps.

'Sorry,' he says, easing up.

CHAPTER THIRTEEN

Welcome to Necropolis.

This is a members-only adult website for those whose fantasies include total power exchange and extreme domination scenarios. It contains material offensive to the vast majority. We make no apologies for what we are, but we do warn you not to enter if such material is not for you.

In Necropolis, there are no limits. In real life, practise safe sex.

Claire signs up and waits while the computer submits her form electronically. A few minutes later the computer beeps. Her membership password is in her e-mail.

'When the police took Vogler's computer in, they went through his hard drive for fragments of erased data,' Dr Leichtman told her earlier. 'They discovered the computer had been used to access more than a dozen hardcore Internet sites.' She handed Claire a slip of paper. 'This is today's homework assignment. Find out everything you can about the people who visit these places. Read about them, talk to them. See if you can figure out what makes them tick.'

'Talk to them? Won't they want to talk back?'

'Of course. You'll have to start thinking about your cover story.' Dr Leichtman looked at her watch. 'I'll be back in a couple of hours to see how you're doing.'

Claire types her password into a log-in screen, and suddenly she's in. The site's divided into different sections: Photos, Fantasies, Lonely Hearts, Chat. A message appears:

> Since you're new, why not sign our
> guest book and introduce yourself?
> Read what some other new members
> have said, or go directly to the chat
> room and say hello.

What to put? She wishes Connie Leichtman was there to advise her. Then she realizes that the psychiatrist is deliberately letting her do this alone. What do teachers call it? Learning by doing.

Evidently the tests aren't over yet. She's had the oral, this is the written.

She types:

> >>Hi. My name is Claire. I'm twenty-
> five years old and I live in NYC.

She takes a deep breath and continues:

> I don't know if I would ever have the
> courage to explore my fantasies for

real, but I would love to share
experiences, dreams and thoughts
with other members.

Within a few moments she has three replies.

>>Hi Claire. Like the photo?

She watches, appalled, as a picture downloads a strip at a time. It's a naked girl, clutching a knife to her stomach, gore and blood spreading everywhere.

But, in truth, it's so obviously posed that, once the picture is fully loaded, it seems no more threatening than a cartoon. She types back:

>>No. It looks pretty dumb to me.

The second reply is longer and more detailed. The writer, who calls himself The Beast, wants her to know that he would love to strangle her, spread her legs and force himself on her as she chokes underneath him. He wants to hear her beg for mercy. He wants to hear her beg for more. She types:

>>I seem to do a lot of begging for
someone who's choking to death.

The third reply says simply:

>>It's kind of quiet right now because
it's the middle of the day — the only
people around are these frat-house
brats. Why not come back this
evening and I'll introduce you to the
grown-ups?
Regards, Victor.

>>Thanks,

she types gratefully. She moves on to another site.

At a restaurant, they discuss sex murders over the dish of the day.

'Get this straight, Claire. Our killer isn't a sado-masochist in the modern sense of the word. But he may well choose to hide amongst practitioners of S&M, because he shares certain of their interests. Where they use bondage as a shortcut to sexual pleasure, he uses it as a shortcut to the things *he's* interested in: humiliation, degradation, the power of life and death over another human being.'

The waiter comes over to pour some more water for them. He smiles at Claire. Dr Leichtman, oblivious, carries on talking.

'Sadomasochism is very interesting, actually. Why is it suddenly hitting the mainstream? It used to be thought that a propensity for masochism was caused by physical punishment in childhood. But strangely enough, it's the Spock generation, the ones who were never smacked, who've grown up wanting to experiment with bondage and control.'

The waiter, fascinated, can't tear himself away.

'Sometimes we can understand *how* a person's sexuality is wired, but not *why*. You ever watch a butterfly trying to mate with a fluttering leaf? Sex crimes are just another example of biological overkill.'

There are white plastic teacher's boards on three of the four walls of the little classroom. Dr Leichtman, Frank and Claire stand beside them, one apiece.

'OK,' Connie says. 'I'm the killer. Frank, you

96

take Vogler.' She tosses a marker pen to Frank, who uncaps it and writes 'Vogler' on his board, just as she is writing 'Killer' on hers.

'What do I do?' Claire asks.

'Nothing, yet. But if we both write the same word – in other words, if there's an overlap – then you write it on your board, too.'

'First of all,' Frank says, 'he's smart.' He writes 'High IQ' on his board.

'Same here,' Dr Leichtman murmurs. 'Claire, that's your first overlap.'

'He's a loner.'

Dr Leichtman nods. 'While over here we've got poor heterosocial skills.'

'His previous relationships have ended badly. And his marriage was heading for some kind of crisis.'

'A history of failed relationships. That's also typical of a sex killer.' Dr Leichtman's pen squeaks on the white surface of her board. 'My turn. We know this killer's highly selective – one might say, a perfectionist.'

'While Vogler's been described as a control freak.'

'If he follows the same pattern as other sex killers, he'll have a highly developed fantasy world which sustains him between killings.'

Frank pauses for a moment. 'Vogler's kind of a fantasist, too,' he says. 'Poetry and all that.'

'OK. Claire, put "fantasy" down.'

Several minutes later they draw to a close.

'So, what do we have?' Dr Leichtman asks.

Claire indicates her board. 'All of those are the overlaps.'

'Which means' – Dr Leichtman walks across,

takes Claire's marker from her and writes on her board the single word 'Claire' – 'in order to attract him, you have to appeal to all these qualities.' She rings the words on Claire's board as she speaks. 'You have to be naive, curious about new experiences, yet appealing to his sense of secrecy. Intelligent, yet not so much that you threaten his desire to master and control you. Vulnerable. A fantasist who can enter and share his private world. Interested in erotica and the dark side of your own sexuality. A perfect victim to appeal to his desire for perfect control. You see? These qualities, and only these, we can justify on the basis of what we know about the killer. Anything else is just a fishing expedition.'

'So you need me to turn this list into a plausible character.'

'Exactly.'

'No problem. It's just like constructing a character from a script, isn't it? Except that here the character comes first. How do I approach him?'

Dr Leichtman caps her pen. 'Leave that to us.'

CHAPTER FOURTEEN

Dear Mr Vogler,

You may remember lending me the enclosed book, *Les Fleurs du Mal*. I met you in Flaherty's about six months ago, and although our conversation was a brief one, I have often thought about it. I apologize for not returning the book sooner, but I've been reading the poems with fascination and didn't want to send it back until I'd finished.

In fact, I should be completely open with you and admit there was another reason I didn't get in touch before. I saw in the papers that your wife had died, and I didn't know what to begin to say to you. I hope that now a little time has passed you are beginning to put some of that behind you. Believe me, I know what it is like to have lost someone close.

Perhaps those experiences of mine are the reason I find so many resonances in Baudelaire. I love his darker, more ambiguous poems in particular. I, too, have 'a thirst for oblivion', and seem to recognize in his writing something of my own particular sensuality.

I have tried to translate several of the poems, though I'm sure you would laugh at my efforts. His words seem to lose so much of their erotic charge in translation.

I would be very interested to know what you think and am enclosing my e-mail address in the hope that we can continue our discussion.

Claire Rodenburg.

'He won't reply,' Frank says.

'He will if he's the killer,' Dr Leichtman says calmly. 'If he's the killer, he'll be drawn to her vulnerability the way a shark's drawn to blood.'

Another lesson – outside, this time, while Dr Leichtman gulps down nicotine from yet another cigarette.

'My first plan of attack is to get Vogler to expose himself through his fantasies. If he's the killer, he'll have an extremely sophisticated and well-developed fantasy life. The killing fuels the fantasies, and the fantasies in turn fuel the desire to kill again. In the right circumstances, and with the right confidante, I believe he could be induced to reveal what he fantasizes about.'

'Why would he do that?' Claire objects. 'I thought we agreed that this guy was smart.'

'Yes, but he's also lonely. He's aware that he's crossed a threshold that separates him from other men. He'll jump at the chance to connect with someone who seems to share his predilections.' She waves the cigarette like a baton as she talks. 'As he reveals more, the details of his fantasies will increasingly come to resemble the actual details of the murder – not surprisingly, since that's the fantasy that sustains him. He'll derive potent gratification from reliving every moment. Even so, I'd expect him to quickly try to move the relationship with the confidante from the verbal to the real. He'll fabricate whatever pretext he thinks necessary to progress to physical intimacy.'

Claire turns to look at Dr Leichtman. 'Physical intimacy? You mean he'll want to sleep with me?'

'Don't worry. We'll have secured the information we need long before it comes to that.'

'But I'll have to . . . seduce him, won't I?'

Dr Leichtman looks at Claire. Then she leans over and kisses her, on the lips. Claire doesn't react.

'Good,' Dr Leichtman says. 'Very good.'

She's made new friends. Carrie, Victor, The Brat, Beethoven and The Marquis.

> >>In pain, elegance is everything.
> There's no satisfaction in trussing up
> a submissive like a steer and booting
> them in the stomach. To the accom-
> plished top, half the pleasure lies in
> selecting a posture or activity in which
> the slightest movement, or the small-
> est change in the cinching of a knot,
> will produce exquisite suffering.

That's Beethoven. Carrie adds:

> >>Absolutely. One of my favourite toys
> ever was a simple plank of wood,

turned edge-on and raised just a couple of inches too high to comfortably stand astride. My bottom had to get on the very tips of her toes to straddle it. Watching her as she slowly grew too exhausted to maintain the position and sank onto the painful edge was a pleasure in itself.

Claire types:

>>'My bottom'? Sorry, I don't understand.

Victor explains:

>> When Carrie talks about her bottom, she doesn't mean part of her own anatomy, Claire. She's talking about her submissive.

>>Ah. Sorry.

This is a world as impenetrable and jargon ridden as the military, she's discovering. The acronyms alone are making her head spin. CP, BDSM, CBT, YMMV. She's plucked up the courage to ask about some of these, though discovering that YMMV means 'Your Mileage May Vary' hasn't actually clarified matters.

As for the conversations about neck snaps, Wurtenburg wheels, top space and pony play, she's floundering.

Carrie says:

>> Tops and bottoms fit together like two pieces of a puzzle, Claire. To us

it's a relationship as natural, and as neat, as the conjunction of male and female in the vanilla world.

>>The vanilla world? Oh, I see. One flavour suits all.

>>Exactly.

Carrie adds:

>>Your innocence is delicious, Claire. Sure you wouldn't like to step into a side window and try out some of my cybertoys? Netsex isn't quite like the real thing, but it can be just as intense.

Victor says:

>>Leave her be, Carrie. Claire is with us this evening purely as a curious observer.

She likes Victor. Although he contributes little to the discussion, preferring to lurk unseen on the sidelines, he seems to have appointed himself her guide to this strange new world, and he's doing a good job of making sure she doesn't get overwhelmed.

>>Sort of, try before you buy,

Carrie sneers. Claire types back:

>>More like look before you leap. Actually, I'm not entirely new to this

>stuff. Someone I knew once was into
it, but I was very young at the time,
and back then it seemed like a bit of
an acquired taste.

>>Is it? Once you're tuned into it,
control is implicit in every relationship.
We simply make overt what others
disregard. You know: 'In love there is
always one who kisses, and one who
turns the cheek.'

That was The Marquis. On an impulse, Claire
types:

>>I prefer Baudelaire myself. 'I have
more memories than if I had lived a
thousand years . . .'

Carrie says:

>>Oh God, not you too.

>>Me, too?

>>Victor's always quoting Baudelaire.
Come on, Victor, strut your stuff.

But Victor, still lurking on the sidelines, says
nothing.

In another room in the same building Connie
Leichtman and Frank Durban sit huddled over a
computer, watching the lines of text scrolling down
the screen.

'She's doing well,' Connie says at last. 'She's
established motivation and background, there's an
implicit appeal for a mentor to show her what to

do and a reason to hang back if things go too fast.'

'I told you she could improvise more than nonsense.'

'If she *is* still improvising,' Connie says.

It's gone midnight when she logs off. Her eyes ache and her wrist hurts from tapping at the keyboard.

Going past the open door of Dr Leichtman's office she hears the psychiatrist call her name. Connie is sitting at her desk, surrounded by paperwork. A cigarette, propped on an ashtray, pours a thick stream of smoke upwards into the cone of a desk lamp.

'You're working late, Claire.'

'I lost track of the time.'

'We don't pay overtime, you know.' Dr Leichtman holds out an envelope. 'But we do pay. Your first two weeks' salary, in advance.'

'Is it a cheque? Only I don't have a bank account.'

'We know. Don't worry. Two thousand dollars, cash.'

Dr Leichtman waits until the younger woman's footsteps have retreated down the corridor before she reopens the file she was working on.

The file is entitled 'Claire Rodenburg: psychological profile'.

Bessie isn't back from the show when Claire reaches the apartment. She checks her watch; it's gone one. Her roommate's probably still working off her adrenalin in a bar.

Claire takes a thousand dollars out of the envelope and fans it across Bessie's pillow. The bills still smell of Dr Leichtman's cigarettes. On the last one Claire writes, with a lipstick taken from Bessie's make-up table, 'RENT!'

Putting the lipstick back, she sees a crumpled business card amongst the make-up bottles. One end has been torn off, probably for a roach. She picks up the card and smoothes it out.

> Alan Gold
> Gold Associates
> Attorneys to the Music Industry

An address in Atlanta.

You sure worked that one out fast, Alan.

I'm a lawyer, after all. It's my job to know when a witness isn't telling the truth.

Sighing, she takes another $500 out of the envelope. Then she copies his address onto the front and seals it.

Across the back she writes, 'Hope things are OK with your wife.'

Seven miles away, on the other side of the river, Detective Durban waits for the flop. 'Hit me,' he says.

It's Mike Positano's turn on the button. 'Queen of spades, five of clubs, ten of clubs,' he says, laying them out.

Frank winces. Across the table from him, Eddie Lowell, a lean man in his early fifties, with hair greying where it hasn't been rubbed away by the worries in his lieutenant's cap band, laughs sonorously. 'Got the nuts, Frank?'

'Family pot,' Frank says disgustedly. 'I'll check.'

'I'll raise five,' Weeks says.

'Calling station Weeks,' Eddie murmurs.

'Did I call?' Weeks demands.

'As good as.' Five bucks wasn't a bet. Five bucks was a spectator's ticket.

'Fifteen dollars,' Weeks says, stung. Across the table, Eddie catches Frank's eye. No expression passes across either man's face, but the mere existence of such a glance is enough to tell both men they're thinking the same thing.

'Raise you fifty,' Frank says. Two minutes later, when Frank's remaining club comes through, Weeks is staring in disbelief as his money vanishes into Frank's top pocket.

'Slow-play bluff,' Eddie says, chuckling. 'Frank's speciality.'

'I'm out,' Weeks says miserably. 'I've lost enough for one night.'

Eddie yawns. 'Me, too. Thanks for the game, guys.'

Frank wants to say, One more game. But he doesn't. That's one of the things you learn, in poker. You never tell anyone what you really want.

So when the thought of going home is like the thought of taking a cold walk in the rain, you don't say anything. You just smile and say, 'See you tomorrow then, fellows. See you in the morning.'

Above the streets of SoHo, Christian Vogler is also awake. Dressed in a silk dressing gown, his face illuminated by the cold white glare of his computer screen, he pecks and taps at his keyboard.

There's a pause while his words are sucked down the thousands of miles of fibre-optic cable that make up his Internet link, then another pause while, from somewhere else in the world, another connection is made. Bytes of data rearrange themselves on his computer screen into words, images and thoughts.

Vogler's nostrils flare. Excitement spreads like a rush of drugs from his cortex into his central nervous system. But his hands stay glued to the keyboard, moving like a concert pianist's across the clattering plastic keys, weaving new melodies that only he can hear.

CHAPTER FIFTEEN

The next day Frank comes to her apartment early.

'Pack a suitcase, Claire. You won't be back for a while.'

'Where are we going?'

'Connie wants you somewhere that's more consistent with your story. We've had a decorator do a rush job for us.'

'A decorator? Hey, I'm going up in the world.'

She wakes Bessie, raiding her closet for emergency clothing supplies.

'Take care of yourself,' Bessie says anxiously. 'Don't let these people freak you out.'

'I won't,' Claire promises. Flicking through Bessie's underwear, she looks briefly at the gun, gleaming amidst lace and cotton. Then, a little reluctantly, she covers it up again.

There are so many things to say. But the policeman's waiting, and for once she can't think of a line.

'Break a leg,' Bessie says softly.

Claire nods.

As she pulls her suitcase down to the waiting car, she feels further from home than she has done for months.

*   *   *

He takes her to a walk-up on West 14th Street, on the fringes of the old meat packing district. Parts of this area have been redeveloped recently.

Not this part.

The apartment is a shithole. Black candles line the walls, beneath mounted animal parts and ripped heavy-metal posters. A battered electric guitar leans in one corner.

'For Christ's sake,' she says furiously, peering around at the fake velvet drapes and the Rothko prints Blu-tacked to the walls. 'Why not go the whole hog and give me white make-up and a Mohican?'

'It cost a lot of money to make the place look this bad,' Frank says mildly. 'You'd be surprised.' He picks up a painted human skull on which a candle has been mounted. 'Maybe they did go a little over the top.'

Wordlessly, Claire plucks the skull from him and tosses it into the trash.

'I'll let you unpack,' he says diplomatically. 'Get your own things around you. It'll feel homier then.'

She doesn't hear him. She's just seen the glass tank in the corner. Something silvery grey is slithering around inside. 'Is that a *snake*?'

'It's just for show, Claire. Kind of like a stage prop.'

She sighs, reaches for the suitcase.

'One other thing,' he says as he turns to go. 'The apartment is wired for audio and video, right? The boys are working on the facilities right now in the apartment downstairs.'

'What are you saying, Frank?'

'Well, the cameras aren't meant to be

operational yet. But they'll be testing the system from time to time. All I'm saying is, if you take a shower it might be best to turn the lights out.'

He comes back at noon and drives her to a small gym in SoHo. There, in a private room, he introduces her to a muscular man called Ray.

'Ray's gonna show you how to defend yourself.'

'Right,' Ray says. 'Just a crash course, you understand.'

When he says a crash course, he really means crash. She hits the mat over and over again, until her ribs ache and her body's black and blue.

But by the end of the session she knows how to disable someone who comes up behind you and puts a ligature over your head; how to maim; what a man's testicles feel like in your outstretched hand, before you start to twist them off, like an apple twisted from a tree.

She remembers stage fights, learning how to duel with blunt-tipped prop swords. It seems like another lifetime.

Who are you?
My name is Claire Rodenburg.
Where do you come from?
I was born in Ferry Springs, near Boise in Idaho. My father died in a plane crash when I was ten. My mother never remarried. I guess I've always had a thing for older men, for rebels.
Go on.
I had the usual high-school boyfriends. I lost my virginity to one of them when I was sixteen. After that, sex came easily. I hung out

with a pretty wild group. But they were never really all that wild, underneath. They all wanted the same things everybody else wanted: me, principally. Then, at college, I had an affair with one of my teachers. He was married.

What was his name?

Mr Furbank.

You didn't use your lover's christian name?

Sorry. Eliot Furbank. That was when I discovered I had a darker side, a part of me that wanted to be forced to go further than I'd ever been before. We couldn't be together that much, so he used to write stuff for me. Fantasies. He'd send them by e-mail, usually, or leave them in my pigeon-hole.

Good, Claire. What happened to him?

His wife found one of the letters. She took it straight to the dean. Eliot was fired, of course.

How did you feel about that?

I was elated. I thought we could finally be together. But he couldn't handle it. He ended up by killing himself. He left me one last note. He – he wanted me to join him.

And then?

Then I travelled. With hindsight, I can see I was just running away from something that had got way out of control.

You were running? Or you were searching?

A bit of both, I guess.

And what were you searching for?

I don't know. I read stuff – 'The Story of O', Anne Rice. After what I'd been through, it seemed a bit tame. But I'm curious. I guess I need a guide.

Don't say that. It's too overt. He'll see your potential for himself. Now, one more time: Who are you?

'I'll be moving into the apartment right below you,' Frank tells her later, in the car. 'If you need anything over the next few weeks, just knock on my door.'

'Is that really necessary? Moving in, I mean.'

'Maybe not yet. But it saves on commuting.'

'Won't Mrs Durban mind?'

'There is no Mrs Durban,' he says gruffly. 'Well, there is, but she's living with a designer now. Some guy who makes wedding cakes and stuff out of cardboard. He earns more in a month than I do in a year.'

'Is that why she left?'

'What makes you think *she* left *me*?'

'Because you strike me as too loyal to walk out on anyone?'

He keeps his eyes on the road. 'She left me because I worked too many nights and I'm grouchy when I don't get quality sleep.'

'So it's not the horrors of the job keeping you awake?' she asks, and suddenly now he does look across at her, his lips thin with anger.

'You've been spending too much time with Dr Leichtman, Claire. Save the psychobabble for her, hey?'

She's silent, puzzled. For the first time she begins to see that those putting this operation together might have different agendas, different plans of attack, perhaps even different objectives.

Frank finishes some take-out and channel-hops on the TV. There's nothing on.

He looks at his watch. It's gone midnight. He wrings one last tumbler of bourbon out of the bottle on the table.

Wandering round the deserted apartment, still festooned with leads and wires which the surveillance boys haven't tidied away, he stops in front of another, larger TV set, dumped incongruously in the middle of the main room.

He turns it on.

This time the remote control surfs, not through the late-night cable offerings and talk shows, but through a dozen different views of Claire's apartment, directly above.

He sees a table with an abandoned deli box, a half-empty bottle of Chardonnay. He hesitates, presses another button, sees the empty bed. He presses again.

She's standing, naked, by the open window, her back to him, looking out at the New York night.

She turns. There's a glass of wine in her hand, mirroring the shape of the dark shadow at the top of her legs. And he swears she must know where the cameras are, know that he's watching, because she looks directly at him and runs her free hand down her body in a slow, lingering caress.

She steps towards him. Her breasts fill the screen, and then she's beyond it.

And though he switches between the cameras for several long minutes, it's as if she's vanished into thin air.

CHAPTER SIXTEEN

She's woken the next morning by a banging on her apartment door.

'What's up, Frank?' she says blearily, opening the door to him.

He shows her the printout in his hand. 'It's from Vogler. We're in business.'

From: 'Christian Vogler' (CV@nyscu)
To: 'Claire Rodenburg'
(ClaireR@colormail.com)

Claire,

Of course I remember you. I seem to recall that on that occasion I was rather rude. I can seem a little distracted when my mind is on my work. I was deeply touched by your kind words, and not a little intrigued by your references to your own life.

Baudelaire is notoriously difficult to translate, but I hope that you find, as I have, that the effort is rewarded. Perhaps, if you are still struggling, you would like some help?

Regards,
Christian Vogler

'Are you sure?' Claire says doubtfully, reading it again. 'He sounds to me like he's just being polite.'
Frank says, 'Or he's being careful.'

From: 'Claire Rodenburg'
(ClaireR@colormail.com)
To: 'Christian Vogler' (CV@nyscu)

Dear Christian (may I call you that?),

Thanks for your e-mail. Re-reading my own letter I worry that I may have come across as a little strange. I suppose I have led a rather un-conventional life, perhaps too unconventional. I guess that's why the words of someone like Baudelaire, someone who has dared to go beyond the everyday, are so inspiring.

I love to imagine myself as his Vénus, receiving all those extraordinary poems, unsigned and anonymous. I wonder if he thought they would shock her, or if he knew she would be turned on by the things he had dared to conjure up?

I say imagine, but in fact I was once in a similar position myself, and I know what it's like being allowed inside someone's mind, being led little by little into their darkest, most bizarre fantasies. It's an amazing feeling.

> I guess some people would call what
> that man wrote me pornography. But
> to me they were as beautiful, and as
> honest, as any poems.
>
> Claire

Dr Leichtman agreed she should continue her acting classes, for the time being.

At the next session, Paul introduces them to mask work. The masks are Japanese, their features saved from mere caricature by the hint of cruelty in the way they're drawn. Hers is the Waif: an innocent, a lost child, with a smile that, though it never changes, seems somehow to be by turns eager and ingratiating, or knowing and coquettish.

Paul talks about them as if the masks, and not the actors, are the real people. When one of the students, having put on the mask of an old man, comes up behind Claire and pokes her with a stick, Paul says, 'He's always doing that, the old fool.'

Rather than act a scene together – there are no eye holes, and they'd have fallen over each other this first time – he has them stand in a row, facing him, as if he's the audience, acting out their roles simultaneously on the spot. The story is that of a landlord who comes to the rice fields and rapes a woman whose family can't pay the rent. The actor wearing the Rich Man mask knocks at an imaginary door; two actors down the line, the Waif opens it. When he rapes her, he has to mime his aggression, and Claire her fear, ten feet apart, without either of them being able to see what the other's doing.

117

Suddenly Claire realizes that, underneath the mask, she's crying. She doesn't know how, or why. It's as sudden and inexplicable as a nosebleed. For her, used to being able to control her tears at will, this sudden lack of control is as unsettling as the tears themselves.

When the scene's over she pulls off the mask and sits down, sucking in lungfuls of air to control herself. At first the others think she's fooling around. Then, one by one, they fall silent.

Paul comes over and squats down, so he's at the same height as her. 'You OK?'

She nods, not quite trusting herself to speak.

'It's like that with the masks sometimes,' he says quietly. 'If they trust you – if you're good – sometimes they make you pay a price for borrowing them.'

On her way back to her shithole apartment, she wanders into an optician's store. She chooses a pair of wire-framed glasses and tries them on, looking at herself in the mirror.

It works, kind of. The Hurt Girl.
She nods thoughtfully at her reflection.

From: 'Christian Vogler' (CV@nyscu)
To: 'Claire Rodenburg' (ClaireR@color-mail.com)

This sounds fascinating, Claire. Perhaps, if you are still in town, we could resume our conversation over a drink?

'We can't risk a meeting yet,' Dr Leichtman says firmly. 'Claire isn't ready, and neither am I.'

**From: 'Claire Rodenburg'
(ClaireR@colormail.com)**
To: 'Christian Vogler' (CV@nyscu)

Thanks, but I'm not actually in the city at present, though I am picking up my e-mails.

I don't quite know why I told you all that stuff about myself. Maybe it's because travelling alone makes me thoughtful, or melancholy, depending on your perspective.

It was a long time ago now, but yes, it was fascinating. Fascinating and terrifying and thrilling, all at once.

Claire

From: 'Christian Vogler' (CV@nyscu)
To: 'Claire Rodenburg'
(ClaireR@colormail.com)

If you are still in need of a shoulder to cry on . . . I have two here, and they're both at your disposal.

**From: 'Claire Rodenburg'
(ClaireR@colormail.com)**
To: 'Christian Vogler' (CV@nyscu)

Thanks. Could I have some arms to go with that?

From: 'Christian Vogler' (CV@nyscu)
To: 'Claire Rodenburg'
(ClaireR@colormail.com)

You could indeed. Anything else you need?

From: 'Claire Rodenburg'
(ClaireR@colormail.com)
To: 'Christian Vogler' (CV@nyscu)

Well, since you ask . . . but maybe that would be too much . . .

From:'Christian Vogler' (CV@nyscu)
To: 'Claire Rodenburg'
(ClaireR@colormail.com)

What? Please, my evenings are long and lonesome at the moment, and I hate to think of you Melancholy in Memphis, or wherever it is you are.

From: 'Claire Rodenburg'
(ClaireR@colormail.com)
To: 'Christian Vogler' (CV@nyscu)

Well . . . I miss those fantasies he used to send me.

From: 'Christian Vogler' (CV@nyscu)
To: 'Claire Rodenburg'
(ClaireR@colormail.com)

In that case, perhaps the enclosed will keep you company on your travels.

<<forclaire.doc>>

CHAPTER SEVENTEEN

'It's all there,' Frank says. For the first time since Claire has known him there's a flicker of excitement on the detective's face. He re-reads Vogler's fantasy for the third or fourth time. 'My God, it's all there.'

Dr Leichtman doesn't answer. The only sound is her pencil tapping against her teeth.

'It's just as you expected,' Claire says to her. 'Everything you said he'd write about. Violence, pain, control.'

The pencil continues to tap.

Frank reads aloud, ' "The musky smell of your arousal fills the room, like the sickly perfume of a rare flower, an orchid that releases its heavenly odours only as it starts to wither and decay . . ." This is weird shit, Connie.'

The tapping stops. Dr Leichtman says, 'He could have gone down to the bookstore and copied that out from any one of half a dozen books in the adult fiction section. It's mildly deviant, sure, but I couldn't put my hand on my heart and say that only a killer would have written it.'

'He hasn't eliminated himself, though.'

'He hasn't, no. Not yet.'

'So what do we do now?'

Dr Leichtman turns to Claire. 'It's possible he's

simply holding back. You need to show him you're tougher than he thinks you are. Write back. Give him something in the same vein, but stronger.'

'You want *me* to write it? Couldn't you?'

Dr Leichtman shakes her head. 'Uh-uh. Why do you think we got you to spend so much time on those websites? It needs to be in your voice – or the voice of the person you're pretending to be.'

Sitting down at her laptop, Claire has to remind herself that she's done harder things than this, that she once went out into the New York streets and sold sweaters made of hippopotamus wool.

**From: 'Claire Rodenburg'
(ClaireR@colormail.com)**
To: 'Christian Vogler' (CV@nyscu)

Dear Christian,

Thank you for the fantasy. It's wonderful. But believe me, Christian, the things you describe are fairly tame for me. The things I like . . . sometimes I scare myself with how extreme they are – God, why am I telling a total stranger this? – Sometimes I look at the things that turn me on, things that humiliate me, that make me powerless and vulnerable and afraid, and think there's something wrong with me or that I'm weird in some way.

I'm only telling you this because I sense that you might actually understand. I'm almost nervous of you writing anything else in case you get it wrong. Perhaps it would be better to say goodbye now, before this takes us any further.

I wrote something myself. Tell me if you like it.

With love,

Claire.

<<forchristian.doc>>

From: 'Christian Vogler' (CV@nyscu)
To: 'Claire Rodenburg' (ClaireR@colormail.com)

Claire,

What a remarkable woman you are turning out to be. I am very much looking forward to meeting when you're back.

In the meantime, you may find the attached a little more to your taste.

<<claire2.doc>>

In the second fantasy he wrote for her, Christian described how he would blindfold Claire and beat her with a belt. He wrote, 'The belt strokes your body. It's a snake, a long black serpent that insinuates itself into the curve of your perfect breasts, the dip of your armpit, the prow of your pubic mound and the swollen, glistening tongue of your sex.

'You're trembling. The snake draws back. But it

has only drawn back to gather power for its bite.

'Just as you are tensing for the blow, you feel something touch your lips: the end of the belt. "Kiss it," I order, and obediently you touch your mouth to the soft, cruel lips of the snake. There is a pause. Then, suddenly, you scream. You have felt the sweet sharp sting of its teeth across your belly and your breasts.

'I say quietly, "One" . . .'

In his third fantasy he described Claire lying on a bed of freshly laundered sheets, surrounded by a dozen candles, like a body laid out on a white stone altar. 'I pick up the candles one by one. They are fat and heavy, like the candles in a church. The flames are shaped like spear points, big and white hot, tipped with inky smoke. Each flame is surrounded by a disc of clear molten wax. I hold the first candle above your motionless body and tip the hot wax onto your skin. You flinch, but you do not cry out. The wax hardens on your soft skin, like a scar.'

In the fourth, he described her being surprised in her hotel room by a cold, mysterious stranger, who ties her to the bed with ropes.

'This is good,' Dr Leichtman says, reading from the screen. 'We're getting a lot of material here.'

'Like what?' Frank asks.

'This stuff with the restraints, for example. He's moving progressively closer to the actual circumstances of the killing. And setting it in a hotel room, that's a very significant overlap.'

'But nothing that only the killer would know. And a lawyer would say that we'd suggested the hotel room ourselves by telling him that Claire's travelling at the moment.'

'Give him time, Frank. On the strength of this, I can already say that Vogler has a sexual deviance that only a tiny proportion of the population would share. The chances that Stella knew two people like that are minuscule. Let the net close slowly. It'll be all the tighter when it does.'

From: 'Claire Rodenburg'
(ClaireR@colormail.com)
To: 'Christian Vogler' (CV@nyscu)

Very nice, Christian. But, I wonder, how much further do you dare to go?

As for meeting, we'll see. I suppose I'm in two minds. A part of me is saying, you must meet up with this incredible person who understands you so exactly. Another part is reminding me that I've been let down so many times before. And, once – well, as I told you, once I wasn't let down, and that was even worse in the end. A long story, and a tragic one, which maybe I'll tell you all about some day.

I read your last e-mail in a cybercafé in Chicago with two very straight college kids on the next machine. If only they could have seen what I was reading! Couldn't wait to get back to the privacy of my hotel room, as a matter of fact . . .

There's a passage from Baudelaire I found in a bookshop here:

Is ours so strange an act, so full of
    shame?
Explain the terrors that disturb my
    bliss.
When you say Love, I tremble at the
    word,
And yet my mouth is thirsty for your
    kiss.

Keep writing me, Christian. Please.
Claire
X

CHAPTER EIGHTEEN

'Today,' Dr Leichtman says, 'we're going to learn how to listen.'

'What?'

'I said, today—' She stops. 'Oh. Ha ha. Very amusing.'

It's the morning of the ninth day, and both of them are wondering what the hell they've got themselves into.

'What I'm going to show you now', she continues, 'are some basic neurolinguistic techniques.'

She puts a chart on the overhead projector. It's divided into two columns, one headed 'Wrong', the other headed 'Right'. She points to the first item.

'First, try to refrain from making judgements. Saying "that's disgusting" or even "that's wonderful" is less useful than a neutral response such as "I see" or "how did you feel about that?" Advice – "why don't you try this?" – is also not so good. Better to make observations: "I can see you're feeling tense" or ... you're fidgeting, Claire. Is something wrong?'

Claire shrugs. 'We covered all this in week one of my acting classes. Except we called it blocking and accepting.'

'I think you'll find this is actually a little different. Now then—'

'How much longer are we going to go on *talking* about all this?' Claire moans.

'My training lasted seven years. I hardly think that nine days—'

'I hardly think that nine days—' Claire parrots. The mimicry of Dr Leichtman's voice is so exact that the psychiatrist flushes.

'That reminds me, Claire,' she says frostily. 'You must tell us when you're having your periods. We may have to structure the operation around your *moody* times.'

Halfway through the afternoon session, Dr Leichtman's pager goes off. Connie pulls it out of her pocket, reads the message quickly, then hurries to a phone.

'Anything exciting?' Claire says when she comes back.

'Sort of.' Dr Leichtman puts the pager down on the desk.

'Well?' Claire says when Connie doesn't elaborate. 'What is it?'

'There's been another murder. The police think . . . it's possible it was the same killer. They'd like me to take a look.' She looks at Claire. 'Want to come?'

'Me?' Claire says, surprised.

'I think it might be useful for you to see exactly what we're up against here,' Dr Leichtman says quietly.

Another hotel. This time it's a cheap flophouse on Second Avenue, among the city's last remaining peep shows and sex cinemas. Judging from the smell in the corridors, it's the kind of place where most of the customers don't stay a whole night.

Claire and Dr Leichtman have to wait downstairs for Crime Search to finish up. Dr Leichtman is visibly agitated. At first Claire mistakes it for nerves, but gradually she becomes aware that it isn't fear the other woman's feeling.

Connie's excited.

She catches Claire looking at her. 'It's rare to get a chance to see a scene this fresh,' she explains.

They're given white paper jumpsuits, to contain any stray fibres from their clothes, and elasticated plastic bags to put over their shoes. Then they're escorted upstairs.

Durban is already there. He watches them as they edge into the room.

'Why's she here?' he says, pointing at Claire.

'I wanted her to come.'

For a moment Claire has the impression that Frank's about to object. Then he shrugs.

'When they found her, this is how she was,' he says, gesturing at the bed. A blanket covers the outline of a body.

'Were the blinds drawn?' Dr Leichtman asks.

'No.'

'Suggests it was still dark when he left,' she murmurs. 'He didn't stay here long.'

Frank puts his hand to the blanket. 'This isn't pretty,' he warns Claire. He pulls the blanket back.

Claire gasps, but no air comes. It's as if someone has sucked all the oxygen out of the little room.

The body on the bed is black and female. It's lying face up, except that it has no face. It has no head, either. Where the neck should be is a bloody stump, a flattened sleeve of skin encasing a slender tube of white gristle.

The policeman pulls the blanket back further. Between the girl's naked legs is a head. Oil gleams in the short, afro hair. The bulging, swollen tongue has been aimed directly at the junction of the thighs.

Claire turns, runs into the bathroom and heaves into the shower.

After a few moments Frank comes after her. 'Sorry,' she chokes.

'Don't be. No-one should get used to seeing this stuff.'

She indicates the puke in the shower. 'Have I—'

'Contaminated the crime scene? Don't worry. We were done in here. Look, if you don't want to go back—'

She shakes her head. 'I'll be OK.' She follows him back into the bedroom.

'See her ears?' Frank says to Dr Leichtman. On either side of the girl's head, two bloody holes have been ripped in her ear lobes. 'The earrings have been pulled off. Same with the navel stud.'

'Taken as trophies?'

'No. Thrown down the john. Flushed, but they were too heavy to get round the bend.'

'Interesting,' Dr Leichtman says. 'Stella's jewellery was removed as well, wasn't it?' She peers at the stump of the neck. 'Did she struggle?' Like Frank's, her voice is flat; a professional monotone.

'The ME's not sure. There are signs of a fight: scuffed walls, a broken lamp.' He shows her. 'Trouble is, in a place like this it could have been that way before.'

'Polaroids?'

'None that we know of.'

'What about intercourse?'

Frank shakes his head. 'One of my colleagues used to work in Vice. He thinks the victim's a hooker. If that's right, and if she's had other clients in the last twenty-four hours, forensics aren't going to be much use.' He shrugs. 'We'll try anyway, of course. Maybe we can track her other customers and eliminate them.' He doesn't sound hopeful. 'What do you think, Connie? Are we looking at the same guy?'

'I'm not sure. On the one hand, it's a hotel room, it's another over-the-top killing, and the jewellery – that certainly seems to indicate a pattern. But you have to look at all the dissimilarities, too. It's a hotel room, yes, but a very different hotel, and a very different set of circumstances. Stella's killer came prepared. He took pains over what he did; he wanted it to be perfect, to match his fantasies exactly. This looks less organized, less controlled.'

'The hotel may have been all he could get, for cash,' Frank says. 'I've had someone check; there are two big conventions in town. There isn't a free room this side of the river.'

'Then there's the fact that he left while it was dark. He didn't even close the drapes. Stella's killer spent time with her. Remember the Polaroids?'

'Maybe he was concerned that the struggle had been heard. For all he knew she had a pimp waiting.'

'OK. But why do something like this in the first place if he can't do it the way he wants?'

'This may have something to do with it.' Frank lifts up the corpse's arm. 'Take a look at that.'

On the palm of the girl's hand something has been written.

The psychiatrist peers in closer. It's been written in black ink on the dark skin, so it takes her a few moments. 'www.pictureman.com. It's a web address.'

Frank nods. 'Looks that way.'

'What makes you sure it's connected to the murder? Some people write things on their hands to remember them.'

'True. But if she is a hooker, anything written on her palm would rub off pretty quickly.' He makes an obscene gesture to make his meaning clear.

'Has anyone checked it out? It's a hardcore site, right?'

'No. No, that's the strange thing. When you type in that address, the computer tells you it doesn't exist.'

Afterwards, Connie takes Claire to a coffee shop, buys a coffee and pours two sachets of sugar into it.

'Drink this,' she says. 'It'll stop you shaking.'

Claire has to hold the cup in two hands to get it to her mouth.

'Images on the screen,' Connie says. 'They're never quite the same, are they?'

Claire nods.

'You acquitted yourself well today,' Dr Leichtman says gently.

Claire finds her voice. ' "Acquitted?" As in, "Miss Rodenburg, you are free to go?"'

'You're always free to go, Claire. Nobody can force you to do this.'

'Is that why you wanted me to come with you?

To see if I'd be scared?'

'To see if you were ready.'

She feels a sudden quickening of her pulse.

Connie says, 'As you know, I've had my doubts about this operation. And I'd like more time to prepare you, much more time. But we haven't got it. Once a killer's timescale – his intervals between killings – becomes accelerated, it never reverts. He's going to kill more often now.' The psychiatrist nods. 'Tell Christian tonight you'll be back in town tomorrow.'

PART THREE

'Certain illustrious poets have long since divided amongst themselves the more flowery provinces of the realm of poetry. I have found it more amusing, not least because it is more challenging, to extract beauty from evil.'

Les Fleurs du Mal, Baudelaire

CHAPTER NINETEEN

Her friend hasn't showed.

That's what you'd think if you saw her, waiting on her own at a table near the bar, trying to make her Virgin Mary last all evening; just another young professional waiting for her date. Perhaps a little prettier than most. A little more daringly dressed. She hasn't come straight from the office, that's for sure.

She's managed to get a table with a view of the entrance, and she scans the door anxiously, waiting.

But when he comes, it's from behind her, pulling up the chair next to hers. She wonders how long he's been there, watching.

He's wearing a dark leather jacket, a fine black cotton polo-neck and khaki pants. He twists the heavy ring on his little finger once as he sits down.

'Claire,' he says. 'How wonderful to see you.' His gooseberry-green eyes lock onto hers. For a moment she has the sensation that he can see everything, that he knows everything, that he can see the wires taped to her skin and the betrayal in her heart.

'Hello, Christian,' she says.

* * *

All afternoon Connie's been making Claire rehearse her cover story one last time. *Who are you? Why are you here? What do you want?*

But Claire has been preoccupied with a rather more practical matter. When she was working for Henry, she used to do each assignment in a different voice or accent. For practice, as much as anything else.

Now she can't remember if the Claire whom Christian Vogler last met was American or English. The cover story is flexible enough to accommodate either, of course. The problem is whether he'll spot the inconsistency.

She's gone for American. Either it's the right choice, or Christian doesn't recall her that well.

'You're even prettier than I remembered,' he says, and leans forward to kiss her cheek.

His leather jacket brushes against her, soft as a cobweb, and she remembers Bessie, a vegetarian, telling her that to get leather that soft they use the skins of unborn calves.

'Thank you,' she says. How would her character react? 'Though actually I'd prefer it if you didn't lie to me, even if it is for the sake of a compliment.'

Too much, she wonders? But Vogler is smiling at her prickliness.

'It isn't a lie,' he says. 'I don't lie about things that matter.'

There's a pause while they order drinks. She touches the back of her head, idly stroking the unfamiliar bristles on the nape of her neck. The hairdresser she went to that afternoon had begged her not to have it cut short, insisting that it would never grow back the same. But she had been adamant, and eventually the hairdresser had done as he was asked. Clumps of damp hair fell around her eyes like snow.

Short hair, like his wife's. A tiny detail, but who could say which tiny detail would be the one that made the difference?

Frank, sitting in the hairdresser's waiting area, had watched her in the mirror, his hard eyes softened with what might have been pity.

As the hairdresser trimmed and snipped, Claire had the feeling that she was crossing at last from Connie's field of influence to the policeman's. From ideas to action.

No more read-throughs or rehearsals.

Show time.

'This is . . . strange,' she begins hesitantly.

'Strange? In what way?'

'To meet like this . . . in the flesh, so to speak, having already been so . . . intimate.' She meets his eye. 'Kind of like waking up next to a stranger and having to talk about breakfast.'

Claire's backpack, casually propped under the glass table, feeds audio and video to the watchers. Outside, in the surveillance van, Connie, hearing one of her own lines fed effortlessly into the script, nods appreciatively.

Frank's right. The girl can act.

Christian's eyes don't leave hers. 'And is that some-thing that happens often? Waking up next to a stranger?'

'Oh, no. I just meant . . . well, yes. Sometimes.' She lowers her gaze. 'More in my wild youth, perhaps.'

'You don't seem that wild to me.'

'Appearances can be deceptive.'

'Not yours, I think.'

Her character gets a little riled at this, at the assumption that he has her neatly boxed up and filed away. 'Oh? And what does my *appearance* tell you?'

He reaches out and gently turns her head sideways, so that he can study her in profile. She can't help it: she flinches, just a little, at the touch of his fingers. He doesn't seem to notice.

'I see someone . . . beautiful, but unhappy,' he says. 'That's right, isn't it?'

'Don't get the wrong idea,' she says tartly. 'I'm not some desperate singleton looking for a man.'

'That's not what I meant.'

'I doubt if there's one person in this room who's done the things I've done.'

' "I have more memories than if I had lived a thousand years . . . ?" '

'Exactly.'

'Sometimes,' he says, carefully, 'the things we fantasize about, we don't want in reality.'

'Sometimes we know what we really want, but we need some help to get there.'

'Most people would say that taboos are there to protect us.'

'You and I are different from most people.'

'That's true,' he murmurs.

She meets the green eyes full on. 'Our fantasies,' she says. 'We have our fantasies.'

After a moment he shakes his head. 'No,' he says. 'Those were yours, not mine.'

In the van outside, Frank and Connie look at each other.

* * *

'Yes. *Your* fantasies. You wrote them.' She's puzzled, aware that a sudden change of mood has taken place, unsure why.

'Of course,' Christian says. 'You told me what you wanted, and I obliged. I'm a translator. I work in other people's voices, other people's styles, all the time. Baudelaire's, for example.'

'But you like Baudelaire,' she says, confused.

'Do I? Oh, he has some stylistic quirks that make him interesting to me on a technical level. That's why he fascinates me: as a challenge.' Christian Vogler takes a handful of pretzels from the dish on the table. 'You mustn't take all that adolescent doom and gloom too seriously.'

'I see,' she says, though in fact she's not quite sure what she sees any more.

'Listen, Claire,' he says, more gently. 'I wanted to meet you because, well, you're right when you say that we have something in common. Like you, I lost someone very close to me.'

'I know. I saw in the papers—'

'I'm not referring to Stella's death, not entirely. I had started to lose her even before that.' He sighs. 'Perhaps if she had lived we could have resolved our problems. It's one of the many questions I'll never be able to answer, now. But my point is that, like you, I know what it is to grieve. And I know how easy it is to let grief destroy you. You feel an overwhelming guilt for being the one who survived. You want to punish yourself . . . or, in your case perhaps, to find someone else who'll do the punishing for you. But there comes a time when you have to let go of your guilt and anger. Life goes on, but only if you let it.'

141

She nods. In all their rehearsals they'd never considered this.

'I brought you something,' he says, and he pulls a little book out of his jacket pocket, pressing it into her hand. 'Here.'

For a moment she thinks it's another book of poetry. Then she sees it's one of those slim volumes of New Age philosophy, the ones you saw piled next to the cash register in bookstores. She looks at the title. *The Little Book of Loss.*

'That book helped me a lot, when Stella died,' he adds.

'Thanks.'

'You're welcome.' He signals to the waiter for another drink.

She tries desperately to think of some way to salvage this, to get the operation back on to the script. 'So you don't want to hurt me,' she blurts out.

'Claire. Oh, *Claire.*' He reaches towards her, stroking the short blond hair on her neck gently with the back of a finger. 'Don't you see? I want to take the hurt away.'

CHAPTER TWENTY

' "Why do we say 'good grief' when something happens to us?"' Claire reads aloud. ' "Is it because deep down we know that grief *is* good, that wounds hurt most when they heal?"' *The Little Book of Loss* flies in an arc through the air, joining the empty pizza boxes in the trash basket. 'Christ! Who *writes* that stuff?'

'It didn't go too badly, I thought,' Connie says. 'For a first attempt.'

'Maybe you should write one of those books,' Claire says sweetly. '*Dr Leichtman's Little Book of Positive Thoughts*.'

'Hey, Claire,' Frank says. 'That's enough.'

'Let's face it, Frank. This isn't going to work.'

'Let's look at the facts,' Frank retorts. 'Has Christian Vogler eliminated himself as a suspect?'

'No,' Connie says firmly. 'He specifically mentioned that he'd been having problems with Stella. That's new information.'

'So maybe he's just being careful. After all, we know our killer's ultra-cautious. It's entirely consistent that he'd be reluctant to incriminate himself.'

'Were you ever a detective?' Claire says. She knows she's being a bitch, but she's still high on adrenalin and anger. She wants applause, she wants to get out there and drink and dance and fuck.

Frank ignores her. 'So what is his game? Perhaps Claire isn't his type after all.'

Connie says slowly, 'Maybe it's a test.'

'What sort of test?'

'He wants to see how determined she is,' Connie says. 'If she can be put off by a paperback of platitudes. You're right, Frank, our killer's clever; he wants to be absolutely sure she's for real before he makes his move. Like a trout nosing a fly before it takes it.'

'Claire?' Frank asks. 'Does that make sense to you?'

She sighs. 'Run the footage again?'

Frank goes over to the machine and rewinds the tape. She watches the video one more time. 'Well . . .'

'What is it, Claire?'

'When I came out of there I was pretty pissed off, so I wasn't really thinking about it as a piece of theatre. But now I look at it again . . . you know, you can always tell when an actor strikes the wrong note. Even if it's nothing you can put your finger on, you just know.' She nods. 'When I look at this tape, I can see it. Christian's *acting*.'

'Which means', Connie says thoughtfully, 'we're going to have to be a bit more subtle than we anticipated.'

Back in the horrible dank apartment, she fires up the laptop Dr Leichtman gave her. The snake, which seems to be nocturnal, writhes in a complicated knot pattern against the glass of its tank.

She has no idea if it's a boy or girl. But, privately, she's started calling it Connie.

Welcome to Necropolis.

She clicks on the chat room. It's crowded tonight: at least a dozen names, most of them unfamiliar.

Victor's there, hanging around on the sidelines again, jumping from conversation to conversation, his contributions short and sarcastic.

For the first time she thinks of his behaviour as being like that of a big cat, prowling. What's he hunting for? she wonders.

Her fingers clatter across the keys.

>>Hi, Victor. How's it going?

>>Hey, Claire. Thought maybe you weren't coming back.

>>Looks like you've had plenty of company in the meantime, though.

>> None of them as fascinating and beautiful as you.

>>So sweet. Actually (hic) I'm a little drunk.

>>While I'm merely intoxicated by your presence.

>>I've had a date, Victor. Such a wonderful man.

>>ITRW?

>>Sorry?

>>I was asking if your date was In The Real World. Not a phrase I use much, actually, preferring to believe this digital domain of ours is at least as real as anything that happens out there in the flawed and imperfect Realm of the Physical . . . But I digress. Your date. You were going to give me the sordid details.

>>Was I? Well, yes, it was ITRW.

>>As you probably gathered, I'm jealous already.

>>What of? I'm tucked up here with you now.

>>True. And I suppose you must be alone. Unless your date is rather more tolerant of VR socializing than any of mine have ever been. Since the night is still young, I take it that nothing happened?

>>Nothing.

>> Your correspondent breathes a big sigh of relief.

>>Victor?

>>Yes, angel?

>>You know the other day, you and Carrie were talking about netsex?

>>Yes?

>> How does that work, exactly?

>> Well – exactly – it's kind of hard to explain until you try it. It's not sex in the literal sense, of course, in that the physical sensations are entirely in your head. But many of us find that bodies are only a kind of narrative device, in any case. A means to an end.

>>Would you like to show me?

A pause, so long that for a while she thinks Victor must have disconnected.

>>I'd be honoured, Claire. The first thing we have to do is get ourselves a little privacy. On the left of your screen you'll see a button marked 'private chat'. Click on that, would you?

>> OK.

>> OK, *sir,*

Victor says, and she doesn't think he's entirely joking.

Sex without bodies, desire without substance, pleasure without form. In this strange new world, thoughts become sensations directly, without the intermediary of flesh.

This must be how it feels to make love to an angel, she finds herself thinking; or to a ghost. So long as you didn't try to compare it with anything that existed in the real world, it was . . . well, different.

>>How was that, hon?

She types back:

>>Good for me.

>>Good for me, too.

>>Now I'm going to be a sexist pig, roll over, and go to sleep.

>>Well, you know what they say. In cyberspace, no-one can hear you snore. I think I'll hang out for a while.

>>See you soon, Victor.

>>See you, Claire.

>>Zzzzzzzz . . .

CHAPTER TWENTY-ONE

But she still can't sleep.

The district in which the apartment is situated is semi-derelict, but the old warehouses and meat-processing plants are home to a variety of low-life nightclubs. There's one called, predictably enough, Meat, just around the corner.

At the club, there's a dealer waiting for customers by the washrooms. Half an hour later, Claire's just another cog in the wired-up beehive of the dance floor.

When she can't dance any more she goes uptown, to the Harley Bar. Brian doesn't look overjoyed to see her. Which is hardly surprising, since her hair is ratty with dried sweat, her eyes are the size of duck eggs and twice as bright, and she's burbling incoherently about saving the world from serial killers.

But, crucially, he doesn't have anyone else to spend the rest of the night with.

And even if he had, they wouldn't compare to her.

It's almost noon by the time she gets back to 14th Street. She's still coming down; her eyes are gritty and her mouth feels like it's full of the stuff flower arrangers use to keep their stems upright.

For a moment, she thinks she's in the wrong apartment.

The walls have been painted cream. The animal skulls and thrift-shop artefacts have vanished. Now there's cheap Swedish furniture, piles of books, bright Turkish kilims. A neat rack of classical CDs – Rachmaninov, Bach, Mozart – instead of a mess of Green Day and Nine Inch Nails. MOMA prints in bleached wood frames instead of the tatty rock posters and Rothkos. And, as if by some wave of a wizard's wand, the snake has turned into a tortoiseshell cat, regarding her lazily from the armchair as if he's lived there for ever.

'He's called Augustus,' Connie says, coming in from the bedroom.

'Really?'

'What do you think, the cat needs a cover name? Of course he's called Augustus.'

'This is much better,' Claire says, looking around approvingly. 'But why the rush?'

Instead of answering, Connie presses a button on the answer machine.

Vogler's voice.

'Claire, it's Christian. I just wanted to tell you how good it was to meet last night.' A pause, and then a laugh, slightly embarrassed. 'Could we perhaps see each other again? No pressure, but if you're free ... Give me a call when you get a minute.'

'Do I call him back?'

'Sure. But first you play hard to get.'

Claire goes to an armchair, pulls off her shoes and puts her feet up on the table. 'I thought that was how men turned into psychopaths in the first place,' she mutters.

'Come on, Claire, get up. We have work to do.'

From: 'Claire Rodenburg'
(ClaireR@colormail.com)
To: 'Christian Vogler' (CV@nyscu)

Christian,

I wanted to meet you last night because I thought you were an intelligent person who wouldn't try to change or judge me. I was wrong. Dismissing the things that turn me on as merely some kind of warped re-action to my grief belittles me and the huge leap of faith I made when I shared the secret of my sexuality with you. In a way I almost feel raped by what happened last night. You'll say that's ironic, given the stuff I like, but there it is. I suppose I should have realized sooner, from your e-mails, that your heart wasn't really in it. But for some reason I didn't.

Damn you, Christian. You started to get under my skin and inside my head, and that's a place I don't let many people go – for reasons that have just been reconfirmed.

I don't want to diminish how good it was. It was great. But I don't think it'll be like that again. Better to say good-bye now, don't you think?

Claire

From: 'Christian Vogler' (CV@nyscu)
To: 'Claire Rodenburg' (ClaireR@color-mail.com)

My dearest Claire,

What a very extraordinary person you are.

Before you consign me to oblivion, will you at least give me one more chance? I'll be in a bar called Wilson's tonight from eight o'clock onwards. It's on Forty-Third, about a block across from Broadway.

If you come, you come. If not, another memory.

The bar is dark and big and almost empty; it's a long sliver of a room which extends back into the block. The walls have been stripped back to the brick, and the only light comes from the candles in jars on each table.

She gets there at exactly eight twenty-five. She sees him sitting at a table towards the rear, reading, his book angled towards one of the candles.

There isn't enough light for the Minicam to get pictures, the technicians who scouted the place had reported. Instead, Claire has a microphone concealed in her bag, transmitting sound direct to the van outside.

When he looks up and sees her approaching, a warm smile spreads slowly over his thin, ascetic face.

'Your last e-mail touched on something that is

particularly important to me,' he begins, 'and that is the question of trust.'

For a moment she thinks, *He knows*.

Then he continues, 'Do you think you can trust me, Claire?'

'The jury's still out on that.'

'I'm not interested in juries. Only in the judge.' He looks at her. 'I have always believed that knowledge doesn't care who has it. But that those who have it must use it.'

'What on earth does that mean?'

'Put your hand over the candle,' he says softly.

She looks down. The candle is inside a glass jar about four inches high, with an opening at the top like a lantern.

'Trust me,' he says.

She puts her hand over the opening and he places his own hand on top of hers, not forcing her, but letting the weight of his hand press hers onto the hot glass.

'Now,' he says. 'Whatever happens, you must not take your hand away until I say you can. Agreed?'

'It'll burn me.' The disc of heat under her palm is already unbearably hot and she winces.

'If you trust me,' he says, 'it will be all right, I promise.'

Together they look at the flame. It looks like a long fingernail, a talon jabbing up at her hand. The pain turns from something that prickles into something that makes her want to throw her head back and howl, a circle of needles burrowing deep into her skin. Her nerve endings are screaming, telling her to pull her hand away. Her eyes water. Her skin is liquefying, bubbling like crackling on a roast.

Then suddenly, the flame gutters. A moment later it begins to shrink. Then it goes out. The pain abates.

'You can take it away now.'

She turns her hand over and looks at it. There's a red disc, like a suction mark, stretching from her little finger to her thumb. No blisters. She puts it to her mouth and sucks it.

'The flame is deprived of oxygen, so it goes out before it burns you,' he says.

'How did you know it wouldn't burn me first?'

'I tried it myself, while I was waiting for you.' He holds up his hand, palm towards her. On it, barely discernible, is a circular mark. 'You have to decide if you trust me, Claire. That's all.'

She touches her hand, still hot, against his cheek. 'I didn't take it away, did I?'

'Come with me,' he says. 'There's something else I want to show you.'

A few blocks east they arrive at an anonymous doorway with a red rope outside. There are a couple of bouncers and a female greeter. The greeter looks at Claire condescendingly, as if she's failed the dress code. Which, since Claire is wearing Bessie's best Prada jacket, is faintly irritating.

Only when they get inside does she understand that, in here, Prada doesn't count for much. In fact, anything made of fabric doesn't count for much in here. In here, the materials favoured by the clientele are leather, PVC and clingfilm. Oh, and skin. They like skin a lot.

Claire's never been to a bondage club before. Her first thought, irrationally, is, *How the hell do they get a taxi home?*

A man walks past her wearing leather trousers and nothing else. In his hand he holds a chain. The chain leads to a small steel ring, embedded in the nipple of a breathtakingly beautiful naked young woman. The word 'SLAVE' has been written on her forehead.

Claire looks around and sees riding chaps, leather harnesses and strange gags that involve some sort of ball contraption inside the mouth. Another man is wearing only a hood that completely covers his face, with just a tube to breathe through.

'Over here,' Christian says in her ear. 'We're in luck. There's an entertainment.'

A crowd has gathered at one end of the room. As he leads Claire to the front, she sees a rough wooden frame, across which a naked girl has been tied. The two men standing alongside her are holding riding whips. The girl's buttocks and back are criss-crossed with weals, like a game of noughts and crosses. The first man brings his riding crop down. Even over the din of the sound system Claire can hear the crack of leather on skin, see the flesh give and ripple as it strikes. The girl whimpers. The crowd cheers and shouts encouragement. As the first man pulls his arm back, the second man, from the other side, slams his whip down. Another mark joins the others on the girl's backside.

Claire watches, appalled and fascinated. The girl on the frame lifts her head and seems to mumble something to one of the men. He turns to the wall behind him and hangs the riding crop on a hook. Only now does Claire notice that the whole wall is covered with implements: coils of ropes and leather restraints, elaborate whips and Chaplin-esque canes, handcuffs and belts. The man takes down a large round paddle. The woman shifts her legs slightly in her restraints. Claire sees the glint of a piercing, deep between her thighs. The man with the paddle starts to beat her with it, faster than before. Her hips begin to quiver. She lifts her head and howls. Only then does the man stop. He goes to her head and makes her kiss the paddle.

When they untie her she remains lying across the frame, exhausted. A small group of the onlookers, excited by the performance, start an impromptu cluster of their own. Some people watch. The rest drift away.

'There's a bar upstairs,' Christian says. 'Or would you rather we went somewhere quieter?'

'So,' he says. 'Was that what you expected?'

They're walking up Broadway now. Despite the warm night, Claire's shivering.

They had anticipated that something like this might happen, of course.

'Oh, I've tried all that stuff,' she says, as non-chalantly as she can. 'Been there, done that, got the T-shirt. It just doesn't do it for me.'

'No, I didn't think it would,' he murmurs.

'It's all so . . . silly, isn't it? So contrived. Besides, in situations like that it's the bottom who's really in control. There are always safe words. Colours, usually: red for "stop everything", yellow for "stop that particular punishment", green for "give me more of that". I bet that was how that girl told her tops to switch to the paddle at the end, which hurts less.'

He nods, clearly impressed by the depth of her knowledge.

'Those places are a bit like going on one of the rides at Disney,' she continues. 'It looks scary, it may even feel scary the first few times, but deep down you know it's all pretend.'

He stops. 'Exactly. That's exactly my point, Claire.'

'What is?'

'You're not looking for some cartoon dungeon-master who's going to beat the shit out of you. Not really. You're looking for someone who's going to hold your hand as you jump together into the abyss.'

'That's right,' she says softly.

'Someone who's going to take you into a place where there are no safe words to yell when it gets scary.'

Behind them, a little way down the street, a pedestrian stops when they stop. And a white van with blackened windows, cruising at walking pace 500 yards behind, pulls unobtrusively into the kerb.

'You mean death, don't you?' she says.

'I mean *trust*,' he says. 'When you trust someone completely, there are no safe words.'

He likes her apartment, he says. It's just the sort of place he'd imagined her living: unpretentious but with impeccable taste.

She excuses the faint odour of paint by saying she's just redecorated.

At the Chinese supermarket on 49th he had gathered ingredients: ginger, five-spice powder, cardamom seeds, fresh beansprouts and, from the huge aquarium that gurgled at the back of the shop, a live crab, its huge front claw bound with tape. On the way back, in the cab, she'd watched apprehensively as the carrier bag containing their dinner tried to scuttle across the seat.

He fills a pan from the cold tap in her kitchen and shows her the painless way to kill the crab, heating it up slowly with the water. Occasionally it bangs its claws against the sides, like an old boxer lashing out with bandaged fists. After a few minutes the room is filled with a thin, high whistle. It's the air escaping from the shell, he says.

While the crab is cooking, Christian takes a step forward and gently takes her chin in his hand. He turns her face towards him. She catches a faint hint of his scent, an unfamiliar, foreign-smelling cologne. Then she feels his thin, hard lips brushing against hers. She kisses him back, letting her body respond to him as well, arching against him, the material of his suit rough against her bare arms and legs.

'I think the trout just swallowed the fly,' Connie murmurs. 'Or should that be the other way around?'

'Looks like they both swallowed something, anyway,' Frank says. He adjusts the contrast on the monitor, cursing it under his breath.

'Take off your clothes,' he says.

On the stove the crab blunders around the sides of the pan, making it rock.

'No,' she says, looking at the floor. 'Not yet, Christian. I'm sorry, but not yet.'

'I don't think he'll resort to force when you say no to him,' Connie had said. 'I think he's got more self-control than that. This killer picks his moment, he controls events rather than reacting to them. But we'll be standing by, in case.'

158

His green eyes are unreadable now, their depths as dark as jade. 'Not on the first date? I didn't take you for someone who lives by rules like those.'

'It isn't that. All this – it's happening so fast. I'm confused. And I've made mistakes before. I've been let down.'

'As have I. But I'm clear about you, Claire.'

'I need more time,' she says. 'Just a little more time.'

'Of course,' he says. He kisses her again. 'As much time as you need.'

He lifts the crab out of the scalding water; shows her how to smash it open with a hammer to scoop out the poisonous brain.

CHAPTER TWENTY-TWO

'It was . . . interesting,' she says.

Frank and Connie look at her sceptically.

'What can I say?' she shrugs. 'He's charming, intelligent . . . quite intense, of course, but I think he's probably less confident than he appears . . . What?'

They're looking at her like two parents who disapprove of their daughter's date.

'How did he seem when he dismembered the crab?' Connie asks. 'Was he excited at all?'

'Sure. So was I. We were hungry and it was delicious. He's actually a pretty good cook.'

'I'm concerned about this,' Frank says to Connie.

'You must understand, Claire, that one of the dangers of this operation is that you might get too involved,' Connie says. 'The moment I see that happening I'll have to call the whole thing off.'

'I'm not getting involved,' she says irritably. 'I'm just saying that, if he's a killer, he's a pleasant, charming killer, that's all.' She feels a slight pang of guilt, remembering the way she had let her body react to Christian's kiss. Or had that just been proof that she was playing her role to the hilt?

'Show her the tape,' Frank says.

Connie puts a videotape into the machine. It's a blurred, grainy black-and-white picture, but Claire can tell what she's looking at: the apartment. The figure in the foreground is Christian, making coffee. The one exiting frame left is Claire.

'At twelve twenty-one you went to the bathroom,' Frank says. 'Now watch what he does.'

Christian turns from the stove and takes two steps across the passage. The image jumps. Another camera picks him up as he enters her bedroom. He opens a cupboard and flicks rapidly through her dresses. Then he goes to the bed and scrutinizes the drawers in the nightstand. He picks up the book she's left there and examines the spine.

He turns, as if listening to something, and moves towards the door. There's a laundry basket by the bed, and he takes something from it, holds it to his face, inhales and puts it back. Seconds later the first camera picks him up again, pouring coffee out of the grinder as Claire enters the frame again.

Claire shrugs. 'So? He was having a look around.'

'He was snooping in your bedroom. He sniffed your dirty laundry.'

'Believe me,' she says, 'I've had worse.'

'Listen,' Connie says. 'We're not showing you this because it proves he's guilty. Far from it. But once again Christian has failed to eliminate himself. All we're saying is, don't let your guard down. Not for a second.'

CHAPTER TWENTY-THREE

Her days have settled into a kind of routine.

In the mornings she goes to the gym, reads play texts at the library, goes to acting class, or sleeps. The police have got her a lunchtime job waitressing at a bar uptown as cover, but the work is hardly onerous. Most evenings Christian comes by and they go out, tailed at a discreet distance by plain-clothes colleagues of Frank's.

She wears a heavy faux-gold necklace with a miniature microphone in the stone and a transmitter embedded in the clasp. It's hideous. The people who want such things are usually rich men, Frank explains, spying on their mistresses.

Sometimes Christian e-mails her more fantasies. Occasionally, before he leaves her for the night, she'll change into the long T-shirt she wears as a nightgown, climb into bed and he'll read them aloud to her, as if he were reading a fairy story to a child. Except that these aren't fairy stories.

Dr Leichtman no longer pretends that one of these fantasies will suddenly betray Christian as the murderer of his wife. It's a longer, murkier game they're playing now, a game of watching and waiting.

Claire has got so used to the cameras that she

forgets they're there. After she's walked through the apartment naked, or staggered through it drunk, or talked to herself, she'll suddenly remember and think, Some cop could have been watching that.

Sometimes her evenings with Christian leave her feeling edgy and frustrated. Then she'll relieve the pressure by going to the Harley Bar and meeting up with Brian as he finishes work.

Once, having drunk rather too many of Brian's bourbon-and-bourbon cocktails, she brings him back to her apartment. Only as she gets through the door, half-finished bottle in hand, does she suddenly say, 'Oh, shit.'

'What's up?'

'Nothing.'

What he doesn't know won't hurt him. And she can always keep the lights off while they're in bed.

He looks around. 'Nice place. It's, er, well—'

'What?'

'It's so tidy. Grown up. I'd expected something less *tame*.'

For that, he gets pushed into the bedroom and ridden till he begs for her to stop.

She's with Christian at the theatre when she bumps into Raoul.

Normally she avoids the theatre, even as a subject of conversation, but Christian has somehow realized that it's a passion of hers. There's a new production at the Circle which is getting rave reviews. It's sold out, but he manages to magic tickets from somewhere.

Standing at the bar in the interval, she hears a voice behind her say poisonously, 'Of course, all that overacting always goes down well with *audiences*. They don't know any better, the sweethearts.'

She tries to turn away, but he's seen her.

'Claire, darling. Isn't it dreadful?'

She should have realized something like this would happen eventually.

'I'm enjoying it,' she says faintly.

'Really? I guess when you haven't worked for a while it must get hard to judge,' he sneers.

'This is Raoul Walsh,' she says to Christian, reluctantly introducing them. 'He plays a singing rat in a musical.'

'A singing mouse, actually,' Raoul says. His eyes narrow. 'Really, Claire, what on earth is that *extraordinary* accent?'

'I've heard the second half is better,' she says, to distract him. 'Wasn't that the bell?'

But Raoul, once started, isn't going to let her get away so easily. 'And talking of funny accents, I saw that barman of yours the other night. What *had* you been doing to him? "I wouldn't call sex with Claire rough, but when she finally got off me I discovered I'd just been circumcised." ' He gets Brian's Australian twang note-perfect. Raoul's friends laugh sycophantically. Christian laughs, too.

He steps forward and clasps Raoul by the shoulders, as if he's congratulating him on his joke, as if he's about to pin a medal on his chest or kiss him on either cheek. Abruptly, Christian brings his forehead down onto Raoul's nose. Raoul folds like a marionette. From nowhere he has acquired a droopy moustache of blood. A woman behind them screams. Raoul, on his knees, salaams gently to the carpet. He chokes. Blood and mucus spray out of his mouth.

'Come on, Claire,' Christian says calmly. 'We're leaving.'

'Not a pleasant fellow,' he says in the street.

'Actors can be so bitchy,' she agrees shakily. She looks round. Two men have followed them out of the theatre. Seeing that she's all right, they fall back. Christian raises his arm for a cab.

'What did he mean?' he says calmly.

'Which bit?'

'About not working for a while?'

'Oh, that.' She thinks quickly. 'I had a brief notion that I might try to be an actress. Raoul and his friends soon made me realize what a stupid idea that was.'

Christian says, 'I think it's an excellent idea.'

'What is?'

'Acting. You need something to give your life a sense of direction, Claire. That waitressing you do isn't going anywhere. You should take a drama course, maybe get some one-to-one coaching. You've got the looks, and the voice. Fourteenth and Third,' he says to the cab driver.

'I can't afford coaching.'

'I'll pay.'

'Christian, don't be ridiculous.'

'What's ridiculous? I can easily afford it.'

'You don't know anything about me. You don't know anything about *us*. I could just take your money. It happens.'

'I know everything about you that I need to know,' he says. 'Total trust, remember? No safe words.'

'I'll see about classes,' she mutters. 'But I can't—'

He interrupts her. 'And why did he make fun of your accent?'

'My mother was English, and that comes out sometimes, and there's a bit of New York in there now,' she improvises.

'They say that's a sign that you have a good ear, don't they? And your French is excellent, too. You'd be a brilliant actress.'

They drive on in silence.

'What he said about that other guy,' she begins.

'You don't owe me any explanations, Claire. Until you decide you want to be with me, who you sleep with is your own business.' He looks out of the window as he speaks, and she knows that he's more hurt than he's allowing himself to show.

'What are you doing this weekend?' he says after a while.

'Nothing much, I guess.'

'Some friends have asked me to visit with them. They have a house down on the coast. I think it would do us both good to get out of the city.'

'OK,' she says. 'I'd like that, too.'

'I've got a lecture Friday at lunchtime. We could leave straight after that.' He pauses. 'Needless to say, I'm not suggesting a dirty weekend. That's still up to you.'

'Thanks.'

There are other words she finds herself wanting to say to him, other explanations she wants to make, but none are within the vocabulary of this character she wears, so she says nothing.

'Listen, Christian. I need to explain something.'

'OK.'

They're in the apartment now, drinking wine. Playing on the CD player is some music of Christian's, something medieval.

'I told you I lost someone close to me.'

'Yes. Eliot. You told me his name was Eliot.'

'I've never really told you how he died.'

'I was waiting until you were ready to talk about it.'

'He was one of my teachers.' She stares into her glass. 'When it all came out he was fired, and his wife left him, and there was no chance of him getting another job. He ended up killing himself. It was . . . it was meant to be a suicide pact. I didn't have the courage then, and I haven't managed to find it since.'

He nods.

'Ever since, I've been like someone standing on the edge of the high diving board: too scared to jump, too uncertain to go back.'

'The *cunt*,' Christian says. She looks up, startled. She's never heard him swear before. He smacks one fist into the other. 'What a despicable, cowardly, self-serving *cunt*. Seducing one of his own pupils, that's bad enough. Making her do the things he made you do, that makes my blood boil. But to lay the burden of his guilt on you as well, that's simply *pathetic*.'

She looks at him, astonished. 'Is it?'

'Of course. Who could do a thing like that? If that man wasn't already dead, I'd want to kill him myself.'

In front of the monitor downstairs, Connie pulls one of her earpieces away from her ear so that she can speak to Frank. 'We're drifting off the script again.'

He shrugs. On the pad in front of him, his pencil has doodled an intricate shamrock of interwoven lines, looping endlessly back on themselves. Dr Leichtman decides it probably wouldn't be a good idea to tell him what that signifies.

Frank looks at the screen. Christian and Claire are kissing.

'And – cut,' Frank mutters.

But the couple on the screen seem to go on kissing for ever.

CHAPTER TWENTY-FOUR

Christian's lecture is in the Maison Française, off Washington Mews. At noon she goes in and asks the bored desk clerk where to find him.

'Room Twelve. Upstairs and to your right.' He glances at the clock. 'He should almost be done.'

She finds the lecture hall. The door is propped open, and she can hear his voice coming through it. She looks in. In the well of a dozen or so rows of banked seats, Christian is standing at a small podium. As a concession to their trip, he's wearing a dark polo shirt and khakis.

She slips into the back row. One or two students glance at her curiously, then turn their attention back to Christian. His voice is as soft as ever, but the actress in her notes the way it carries easily to the corners of the room.

'We cannot hope to understand Baudelaire', he is saying, 'until we realize that we cannot judge his attitudes, and particularly his attitude to women, by the standards of the present. "*Moi, je dis: la volupté unique et suprême de l'amour gît dans la certitude de faire le mal*" – "I say that the supreme pleasure of sex lies in the possibility of *evil*." For Baudelaire, women are not simply individuals, but idealized representatives of their sex, symbols both of perfection made flesh, and the impossibility, in this corrupt world, of perfection proving to be anything more than a brief illusion.'

Catching sight of Claire, he acknowledges her with a nod and the slightest of smiles before continuing:

'Thus, in poem seventy-one, he says of his mistress:

> When she had sucked the marrow from my bone
> I turned to her, languid as a stone,
> to give her one last kiss . . . and saw her thus:
> a slimy rotten wineskin full of pus.'

Several male students exchange grins. One mutters delightedly, '*Way* gross, man.'

'This conflict was apparent in Baudelaire's life, as well as in his poetry,' Christian continues, apparently oblivious to the response his quotation has provoked. 'You may remember the famous letter of rejection he sent to the Vénus Blanche, in which he said'– for the first time Christian consults his notes, slipping a pair of spectacles onto his nose and removing them when he has finished the quotation – '"You see, my dear, a few days ago you were a goddess: so noble, so inviolable. And now here you are, a woman . . . I have a horror of passion, because I know too well the horrors into which it can tempt me."'

Claire suddenly realizes something she's never really noticed before: Christian is an extraordinarily charismatic performer. He has this audience in the palm of his hand.

'For Baudelaire, sex is not a physical itch but a metaphysical yearning. Not some mindless aerobic exercise, but a connection, however transitory, with the terrible dark mysteries of the universe. Like all mystics, he is, of course, doomed to disappointment. The achievement – the heroism – lies in the attempt.'

Even before Christian has finished speaking, a hand is in the air. A girl, seated near the front with a purple laptop open in front of her, says fiercely, 'You're saying that he treats women as sexual objects. By putting him on the syllabus, aren't you helping to dignify his views?'

Christian begins to deal with her point, courteously and methodically. The other students, rightly taking this as the end of the lecture, pack up their notebooks and laptops and begin to slide out of their seats.

Claire waits until the girl and Christian are done. Eventually the student leaves, mollified, and Christian comes over.

'Let's go,' he says. 'Do you have a bag?'

'It's downstairs.'

'We'll pick it up on our way to the parking lot, then.' He seems almost jaunty at the prospect of a weekend away.

'You've got a car?'

'Absolutely.'

The car is a pre-war Citroën, a vast and temperamental antique, which objects with a crash of its stick-shift gears to being subjected to the Friday afternoon crawl south through the Lincoln Tunnel. There's no CD player, and the radio still has the original valves in it. She's amazed that it picks up American stations – somehow REM sounds strangely profane, coming through circuits that were built for the sound of Piaf and *Le Jazz*.

The white van has to drive very slowly to keep from catching up.

His friends' house is about four hours due south of the city. The Citroën's suspension isn't its strong point, and by the time Christian pulls the car onto a tiny unmade track off the main road, her back is killing her.

She's already established that the people they'll be staying with, Philip and Ellen, were friends of Christian's and Stella's. She's not quite sure what it signifies for Christian to have asked her along this weekend, but she knows it isn't something he would have done lightly.

The house is a big, rambling clapboard house, overlooking a secluded rocky bay. It's full of bleached wood and pale blue furnishings, as well as many canvases of the views from the headland. Ellen is an artist; and to Claire's eye quite a good one.

Ellen and Philip greet Claire with a friendliness that doesn't quite disguise their curiosity.

'So you're the girl who's persuaded Christian out of his shell,' Ellen says with a smile when Christian's back is turned. 'It's really good to meet you. He's been refusing to tell us anything about you.'

As they bring their luggage in from the car, another couple look up from the big kitchen table, where they're shucking peas into a bowl.

'Christian, you remember Hannah and Saul, right? Hannah, Saul, this is Claire,' Ellen says. Hannah and Saul smile a welcome.

'And those are their kids in there, watching TV. The house is really full, I'm afraid.' Ellen points to a door. 'You're in there. Just dump your stuff and come grab a drink.'

The room contains a double bed and a breath-taking view of the ocean. Ellen's red setter, Morgan, comes in through the open door and jumps up onto the bed.

'I'll sleep on the floor,' Christian says quietly. 'I'm sorry, I thought I'd made it clear to her—'

'It's no problem,' she says, shooing the dog off the bed. 'Looks like I'll have Morgan to protect my honour anyway.'

Dinner is a relaxed affair – mussels from the beach, seabass that Philip caught himself, and a salad with the peas. Christian was right: it's good to get out of the city, and it's good to be here, drinking Puligny-Montrachet with these educated, intelli-gent, liberal people, who draw her into the conversation without prying too much or con-descending to the fact that she must be nearer in age to Saul and Hannah's kids than she is to them.

After the fish, Saul excuses himself to make a phone call. Philip calls after him, 'Don't bother try-ing with a cellphone. It won't work around here.'

'It won't?'

'Nope. None of the networks work on this stretch of coast. There's a landline in the study.'

Claire, fingering her necklace, wonders if that means her mike isn't working, either. Excusing her-self, she goes to the bathroom and opens the little window that opens on to the road at the front of the house. She turns off the light so that she can see better. Outside, the sky is almost black, the clouds cobwebbed where the moon is trying to break through.

'Frank,' she says quietly, 'if you can hear me, will you flash your lights?'

She waits. No lights interrupt the darkness. 'Frank?' she whispers. 'If you're out there in your car, flash your lights, or sound your horn, or anything. Just give me a signal that you can hear me.'

A sudden knock on the door makes her jump.

'Claire?' Christian says. 'Are you OK in there?'

'I'm fine.'

'I thought maybe you'd eaten a bad mussel.'

'I'm fine, really. I'll be out in a minute.'

Before she closes the window she scans the darkness one last time.

That night they open the windows to let in the distant respiration of the ocean. Christian wraps himself in a blanket and lies down near the window.

She lies awake, listening. After a while, she forces herself to make her breathing echo the rise and fall of the sea.

Eventually she hears him get to his feet and pad across to the bed. She feels the bed rock as he eases himself in beside her.

An arm reaches around and insinuates itself into the tight space between her arm and chest.

Her heart thudding, she feigns sleep.

They lie like that for a long time, until she realizes that Christian's asleep himself.

CHAPTER TWENTY-FIVE

They get back to the city late on Sunday night. On Monday, she's woken by Frank at 9 a.m.

'Wake up, Claire. You need to see this.' He tosses a newspaper onto the bed, then goes to the window and yanks on the blinds.

For a few moments she can't even remember where she is. Groggily, she picks up the newspaper and automatically turns to the theatre section.

'Not there.' He pulls it from her hand and refolds it. '*There*.'

The front page; second item.

DOTCOM KILLER CLIMBS ON NET BANDWAGON.

Website claims to be murderer's cyber-shrine. Mayor condemns lack of online regulation.

Using the internet for banking or to purchase books may now be commonplace, but a new site demonstrates that the World Wide Web also has more macabre capabilities. Pictureman.com claims to show photographs taken by the killer of Pearl Matthews, a twenty-nine-year-old sex worker whose decapitated body was discovered in the Happiness Hotel off Second Avenue last month.

Initial suggestions that the pictures might be leaked from the coroner's archives seem to be disproved by the way the position of the victim's body and head vary from photograph to photograph, suggesting that the killer deliberately posed them and then recorded his gruesome activities.

The Mayor's office immediately condemned 'the unregulated Wild West that is the World Wide Web', and called for proper controls to be introduced. 'What's the use of cleaning up Times Square when the pornographers can relocate to our teenagers' bedrooms?' a source close to the Mayor demanded. 'Our office will be pushing the police to close this site and bring the killer rapidly to justice.'

'Shit,' she breathes.

'Shit is right,' Frank agrees. 'Shit in a trench, and I'm standing right in it.' He looks around. 'Where's your laptop?'

She nods at the corner.

He types in the website address and reads off the screen, ' "Welcome to pictureman.com. You are visitor number 39,584." People are going crazy for this thing.'

She gets out of bed, hugging herself in the thin T-shirt she's wearing, and comes across to take a look. 'Why don't you close it down?'

'Oh, sure. We've traced the server. It's based in Senegal, where they rent disk space, bandwidth, whatever they call it, to a free e-mail service in Australia. Which gives its members a certain amount of space to build their own sites. The guys in the Senegal police department don't answer the phones, it's the middle of the night in Australia,

176

and even if it wasn't there's no guarantee they'd agree to take it off. They make their money by selling advertising space. The more people visit the site, the more they'll make.' He clicks again. 'Over fifty thousand now.'

'Are there any links to Christian?'

'Connie's looking at it.' He gets to his feet. 'We need you over in Queens. There's a meeting in half an hour.'

She gestures at the T-shirt. 'I'll get dressed.'

To her surprise, he doesn't get out of her way.

For a few seconds he looks at her, as if unsure of himself. Then, abruptly, he says, 'You're not shy, Claire.'

'What do you mean?'

'You walk around here with no clothes on all the time. You—'

'You watch that, do you?' she says angrily.

'Hear me out. I watch you because it's my job to make sure you're safe. Christian could turn up here at any time, have you ever thought of that? My point is, you're not ashamed of what you are. You brought that boyfriend back here last week—'

'You were watching *that*?' she cries. 'What about my privacy?'

'Listen,' he says. 'Listen. Of course I didn't watch – any more than I needed to. But I saw enough to tell me that you're not inhibited. You're an actress. You've done nude scenes before, right?'

'Oh no,' she says, suddenly seeing where this is going. 'Oh no. Don't ask me to do that.'

'If you don't sleep with Christian,' he says, 'we're still going to be playing charades this time next year. And frankly, we don't have that long. If we don't get something in the next couple of weeks, Christian will be crossed off the list, and you'll have to vanish.'

'What do you mean?'

'We'll send you back to England, business class, with some money in your pocket.'

'What about my green card? You promised—'

'To get you a card if the operation came off. But if we have to *abandon* it, that's a different scenario. We can't have Claire Rodenburg, English actress, making headlines on Broadway. It would alert Christian unnecessarily.'

'If he's guilty.'

'If he's guilty. Which we'll never know unless we find some way to get under his skin.'

'That's true,' she murmurs, almost to herself. 'I'd never know.'

'If privacy is an issue,' he says, 'we could turn the cameras off and just use the mikes. I know it's not ideal, Claire, but it's all I can offer you.'

'What does Connie say?'

'Connie thinks I'm right.'

'The part demands it, huh?'

'You know I wouldn't ask unless it did.'

'I'll have to think about this.'

'Don't think too long,' he says. She hears an echo of her drama teacher. *Don't think. Act.*

'All right,' she says. 'I'll do it.'

'You've asked her to do *what*?'

'To sleep with Vogler,' Frank says calmly. 'And she's fine with it. Aren't you, Claire?'

'More or less,' Claire says uncertainly. 'Though you did give me the impression that you'd already discussed it with Connie.'

'We discussed the general approach.'

'We did not!' Connie spits.

'Claire, would you, uh, give us a moment, please?'

She turns to go.

'Stay,' Connie says icily.

She stays.

'I want Claire to hear this,' Connie says. 'Let me take you back a few weeks, Frank. I undertook to gather some psychological material which would help to eliminate or implicate a suspect. Snakes and ladders, remember? You're talking about something quite different: a honey trap. And that's not only unethical, it's also highly dangerous.'

'No more dangerous than what she's already done.'

'Remember the previous girlfriend, Frank? The one who Christian played death games with? This isn't going to be some soft-focus Hollywood love scene. There's no saying what Stella's killer might do in a sexual situation.'

'Well, if he tries to kill her, we'll know he's guilty.' He glances at Claire. 'Don't worry. We'll have armed cops standing right outside. If he kicks up rough, we'll shoot him.'

'Shoot him? Dear God.' Dr Leichtman looks exasperated. 'This is insane.'

'Look, Connie. These people you study, they're not figures in some textbook. They're out there on the streets. If you want to catch them, you have to get your hands dirty.'

Claire says, 'Like blowing up a bomb.'

They both look at her. She says to Connie, 'You remember you compared them to unexploded bombs? Well, when they find a suspect package, they don't always open it up and snip the wires.

Sometimes they just stick some more explosive under it and blow it up. I guess sometimes the crudest ways are the most effective.'

Connie says incredulously, 'You really don't think he did it, do you? That's why you're agreeing to this. You think he's everything he claims to be.'

Claire flushes. 'But have *you* ever thought that he might actually be innocent? Have you? What would an innocent man do, faced with someone who was demanding all this weird stuff? Wouldn't he go along with it, if he could? Wouldn't he *pretend* to be interested in all the things she's telling him she likes?'

'Why would he do that?' Dr Leichtman says.

Claire mutters, 'If . . . if he thought she was someone special, underneath. Someone who was really worth it. That's why he'd pretend.'

'Frank,' Connie warns.

'Yes?'

'You can't do this. This girl is getting way too involved.'

'Maybe,' Frank says wearily, 'but she's the only girl we've got.'

CHAPTER TWENTY-SIX

She walks the streets of New York for hours, not buying anything, just wandering. Frank's right: she has few inhibitions about the act itself. Years ago she learned to see her body as a thing apart, a lump of raw material, a *resource*.

She thinks of actors who have gone far, far further than this, turning themselves into bloated monsters for the duration of a shooting schedule, or living in a wheelchair to play the part of a paraplegic. By comparison, what she's been asked to do is nothing very much.

If she has reservations about this next step, it isn't for her sake. It's for his. She's afraid that if she lets Christian make love to her, he'll become even more entangled in Dr Leichtman's web.

Connie's right: she's too involved, and in a way she never anticipated. Looking back, she isn't even sure when exactly it was that her allegiances became so muddled.

Yet if she pulls out now, she'll lose Christian completely, and that's something she doesn't want to do.

Mid-morning, she finds herself passing by the Drama Bookstore. She hasn't been in here for, well, only for a few weeks, but already her previous life seems to be receding into the past, as though those memories belong to a different person.

She goes in and wanders over to the scripts section. There are armchairs, and she drops into one with a sigh of relief. She's picked a copy of Albee's *The Zoo Story* from the shelves, and she's soon lost in the play, speaking the lines in her head.

Ten minutes go by. She's been dimly aware of other shoppers around her, but it's only now, alerted by something at the edge of her vision, that she raises her eyes and sees someone she recognizes.

He's been working his way along the shelves until he's standing quite near her, so she knows she's not mistaken. A thin, weasel-like face. For a moment she wonders if he's from her acting class. No, not that. A production in England? And then it comes to her. She's looking at the child rapist she saw being hypnotized by Connie.

She studies his face, making absolutely sure. Sensing her gaze, he turns and catches her looking at him. Smiles, says, 'Hi,' and turns back to the shelves. A second later, he glances back at her book.

'Great choice,' he says conversationally. 'Man, I love that play.'

She wonders why he doesn't recognize her, too, then remembers that he never had a chance to see her. She saw him on CCTV.

'I'm sorry,' she says quickly. 'For a second I thought I'd met you before.'

'Happens all the time,' he says.

He smoothes his hair back, for all the world like

someone who thinks he's getting lucky. 'People see you on TV, they think you must live next to them,' he explains.

'Right.' He must mean his trial, she thinks.

'Maybe you caught me in the Apple computers spot,' he says.

She frowns. 'You're an *actor*?'

'Sure,' he smiles.

'You weren't ever in prison?'

'Hey!' he jokes. 'My ex-wife thinks I should be, but . . .' The words die on his lips. He looks at her again. 'Shit!' he says urgently and begins to run.

He runs out of the store, scattering the other shoppers, and she follows him as best she can. He's darting through the traffic, running for his life. She tries to catch up, but she's not as fit as he is, and there's no way she's fast enough to reach him.

A cop. There's a cop directing traffic at the intersection. Once more she plunges into the traffic, dodges trucks and tugs at his arm. 'That man's an escaped convict,' she gasps, pointing.

'What man?' the cop says, peering.

But there's no reply.

By the time the cop's turned around she's realized her mistake and has vanished into the crowd.

'Hey!' the cop calls. 'Hey, lady!'

Shrugging, he turns back to the traffic and blasts some more Manhattan pollution through his whistle.

It takes an hour in the drama bookstore, looking through *Spotlight*, the actors' register, before she finds his face.

Eric Sullivan. Minor parts in a couple of TV

movies and a few commercials. But indisputably an actor, just as he said.

She takes a cab back to the office in Queens. She still has her pass, which gets her into Reception. The corridors are deserted, as usual.

She barges into Connie's office. The psychiatrist is in conference with her secretary and half a dozen men in suits.

Claire has time to notice that the secretary seems to be addressing the meeting from beside a monitor on which a tape of Claire herself is showing, before the presentation comes to a halt.

'Claire, this is a surprise,' Dr Leichtman says coolly. She reaches across and switches off the tape.

'What happened to the convict?'

'What convict?'

Claire slams the page she's ripped from *Spotlight* onto the table. 'The one I saw in here being hypnotized. The child molester. The one you said had a long way to go before he was released. The one I just met in the drama bookstore.'

For a moment even Connie seems lost for words. She says slowly, 'Claire, you of all people should understand the importance of good theatre. We thought it best that my authority be clearly established from the start.'

'What authority?' She looks around the room. 'Who are all these people?'

The man nearest to her gets to his feet and extends his hand. 'Paul Ashton, Claire, FBI. I have overall responsibility for Operation Magnet.'

'What's Operation Magnet?'

No-one answers. She looks from face to face. 'I thought Connie was running this.'

'We felt it best to restrict the number of people who have direct access to you, Claire. Dr Leichtman was chosen to be your handler—'

'My handler?' She shakes her head. 'I'm not a *dog*.'

Connie says, 'These people are my colleagues, Claire. I called this meeting because I wanted their advice. This is, by its very nature, a collaborative operation. Operational decisions are the responsibility of the New York Police Department, who are operating under – how shall I put this? – short-term local pressures, which may have influenced their judgement. We were just discussing whether we can really allow this operation to go ahead under the . . . changed circumstances which Frank's suggesting.'

'It isn't up to you, though, is it? It's up to me.'

'We can't guarantee your safety,' the psychiatrist says gently.

'You never did.'

The woman she had known as Connie's secretary clears her throat. 'Uh, Claire, some of us take the view that this operation is becoming increasingly *random*. That proper controls are no longer in place.'

'Random?' Claire says. 'Random?' She shakes her head in disbelief. 'Christian and I aren't *data*. We're not some mould you've spawned in a test tube. These are our lives you're messing with.'

Connie says, 'This website the killer's set up. We think it's a very worrying development.'

'You don't say.'

'Listen to me, Claire. Every serial killer thinks of himself as a kind of performer, acting out a personal psychodrama. Like any performance, it's incomplete without an audience. That's why many serial killers pose their victims' bodies: they get a kick out of imagining the reaction of whoever finds them. Our killer's found a way of performing to a huge audience. It's going to be an immense thrill for him, and probably an addictive one. He's going to want to do it again.'

'All the more reason to catch him, then.'

'And all the more reason to be professional about how we do it.'

An echo in her head: *I'd committed the cardinal sin, you see. I'd been unprofessional.*

'Fuck you,' she says. 'Fuck *you*.'

She slams the door on her way out. As she goes past Reception, she says to the girl behind the desk, 'Hey, honey. Who's your agent?'

'Eileen Ford,' the girl says automatically, then stops, confused.

Model, Actress, Whatever. New York is full of them.

She phones him at his apartment. When she hears the familiar soft, precise voice, she simply says, 'The answer's yes. Tonight.'

The man gets to the woman's home quite late. He's brought her flowers – lilies and tulips and great curling claws of twisted willow.

'Oh, thank you,' she says, taking them. 'They're beautiful. I'll get a vase.'

'Take off your clothes,' he says gently.

'I should get them into some water.' She starts to turn away, but he stops her with a touch.

'Take off your clothes. I want to see you naked.'

Meekly, she allows him to reach up and

unthread the earrings from her ears, unfasten her necklace – Frank's necklace – and slip the first of her blouse buttons through its eyelet.

As he reaches into the small of her back for the fastening of her bra, she says self-consciously, 'They're too small.'

'They're perfect.' He cups each naked breast briefly, bending to take each nipple in turn between his teeth.

The button of her trousers cracks like a plate between his fingers. Her panties make a frail figure of eight around her ankles. She steps out of them. For a moment they tangle on her ankles, and she has to tread them off, as if she's miming walking upstairs. Then she's naked.

'So,' he says, looking at her.

'Will I do?' she jokes self-consciously.

'Don't joke,' he says. 'Don't ever joke about this.'

There's a feeling in her stomach, as though she's hurtling up a skyscraper in an elevator.

For a long moment he looks at her. Then she steps forward to unfasten his shirt. His chest is covered with sleek curls, like a bull's forehead.

When she frees his penis he gives a sigh, and for a moment she holds him softly, feeling the delicate, trembling beat of it, the blood-twitch. She's shivering, too, though whether from nerves or cold or something else entirely, she couldn't have said.

Then he starts to kiss her, gently at first, and something starts to melt inside her head, some barrier that gives way and floods her brain with pleasure. And then the melting sensation spreads from her head to the rest of her, and she gasps as he pulls her to the ground, letting him position her where he wants her, letting him seize her, letting him impale her on his cock, pulling up her knees so that he can gore her with it in sharp, savage thrusts, the way a horse's underbelly is gored by the horns of a bull. She cries out, breathless and dazed, and he pushes himself deeper inside her.

In the apartment below, Weeks rubs his hands together. 'Will you look at what she's doing now? How many copies of this you gonna make, Frank? I'll take a dozen for the boys.'

'Leave it, will you?' Frank says quietly.

'What, you don't want a souvenir?' He nudges Positano. 'I think maybe Frank wants this one all for himself. Something to while away the long nights. That right, Frank?'

Abruptly, Durban reaches forward and turns off the picture. 'I said we'd just use the mikes.'

'Right. As if she cares. She's a pro, Frank, and the profession we're talking about here ain't acting.' He reaches out and turns the picture back on. 'How do you tell if a woman's faking an orgasm?'

'I don't know,' Positano says, 'how do you tell if a woman's faking an orgasm?'

'Who cares?' Weeks says and laughs. 'Neat, hey? Australian joke. Who cares.'

But Frank Durban, watching the bodies on the screen, does care. Frank cares very much indeed.

Later, they lie on the floor, too exhausted even to crawl to a bed, sharing wine amongst the debris of their clothes.

'There's something I want to say to you,' he says softly.

'What?'

'You know the other day, you were asking about my wife?'

Down in the observation room, they fall silent and gather round the screen.

He rolls over onto his front, touching her nipple curiously, turning it this way and that between his fingers, as if she were a radio that had to be tuned to the precise, elusive wavelength he required.

'If Stella's death taught me anything – left me with anything – it's a horror of secrets.'

She speaks to the ceiling. 'Do you have a secret, Christian?'

'Yes,' he says. 'Just one.'

She waits, as she's been taught. *Silence is the best interrogator.*

'I have a confession to make, Claire,' he begins. 'Ever since we met—'

Is it her imagination, or can she hear feet creeping towards the door, safety catches being cocked, a burst of two-way radio hastily muffled in a coat?

'Wait,' she says. *Got to give them time to get into position.* 'I need some water.'

She gets up, naked, and goes into the bathroom. The face that stares back from the mirror is a mask. She runs the tap and splashes her face with water.

'OK,' she says, coming back beside him. 'What is it you want to say?'

'I need – I think you should know . . .' He looks at her arms. 'You've got goose bumps.'

'I'm fine,' she whispers. 'Go on.'

'What I'm trying to tell you is that I'm falling in love with you.'

And the air leaves Claire's lungs in one long gasp, an involuntary sigh of gratitude and relief.

CHAPTER TWENTY-SEVEN

The second time is, mercifully, gentler. He makes love to her with infinite slowness, one hand cupped behind her head so that he can stare into her eyes.

His own eyes remind her of photographs of gas clouds in space, a glowing green phosphorescence that, up close, dissolves into shadows and streaks of light.

She realizes that he isn't fucking her to come himself, but to make her come, to make her lose control for him. The thought of being observed so minutely in orgasm frightens her, and she tries to hide from him, to blank him, to force the crisis away. But it only has the effect of making it stronger. When it comes, it crashes over her like a wave, churning and tumbling her in its rip, so that, for what seems like an eternity, she is lost, a mewling, wailing castaway, her face flecked with spittle and phlegm.

He nods, slowly, as if she has at last told him the truth.

Afterwards he carries her to the tub and washes her methodically, soaping every crevice, his fingers probing the folds of her skin. He shampoos her hair, working the suds in with his hands. She watches in the mirror. Her head is thick with foam, like a meringue.

He reaches down a lather-mittened hand to her bush, soaps it as he soaped her hair, spreads her with soapy fingers and finds her clitoris yet again. It stings, and she moans, sore, for him to stop. He shushes her, forcing her to climb the hill of her pleasure with him one more time.

The debrief is a quiet affair. For different reasons, she guesses, neither Connie nor Frank want to meet her eye.

Outside, car horns shoulder their way through the morning rush. A hydraulic compactor truck snorts and hisses below her window, then moves on. She sits, her fingers playing with her hair, only half listening as they talk about someone called Claire Rodenburg.

'What we've got to be absolutely clear about,' Connie is saying, 'is what we want to happen and how we intend to control events to achieve that outcome. We'd hoped for a pillow-talk confession, but it seems that moment has passed. I think you have to question whether subsequent pillow talk is going to produce material that's any more revealing.'

'What's on your mind, Connie?' Frank asks.

Claire watches sunlight diffracting through the glass of Evian on the table. A disc of light on the ceiling becomes an ellipse, an oval, then fattens once again into a disc. She looks down. Although Connie is still talking, the policeman's eyes are looking at her, Claire. She stares at him until he turns his gaze away.

'As you know, I had my doubts about the path we're going down. Now that we're here, though, we should consider how to use this clearly intense relationship that's developing to best effect.'

'What do you suggest?'

'I think we should change the script. Christian's someone who demands complete loyalty, complete submission. If he is a killer, it's because he feels he's been betrayed by women. I suggest that we let him believe Claire feels the same way about him as he feels about her, and then have her betray him.'

There's a short, stunned silence.

'You mean, with somebody else?' Claire says incredulously. 'You want to make Christian think I'm being unfaithful?'

'Why not? If he's as hooked on you as he appears to be, he'll want revenge. For an ordinary man, that might take the form of a slap or a torrent of filthy language. If he's a killer, he'll try to take your life.'

'It's a high-risk strategy,' Frank says.

Connie shrugs. 'You're the poker player, Frank. Stakes too high for you?'

'Of course not,' he says.

'Not for him either. So we'll just have to keep raising them until someone folds, right?'

'Not yet,' Claire murmurs.

'What was that?' Connie asks.

'Not yet. Don't do it yet. It's too soon. He's not . . . he's not really in love with me yet. Not as much as he will be.'

'Claire's right,' Frank agrees, getting to his feet. 'We should give him a little more time, get him really hooked. And if, in the meantime, he eliminates or incriminates himself, we'll avoid a potentially dangerous confrontation for Claire. Let's do it her way, Connie, at least for a few more days.'

That evening she phones Brian the barman, and tells him she's going to be away for a little while. An acting job, she tells him. A last-minute place on a tour, replacing someone who got sick.

CHAPTER TWENTY-EIGHT

Harold J. Hopkins, proprietor and director of the Crossways Funeral Parlor, looks at the young man in front of him and says, 'Where else have you worked, Glenn?'

Glenn Furnish says politely, 'Well, sir, you'll see from my résumé that, since I qualified as a licensed mortuary technician, I've worked in Houston, San Antonio and New York City. I've also worked in several establishments in Europe. I didn't put them on the résumé because I figured that wasn't relevant professional experience.'

'They do things different over there, I guess.'

'In the mainly Protestant countries, yes they do, sir. They don't have a tradition of embalming, let alone cosmetology. As you'll see from my résumé, cosmetology is my major area of professional interest.'

'Right,' Harold says. He likes this young man. He likes the way he speaks seriously, in a low voice. He likes the way he's worn his funeral suit to this interview. He likes the way he calls Harold 'sir'. In Harold's view, a young man who shows the proper respect for an employer will probably show the proper respect for the deceased.

Harold thinks briefly of his own son, not much

older than the young man in front of him. Showing respect had not been Mervyn's forte. In retrospect, it might have been a good thing that Mervyn had refused to follow his father into the family business. It might only have been storing up trouble for the future.

'Sir?'

He drags his attention back to the young man.

'Sir? I'd be happy to work a trial period, if that would help you decide between myself and the other applicants.'

'Oh, well. Matter of fact, there aren't any other applicants. I just posted that job notice last Friday, and you're the first person to reply. So I guess the early bird catches the worm. How soon could you begin?'

The young man allows a brief smile to touch his lips. 'I just need a couple of days to find somewhere to live. And thank you, Mr Hopkins, sir. You won't regret this decision. I believe I'll be useful to you, and I hope to learn a great deal from watching an experienced professional like yourself at work, sir.'

Harold Hopkins waves away the compliments, faintly embarrassed. 'Nonsense. It's you who'll be teaching an old practitioner like me what the latest ways of doing things are. And there's no need to call me sir. Harold will do just fine.'

Two days after his interview, Glenn Furnish reports to the Crossways Funeral Parlor. Harold gives him a tour of the facilities and introduces him to his wife, Ellen, and their daughter, Alicia, who also works for the business, and to Joel, Harold's business partner. He makes a good impression on all of them. But it's in the prep room that he and Harold linger the longest.

'Adjustable cot, aspirator pump, embalming machine,' Harold says, indicating the room's various features. 'Ventilation in the table. The hearse can back right up to those doors.'

Glenn compliments him on the efficient set-up and Harold makes a self-deprecating gesture. 'We may look like a hokey operation, Glenn, but that's an impression we work hard to foster. Folks prefer it that way. We actually have over a dozen clients a week pass through here.'

Glenn nods, clearly impressed. 'Which embalming solution do you use?'

'Formalin. Low index, usually, to keep down the odour. Why?'

'A lot of people are switching to Sorbent. We used it in Houston. It's less toxic than Formalin.'

'Sorbent. I think I read something about that.'

'I could order some in, if you liked,' the young man suggests.

'That's a good idea. Why don't you do that?'

'Not that I meant to imply there's anything wrong with formaldehyde-based solutions, you understand. The last thing you want is some young hothead coming in here and telling you to change everything.'

'No, Glenn, don't apologize.' Harold Hopkins looks kindly on his new employee. 'There's going to be a lot of stuff I need to catch up on. You see anything around here that could do with updating, I'd like to know what you think.'

That afternoon, Harold and his new assistant ride out to a local retirement home to pick up the body of one of the residents. Retirement home calls are one of the hardest duties a mortician has to perform, and Harold intends to keep a close eye on his protégé to see how he handles this one.

He's glad to note that Glenn doesn't say much on the ride out. Harold knows that many morticians like to laugh and joke on the drive over, then suddenly switch on their serious faces when they get to work. He's even heard it said that a mortician needs to be light-hearted sometimes around cadavers as a way of letting off steam. But he doesn't agree with that, and he's glad Glenn Furnish doesn't seem to operate that way, either. That was why Harold had gotten so mad at Mervyn, for taking the hearse into the McDonald's drive-thru that time. It didn't matter that the vehicle was empty. What mattered was that people expect the highest standards from those who handle them after they've departed.

He's glad to note, too, that Glenn doesn't immediately turn the hearse around and back it into the retirement home gates when they arrive. As Harold used to say to Mervyn, morticians aren't refuse collectors. Drive in frontways, and we'll see about loading the client when the time comes.

The director, a capable lady called Margot Wingate, is waiting for them by the front door. Harold has worked for her many times in the past. He introduces Glenn, then the two men follow her to the room of the deceased resident. This was the main reason retirement home calls were hard. You basically had a lot of elderly people who all knew why you were there – those that still had their faculties – and who were probably wondering if they'd be the next to go. Harold always likes to find time to talk to any of the elderly folks who want to come and chat as he makes his way to the deceased's room. Sometimes they'll just want to make a joke about it not being their turn yet, but sometimes they want to be serious and talk about the deceased, particularly if it was a friend. You had to strike a balance between getting to the room quickly, without making a big fuss about your presence, and being polite. Once again he's pleased to notice that Glenn Furnish has been well trained, and talks to the residents in the same polite but solemn manner as Harold does.

The body is that of an old lady, still lying peacefully in the bed where she passed away. 'I've taken off her catheter,' Margot says. 'She's ready to go.'

Harold looks first at the space between the bed and then at the door. 'I think there should be ample room for our cot in here, Glenn.'

While Glenn goes back to the hearse for the trolley, Margot says, 'He's new, isn't he?'

'Today is his first day. But he's had a great deal of experience. And he seems to me to have the correct attitude.'

'How'd you find him?'

'On the Internet, as a matter of fact. There's an industry bulletin board just started for vacant jobs. I thought I'd give it a try.'

'He'll do well,' Margot says. 'The old folks like him, anyway.'

'Yes.' Harold smiles at her. 'So many outsiders don't realize. Being a mortician is a people business.'

Glenn returns with the cot, and together the two men lift the body of the old lady into the zippered sleeve. Glenn starts to do it up, but Harold stops him.

'Now this is perhaps an instance where I might give you some advice, Glenn. Although we'd normally remove a body with the zipper up, in a retirement home we sometimes do it a little differently. You see, some of these old folks may be too infirm to come to the funeral, so we like to give those that want to the opportunity to come and say their goodbyes as we proceed to the hearse.'

Glenn nods thoughtfully. 'That's a wonderful thought, Mr Hopkins, and I sure am glad you shared that with me.'

'Harold, please,' Harold says, arranging the zippered bag so that it frames the old lady's face attractively.

CHAPTER TWENTY-NINE

She arranges to meet Henry in a bar at lunchtime. Then, remembering the problem with Henry and bars, she changes it to breakfast at a diner.

He looks older than the last time she saw him. The lines on his face have deepened and the bags under his eyes have filled with fluid. Even at this hour, she can smell the stale alcohol on him.

'I thought you'd forgotten me,' he says as she slides into the booth.

'I know, I'm late. I'm sorry.'

'That's not what I meant, Claire.'

She looks at his once handsome face, the hurt in his eyes, and thinks, *Not you, too. Don't make me carry your pain as well.*

Gently she says, 'I've been preoccupied.'

'A boyfriend?'

She shrugs.

'I hope he knows he's a lucky man.'

'I need your help, Henry.'

'Why's that?'

'Remember a client called Stella Vogler?'

'Of course. Firstly because she was attractive, secondly because she was killed, and thirdly because she was just about the last damn client I ever had.'

'Christian Vogler is the main police suspect. I'm helping them to find out if he did it.'

He looks at her in a strange way. 'How?'

'Like before, sort of. As a kind of decoy.'

He whistles.

'The thing is, I'm not sure he did it.'

'The cops have no proof?'

She shakes her head. 'This operation . . . there's something strange about it. There are these crazy FBI psychologists holed up in a building in Queens. There's a cop who's . . . well, I think he's jealous of Christian and me. I think he may *want* Christian to be guilty just to get him away from me.'

He nods. 'What can I do?'

'I need a good investigator.'

'And you thought maybe I could recommend someone?'

She smiles. 'I thought maybe, if you're not too busy, you might help me out yourself.'

'I'm not a good investigator,' he says flatly, and she knows better than to lie to him.

'Maybe not. But you're cheap. And, well, it sounds crazy, but I know that you're who you say you are and not an actor.'

'What do you mean, not an actor? I have eighty-seven programme credits to my name.'

'I mean, not an actor now. Everyone else I speak to somehow turns up in *Spotlight*.'

He thinks for a moment. 'OK,' he says. 'What do you need investigated? Though I have to tell you now, if it's a missing pet, you're on your own.'

'Christian had a previous girlfriend. I don't know her name, but it shouldn't be too hard to find her; they were engaged for a while.

Apparently she accused him of drugging her and using her in some kind of passive sex ritual. It's the only real lead the police have. If she's lying . . . And then there's Stella. I want to know why their marriage ran into difficulties.'

'Real detective work, in other words?'

'Real detective work. Will you do it?'

'For a dame like you,' he says, 'I'd sunbathe naked in an erupting volcano.' He winks. 'See? I still know all the lines.'

She does the legal research herself.

At the public library she buries herself in law books – first year students' textbooks to begin with, then, as she finds the references she's after, casebooks, books of precedent and international law.

It's the end of the day by the time she tracks down what she needs.

That night, she meets Christian at a bar on Mercer. It's just round the corner from his home.

'Do you want to come back?' he asks at the end of the evening.

And she knows she shouldn't – since she's been told the necklace microphone has a limited range – knows she ought to entice him back to her apartment, with its cheerfully anonymous Swedish furniture, its drawers full of underwear she didn't even buy, its cupboards full of watchers and policemen and lies.

'It's a bit soon for that,' she stalls. 'You know, the place you shared with your wife.'

He flinches. 'Of course. Let's go to yours.'

* * *

Back at the apartment, he shows her a game.

She has to lie completely still while he traces the letters of the alphabet on her clitoris with his tongue, and say each letter out loud as he does it.

To begin with it seems easy, almost non-sexual, as simple as charades or any other guessing game. But gradually, the act of concentrating so hard on the tiny sensations heightens them unbearably. The anticipation itself becomes something exquisite, each tiny movement etching itself onto her nerve endings almost before it happens. She has to clench her legs to stop herself from pushing against him, demanding more.

When they get to Z her whole body's shuddering, waiting for him to take her with his tongue and whisk her into oblivion.

'Wait,' he breathes, and starts to write something else. The letters aren't in order now. She realizes he's spelling something out, letter by letter.

'Could you tell what it was?' he asks, much later, when they're lying on the floor.

She shakes her head. 'I couldn't concentrate by then.'

Which is a lie, because she's actually pretty certain that what he wrote with his tongue on her body was this: *I want you for ever.*

He stays the night, so it's late morning before Connie and Frank can talk to her.

She opens the door to them, says, 'Oh, it's you,' and walks back into the living room, leaving them to follow.

'You don't seem very pleased to see us,' Connie says. She fishes in her pocket for a pack of cigarettes and puts one in her mouth.

Claire reaches across and pulls it out, tossing it onto the table. 'Actually, I'd rather you didn't smoke in this apartment. And no, I'm not pleased to see you. I didn't get much sleep.'

'Neither did we,' Connie says meaningfully.

'You've come to inspect the sheets, have you?' Claire mutters.

'Claire, look. Last night was good—'

'For me, too, honey,' Claire interrupts.

'—in many ways. But to be honest, we're not getting the *momentum* we were hoping for.'

'It was pretty momentous from where I was standing,' Claire drawls. 'And lying, and crawling, and kneeling, for that matter.'

Connie ignores her. 'He's not opening up any more than he was. In fact, now that you're spending less time talking, we're probably getting less material than we were before.'

'And that's a problem?'

'What do you think, Claire?'

She shrugs insolently.

'Let me put it this way,' Connie snaps. 'He's hardly going to confess when he's got your pussy rammed into his mouth.'

'Do I detect a note of jealousy?' Claire murmurs. 'Is the psychologist perhaps in need of a little therapy herself?'

Connie makes an exasperated gesture. 'Claire, I understand the conflicts you're experiencing. On the one hand you feel used and soiled by this operation; on the other, this man seems to be offering you love and self-esteem. But if the operation is to be of any use at all, you've simply got to park those feelings and get on with the job.'

'But is it?'

'Is it what?'

'Is the operation any use?'

Frank shoots Connie a warning glance.

Claire goes on, 'I went to the law library yesterday and found out some interesting stuff. Ever heard of Kessels versus The People, a Supreme Court ruling from 1984? No? Well, let me give you the gist. Any recording made without the knowledge of the suspect and without the suspect's agreement cannot be admitted as testimony.'

'That's true,' Frank admits.

'So what's all this for?' she hisses at him. She gestures at the walls, at the microphones, the cameras, the invisible wires that surround her like a filigree cage. 'Why am I doing this?'

'Wait. Yes, you're right. If Christian confessed on tape, it wouldn't necessarily be admissible. But it *could* be used in interrogation. And, crucially, it would enable us to prove within the department that he is a viable suspect.'

'And my role ends up on the cutting-room floor.'

'Claire,' Frank says. 'What you're doing is invaluable. He's ready to crack, I know he is. All you've got to do is push a little harder.'

'I need to take a shower,' she says abruptly, getting up.

'You already took one,' he says without thinking.

She shoots him a furious look and slams the bathroom door.

That afternoon, she closes all the curtains and sits in the dark, watching the TV with the sound turned up high.

'What's she doing up there?' Weeks asks, when he

comes to take over from Frank at the end of the afternoon.

'Nothing much. Watching reruns of old movies, from the sound of it. Crying. Walking up and down.'

'Well,' Weeks says, thumbing between channels, 'that's star temperament for you.'

She logs on to Necropolis. The glow of the screen is the only light in the room.

>>Victor?

>>Claire. I was hoping you'd come back.

>>Victor, I need a favour.

>> Anything, my angel.

>>You're not going to like it.

>>Try me. I'm surprisingly broad minded, for a pervert.

>> I want to meet you. Properly, I mean. ITRW.

There's a long silence. She can almost hear the hum of telephone wires, the low-level buzz of inter-ference, the whistles and beeps of modems as their silence bounces across satellites, streaks from com-puter to computer, crackles down the endless telephone cables that line deserted highways.

>>Victor?

>>Is this a date, Claire?

207

She thinks how many men she's led on, how many men she's acted for, become a chimera, a figment of their dreams.

>>Sorry. Just friends. But believe me, it's important.

Another long pause. Or just some random time lag at the server?

>>Where are you?

>>New York. You?

She waits.

>>Near enough.

>>Where's good for you?

>>There's a cyber café in the East Village, on St Mark's Place. I could meet you there at seven.

>>How will I recognize you?

>> Log on to the site. I'll tell you then.

>>Thanks, Victor. I wouldn't ask unless I had to.

>>I know that, babycakes.

CHAPTER THIRTY

She gets to the café fifteen minutes early and settles herself at a PC in the corner.

Next to her, two Japanese girls are engaged in earnest cyber-chat. A businesswoman types a report energetically, banging her keyboard with two fingers. A teenager is playing a computer game.

There's a smattering of tourists; an older guy with a ponytail who looks as if he's writing code; a woman in a leather jacket with a pile of books next to her; some students, working, and a shifty-looking guy in a long raincoat, fiddling with a coffee mug that's already empty.

She logs on and asks:

>>Victor, you here?

>>I'm here, Claire.

>>Here in the website or here in the café?

>>Both. Tell me what you look like.

>>I'm twenty-five. I've got short blond hair. I'm wearing a black sweat top from Gap and Levi's. I'm in the corner.

>>You didn't tell me you were beautiful.

She looks up. The businesswoman smiles ruefully.

'But would you ever hurt anyone?'

Victor, whose real name is Patricia, says, 'In my fantasies, I dream about sexual domination. But I also dream about world peace, living with Kate Moss and being a professional guitarist. I acknowledge my obligations to society, Claire. I want to live amongst people, and that means that, like anybody else, I have to regulate my wants.' She shrugs. 'It's true that good submissives are hard to find, particularly if you're a fat old dyke. But my straight friends don't seem to have it any easier.'

Claire nods.

'Tell me what this is about,' Patricia suggests.

Claire holds back some of the details, but even in outline it's a pretty weird story.

'What are you going to do?' the other woman asks when she's done.

Claire sighs. 'I don't know. I just want to be certain one way or the other, I guess.'

'Then why not stick with the plan? Work with the police until they either arrest Christian or eliminate him?'

'When I started this thing,' Claire says, 'it seemed . . . crazy, but possible. Now, I'm not so sure.' She thinks for a moment. 'You know, until I did that stuff for Henry, I never understood how much control a woman has over a man, how easy it is to insert yourself into their fantasies. I'm convinced Christian was pretending to be into all this weird stuff just to keep the relationship going.'

'Speaking as someone who's into that weird stuff myself, I'd say he's a pretty lucky guy.'

'Sorry. I didn't—'

She brushes Claire's apology aside. 'Don't worry, I know what you meant. So how can I help, anyway?'

'According to the police, Christian visited Necropolis. I'm just wondering if there's any way of checking up on that.'

'He's unlikely to have used his real name. Even if I've come across him, how would I know?'

'Well – you both have an interest in Baudelaire, if that helps.'

'Hmm.' Patricia thinks. 'There was someone. It was a while ago now. Last fall? She called herself Blanche.'

'She?'

'Yes. Which isn't to say she was female, of course. Gender distinctions aren't very rigid in Necropolis, as you've probably gathered. Men pretend to be women, women pretend to be men. After a while it stops mattering. You just accept people on their own terms.'

'So you couldn't speculate whether Blanche was really a man or a woman?'

'No, only that she was definitely interested in her submissive side. And she made some references to a husband, though that might just have been a smokescreen.'

'No,' Claire says slowly. 'No, I don't think it was. That wasn't Christian you were talking to. Whatever else he might pretend to be, I don't believe he'd ever pretend to be a submissive. That was Stella, using Christian's computer. The name gives it away: Blanche. Baudelaire's biographers called one of the women he was in love with – the woman he worshipped – his *Vénus blanche*. I think Stella got fed up with being worshipped. Necropolis offered her the chance to get away from all of that, even if it was only as a fantasy.'

'There's something else you ought to know,' Patricia says. 'When you logged on to Necropolis, you probably didn't realize, but those public areas aren't all there is to it. There's a part that even members can't find unless they've been told about it. A kind of inner sanctum.'

'How do you mean?'

'On one of the chat pages, there's a link that doesn't have any text or pictures. But if you know where to put your mouse cursor, and you click on it, it'll take you to a MUSE.'

Claire frowns. 'A Muse? What's that?'

'A Multi-User Simulated Environment. Geek-speak for a virtual world, somewhere that exists only on a network. To give you an example, if you type the command to walk into a room, the computer will tell you what the room looks like, what objects there are in it and who's in there. So you can talk to people, but you can also move around and even create your own rooms and objects. The MUSE in Necropolis is called Tartarus.'

'Should I know what that means?'

'In classical mythology, Tartarus was the region of the dead.'

'I get it,' Claire says, nodding. 'The underworld. The next level down.'

'I guess. Anyway, the reason for the long ex-planation is that Tartarus is where the heavy stuff happens.'

Claire looks at Patricia. 'What do you mean, heavy stuff?'

'Trading.'

'In what?'

'Pictures, mostly.'

'We're talking illegal pictures here, right?'

'Try not to judge us too harshly, Claire. For some of us, Necropolis is all we have.'

She touches Patricia's arm. 'Sorry. Go on.'

'Everyone in Tartarus uses a code name, different even from the false name they use in the main Necropolis area. It's sort of like an extra protection. Anyway, there's one particular character who always has really, really freaky pictures to sell. I'm not into that stuff, believe me. But there are people who are.'

'What's this person's name?'

'He calls himself Charon. It's from Greek mythology, too, I think. Charon was the ferryman who took the dead across the river separating them from the underworld. You had to pay him; that was why they used to put pennies on the eyes of the corpses.'

'And you don't know who he really is?'

Patricia shakes her head. 'But when I had that chat with Blanche, Charon was there, too.'

'So he might have approached Stella afterwards.'

'It's possible.'

'And if they made contact – if this guy Charon is the killer – that might be how he fixed on her as his next victim.'

'Well, it's possible, isn't it? It's pretty obvious that you don't give out your name and address on the net, of course. But it's also surprisingly easy to find out those sorts of details. There are sites which let you search public records and voting registers. Then maybe there's some other site somewhere with a photograph of her. It happens. I found my old high school yearbook on the net the other day.'

Claire nods thoughtfully.

'Will you tell the police?'

'Sure, I'll tell them. But I don't think it'll change anything as far as they're concerned. There's no proof, is there? Nothing that eliminates or incriminates, as they keep putting it.' She sighs. 'It's not that I'm not grateful, Patricia, but I'm going to need more than this, much more, if I'm going to get them to stay away from Christian.'

Later, on the way out, she brushes past the seedy-looking man in the raincoat and whispers, 'It's more convincing if you turn the computer on, Detective.'

In contrast to the sleek, bright functionalism of the cyber café, she meets Henry in a bar on the Upper East Side, a serious drinker's hangout where the barman leaves the Guinness to settle, in the approved manner, before he tops up the glass, drawing a shamrock in the froth with the last few drops.

For once, though, Henry's drinking lime and soda.

'The bottom line,' he tells her, 'is that this woman – Jane Birnes, her name is – wanted to marry Christian pretty bad. If you want my opinion, her biological clock had gone off and he seemed like a good choice to be the father of her children. Then, about a month before the wedding,

Christian decides it's not going to work. At which point, not surprisingly, she goes crazy. I talked to the doorman at his old apartment block. They had to get a restraining order to stop her hanging around the lobby, screaming abuse and slandering him to the neighbours. If you ask me, she's been waiting for a chance to get even ever since.'

'Would the police know this?'

'Well, I'm hardly a big fan of New York's finest, but a restraining order? They must have known.' He looks at her shrewdly. 'Unless they chose not to know.'

She sits, lost in thought, her drink untouched.

CHAPTER THIRTY-ONE

As Harold has predicted, Glenn Furnish is a big success. If he had been impressive at the retirement home pick-up, he has turned out to be remarkable in the prep room. He treats the cadavers with a dignity and respect that is greatly to Harold's liking, yet he's also a quick and capable technician.

The body is first stripped, sprayed with fungicide and washed with disinfectant soap. Then, unless it's an autopsy case and the internal organs have already been removed, the inner cavities have to be purged of what Harold refers to as 'nasties'. After that, a trocar – a long embalming needle – is inserted into an artery and connected to the aspirator pump, with another needle and a waste pipe going into a vein. The blood is pumped out of the cadaver's circulatory system, usually under pressure, since it will have solidified somewhat after death. Only when aspirating and purging are complete does embalming take place. Antibacterial solution is pumped around the veins in place of aspirating fluid, and finally sprayed, in a weaker, or lower-index, solution, over the corpse's skin.

The purpose of embalming, of course, is not to preserve the body for ever, but to ensure that it remains in a reasonable condition for viewing by the deceased's relatives. Embalming, as Harold likes to say, is only the first step in the wider science of cosmetology, and it's at this that Glenn Furnish particularly excels. He's full of bright ideas, such as adding Downey, a fabric softener, to the spray solution.

'Fabric softener?' Harold had said, puzzled. 'You mean to keep the coffin clothes looking good?'

Glenn Furnish hadn't laughed at his ignorance. 'No, Harold. Modern fabric softeners contain a glycerol-based humectant which will help prevent the dermis from drying out.'

Harold noticed his employee's cosmetic skills at their very first embalming together, when they had been preparing the body of the old lady from the home. Harold had been suturing shut the old lady's lips, and explaining his thoughts to Glenn.

'You know, the lips are really the most important part of the whole process. After the eyes are closed, it's from the expression on the lips that people try to work out whether she died peacefully or not. Now, you and I know that the normal expression of a cadaver is kind of a cranky one, because the skin dries and pulls the lips back from the teeth. But most folks don't know that, and what they'd really like to see on the face of their loved one is just a little hint of a smile. Not a big cheesy grin, or like someone's cracked a joke, but a kind of restful, satisfied expression. So when I sew the lips shut, I like to just make it a little tighter in the corners.'

'Superglue is better,' Glenn said.

'I'm sorry?'

'A lot of younger morticians now use superglue

to fix the lips. That way you can be sure there won't be any thread visible. And as for that smile, it'll look even better if you fill out the top lip with a little putty. May I?'

He showed Harold how to use the putty gun to lift the corners of the mouth, and Harold was damned if it didn't look more natural than when he did it with a needle.

Harold has never been particularly strong on cosmetology, leaving that side of things to his wife and, latterly, to Alicia. Soon Glenn is taking charge of all that. He rubs skier's lipsalve on the corpses' lips to keep them soft, and packs cat litter in their chest cavities to fill out the empty lungs. He inserts cotton pads, soaked in insecticide, deep into the nostrils to make it look as if the deceased has just inhaled one last good breath. He fills in sunken parts of the dermis with putty and seals the incisions with invisible sealant. He sprays the corpse with SkinTone, to give it the appearance of being in the pink of health. And only then does he start work with the make-up box, applying layers of foundation to the wax-white skin, lipstick to the bloodless lips, coloured Cutex to the drained fingernails. At this stage, if the deceased is a woman, he will often take advice from Alicia, Harold's daughter, and the two of them will try as many as three or four different combinations, discussing their ideas in low voices, and cleaning off their errors with cleansing cream before finally deciding on the right one.

If Glenn has a fault, Harold decides, it's that he has favourites among the dead. As early as the second week, Harold notices that he has an aversion to the obese, particularly obese men.

Entering the prep room when Glenn is working on one such cadaver, Harold sees that he has inserted the aspirator needle into the carotid artery, just below the ear, with the exit trocar coming from the jugular. Normally this would be frowned upon, as the general rule is not to perform any unnecessary interventions on the face. Harold passes a comment to this effect.

'I couldn't find an artery anywhere else,' Glenn says. He's sweating, despite the cool of the heavy air-con. 'Musta turned him over at least a dozen times. He hasn't got a single good artery left. No wonder the fat bastard stiffed it.' He slaps the corpse's wrinkled flesh irritably.

Harold stares. He can't believe the normally mild-mannered young man has used such language. 'Glenn,' he says finally, 'you're doing really well here, and I wouldn't like you to think we're anything other than delighted with your work, but personally I like to consider the prep room a sacred space, almost a consecrated one, where the deceased are treated with the courtesy we would give to God in a church. For those reasons I don't feel comfortable with swearing in here.'

The young man immediately apologizes.

'Well,' Harold says, 'don't mention it. We all get a little stressed from time to time.'

Nothing similar ever happens again, though Harold notices that Glenn seems to avoid the fat ones after that.

If Glenn doesn't like obese cadavers, though, he is the opposite when it comes to making up the bodies of any young females that pass through their hands. There's one in now, a twenty-one-year-old car-crash victim. Her face is a mess, and she's clearly going to need a lot of work before she'll be in an acceptable state for the viewing casket. In fact, Harold has already had a quiet word with the grieving parents and suggested that a closed casket might be necessary. But when he mentions this to Glenn, the young man says, 'Well, let me see what I can do, Harold.'

After the embalming, Glenn gets out his putty gun, his tube of superglue and the invisible incision sealant. He's still working when Harold goes home. Harold looks in on the prep room and finds the young man kneading conditioner into the girl's hair.

Glenn hears him at the door and looks up. 'Petrol in her hair,' he says almost tenderly.

Harold's house is right behind the funeral parlour, so he doesn't feel too bad about leaving Glenn there on his own. But it's nearly eleven before he hears the young man's car driving off.

The next morning, Harold's the first one in, so he goes to the prep room to have a look at what Glenn's done. He's got to admit that the young man has a remarkable aptitude for this work. The girl's face has been totally rebuilt, the work disguised with invisible sealant and SkinTone, so that if you didn't know better you'd think she had barely been damaged. Harold has been around corpses all his life, and it's a long time since a body spooked him, but this girl looks so gentle and restful that he crosses himself and says a short prayer. While he's standing there, he hears a faint noise, like a moan, coming from the girl's throat.

Harold J. Hopkins jumps.

Then he smiles. It's been a while since a cadaver

caught him out like that. And it's only because Glenn's work is so darned lifelike that he's been startled now.

Opening the lid of the autoclave, he selects a freshly sterilized pair of curved steel forceps. Then he goes over to the girl and gently inserts the forceps down her throat.

As he expects, they meet no resistance. Glenn has just forgotten to cork the windpipe. Gaseous build-up, exiting through the voice-box, has made it seem as if she's moaning. He goes to the storage unit, finds a wide, thick cork and eases it down the cadaver's throat, tamping it with the end of the forceps until it's jammed good and tight.

Easy mistake to make. Quite reassuring, in a way, to know that Glenn isn't perfect. Sometimes he makes Harold feel, well, not stupid, exactly, but just a little bit *slow*.

All the same . . . an easy mistake to make, yes, but also an easy mistake to fix. Every time Glenn leaned on her chest she'd have made a little sound, like air being squeezed through an accordion. How could he not have noticed?

But it had been late when the young man had finished, and he would have been dead beat. He'd probably been meaning to do it last thing and then forgotten all about it.

Harold puts the tiny incident out of his mind.

CHAPTER THIRTY-TWO

'I don't believe he did it,' she says.

Frank sighs. 'I've told you, Claire. Unfortunately your opinions don't constitute evidence.'

'The stuff about the picture trading at Necropolis—'

'Is hearsay, not testimony. You know that.'

They're in the apartment, getting her ready for another date with Christian. He's arranged to meet her in a restaurant, so she's being equipped with an array of surveillance devices in addition to the necklace: a transmitter pinned invisibly into the hem of her skirt and a tiny video camera in her bag.

Frank's on his knees, talking through a mouthful of pins, fixing the microphone in place. For a moment Claire's reminded of a parent, pinning up a child's school dress. She shakes her head and clears the half-memory away.

'I want to ask him about that previous girlfriend you found,' she says doggedly. 'I want to hear his side of the story.'

'That's not a good idea,' Frank warns. 'If and when we arrest him, we don't necessarily want him to know we know about that. Besides, how would you explain that *you* know?'

Connie, watching from the other side of the room, says, 'This has gone far enough.'

'What has?' Frank asks.

'I've made my decision, Frank. We're closing this thing down right now. I should have made this call two weeks ago.'

Frank pulls a pin from his mouth. 'This isn't your operation, Dr Leichtman. Strictly speaking, you don't have the authority to stop it.'

'And just what authority do you have for continuing?'

He doesn't reply.

'Look at you,' Connie says scathingly. 'What a pair you make. One of you gambling everything that Christian's guilty, one of you gambling everything that he isn't. Even if I can't make Detective Durban see sense, Claire, perhaps you will. Take that equipment off and let's walk out of here.'

Claire hesitates, unsure.

'Let's go,' Connie says. She walks to the door and holds it open, waiting.

After a moment, Claire shakes her head. The psychiatrist shrugs and closes it sharply behind her.

Frank, still fussing with his pins, says without looking up, 'She'll be back. This is tough on her as well, you know.'

Claire feels a sharp pain in her thigh. One of the pins has pricked her. A tiny berry of blood swells, plump and round, on her skin.

'Oops,' Frank says, smoothing it away with his thumb.

She gets to the restaurant early, so the cops can run a soundcheck on the equipment. She sits there, muttering to herself like a bag lady, reciting some monologue she learned long ago.

The waitress, bringing her a spritzer, smiles uncertainly.

Christian shows punctually at seven, his shoulders damp from the rain. 'This is for you,' he says as he sits down. He hands her a package.

It's a square box, a little bigger than a CD case and perhaps twice as deep. She opens it. Inside is a necklace, or, to be more precise, a torc, a solid neckpiece of thin silver. In the centre is a small design of some kind.

'My family crest,' he says. 'Look.' He shows her the signet ring he wears on his little finger, on which the same design is etched.

'But, my God,' she says, 'you can't give me this. It must be an heirloom.'

'Of course. That's why I want you to have it.'

She lifts the delicate crescent out of the box. 'It's beautiful.'

'You won't mind taking off that one you always wear?' he asks anxiously.

'This?' she says, fingering Frank's faux-gold monstrosity. 'I won't mind if I never see this again.'

He reaches up, unfastens the heavy chain and stuffs Frank's necklace in his pocket. He touches her bare neck, softly, with his fingers, before putting the torc on her. He has to bend it open slightly, like a stethoscope, to make the gap big enough. She feels the unfamiliar metal close around her neck like a collar and reaches up to touch it.

'But this is too precious,' she protests. 'You can't give it away.'

'I'm not giving it away. I'm giving it to *you*.'

'You know what I mean. Let me take it on loan.'

'No,' he says firmly. 'You either accept it or you don't.'

She understands from his voice that, if she accepts, she will be accepting more than a piece of metal.

'Next week I have to go to Europe,' he says.

'Oh.' She hadn't expected this. 'How long will you be gone?'

'Two weeks. Maybe more.'

'Is it a conference?'

'Some lectures. Does it matter?'

'Perhaps I could come with you.'

He smiles at her. 'Don't be crazy. You'd never get back through Immigration.'

'Oh. Of course.'

'So I'll see you when I get back.'

'Christian?'

'Yes?'

'When you went away before, when you were married to Stella, were you ever unfaithful?'

'Never.' He adjusts the torc. 'I told you. I don't do casual relationships.'

She says in a rush, 'The police thought that you and she . . . that you might have killed her, didn't they? That's why they put you on the news, to see if you'd crack.'

He waves at the waitress for a menu. She notes the way his eyes run, briefly, down the length of the girl's body. It's not a furtive look, just a frank assessment. When the waitress comes over, he doesn't give her a second glance.

'The police? Of course they suspected me. Statistically, the husband is always the most likely perpetrator. And they were too stupid and too unimaginative to pursue anyone else.'

'Did you love her?'

'Yes, I loved her. But I'm also glad she's dead. That's not a nice thing to say, is it?' He slides his fingers between hers. 'But if Stella was still alive, I wouldn't be here with you. Now, enough questions. Let's order.'

'There was something else,' she says. 'A girl called Birnes. Jane Birnes.'

He frowns.

'She said you were engaged to her.'

'Oh, of course. *Jane*. But that was a long time ago, and we were never engaged.' He laughs, amused by the thought. 'She was unbalanced. How on earth do you know about her?'

'A friend of a friend,' she mutters.

Shortly before they leave the restaurant, she excuses herself and goes to the restroom.

When she returns he says, 'Your dress is ripped.'

She glances down at the torn hem. 'I caught it on the door. Shall we go?'

In the surveillance truck, Frank hears flushes, reverberation and the banal chat of two women bitching about their dates.

'She's dumped us in the john,' he says wearily.

'What about the camera?' Positano asks.

The technician plays with the focus. A woman's shoe comes into view and the sound of running water fills their headphones.

'The view from the trash can,' the technician suggests.

A hand picks them up, shakes them and drops them in a plastic refuse sack.

'That'll be the restroom attendant,' he adds helpfully.

'What do we do now?' Positano asks.

'Nothing,' Frank says. 'We know where they've gone.'

Even though it isn't far to Christian's apartment, they're quickly drenched by the sheeting rain. Christian goes off to look for dry clothes and champagne while she walks around, touching things curiously. The apartment is vast and dark, filled with Moorish antiques, old leather-bound books, a few modern artworks – mostly female nudes – and shelf after shelf of French and Spanish literature. It smells the way he does, a musty scent of cedarwood and leather, overlaid with spice.

There are no photographs of Stella. She realizes he must have gone through the place removing all traces of her in preparation for this moment.

Indeed, there's a photo of Claire on a table, one she hadn't even known he'd taken, of her walking down the street, the other faces around her reduced to a blur.

She stops in front of a small marble sculpture, around ten inches high. It's a female nude, the polished stone as smooth as glass. The statue stirs something in her memory, some association she can't quite retrieve.

'Here,' he says, returning. 'Put this on.'

He hands her a robe, a long Arabic *djellaba*.

'Was it . . . your wife's?' she says, undressing. He watches her, uncuriously, as she steps out of her underwear and tries to wrap herself in the rough-textured cloth.

'Not like that,' he says. 'Like this.' He shows her

how to arrange the folds of the robe, like a toga. For a moment he doesn't answer the question, then he says, 'Does it matter?'

'No,' she says. She catches a faint echo of another scent trapped in the rough weave, something lighter, more feminine than his.

'Good,' he says. He slips his hand under the fabric and cups her breast. 'Bend over.'

She rests her arms on the table in front of the statue. She feels him lifting the robe up to her waist, tucking it carefully so that it stays there of its own accord. A finger, wet with champagne, trails down the cleft of her buttocks, from the base of her spine to the start of her sex. She feels him linger on the puckered opening of her anus and tenses involuntarily. He laughs. She hears a chink as he slips his belt through the loops of his trousers.

'Trust me,' he says.

She waits, apprehensive but aroused. The belt strikes with a lazy crack across her right buttock. Fire fizzes down her nerve endings, cascades of sparks that sizzle and shimmer in her head. Pain follows a moment later, a sting that makes her yelp. The belt falls again on the other cheek, and she wails again, louder.

He pauses, and she doesn't move, her head still buried in her arms. She understands that if he's angry, if he needs to hurt, it's not her his anger is directed at but the previous occupant of this robe, the one who left him when she died. He hits her again, and she sways to catch the next one, grunting as if she's being fucked. Another blow, and her cry this time is one of pleasure as well as hurt. She can feel the heat, but can't tell if the dampness on her damaged skin is perspiration or blood. She finds she doesn't care. She would never have believed it, but she is going to come from being hit, is going to climax without so much as a touch on her clitoris, but only if he doesn't stop, only if the fire and the pain keep coming. She tells him so, or tries to, and though the words won't come out right he seems to understand.

'Jesus,' Frank mutters. 'This sounds painful.'

It's gone midnight, and there are too many people crammed into the truck parked outside Christian's apartment. The air is rancid with bodies and the smell of stale take-out.

The input from the necklace in Christian's pocket is turned up full. There's some hiss, and an occasional crackle of cab-controller interference, but the sound of leather hitting flesh is perfectly audible, as are the sounds Claire's making in response.

No-one in the van says anything. Frank pulls a tissue out of his pocket and dabs at his forehead.

Christian carries her to the big double bed and takes a mouthful of champagne. He encircles a nipple with his mouth and sucks on it gently. Bubbles nibble at her sensitive nerve endings.

Still holding the liquid in his mouth, he pulls away and dribbles some over her belly and thighs as he kisses his way slowly down to her poor, bruised sex.

First his tongue, slippery with champagne. Then, as he pulls all of her into his mouth, there's a sudden tingling, burning sensation as the bubbles nuzzle blindly into every crevice and fold. It's as if her labia has been invaded by a thousand tiny bees. 'Oh, Christ!' she says, grabbing his head. 'Christ!'

She hopes his apartment either has good sound-proofing, or that the neighbours are out.

CHAPTER THIRTY-THREE

She leaves at dawn, just as the city is waking up. It's a beautiful morning. Squirrels play tag up the trunks of trees, darting among the feet of the early-morning joggers.

She walks amongst them, lost in thought, a figure moving at a different speed to the rest of the world.

In the van, Frank pulls off his headphones and rubs his eyes. 'She's out of there. Let's go.'

Together with Connie, he walks to the door of Christian's building and presses the buzzer.

Christian's voice comes through the intercom. 'Who is it?'

'Durban.'

The door hums.

They go up. Christian is in his bathrobe, sipping black coffee.

'Hey, Chris,' Frank nods. 'How's it going?'

'OK.' Vogler looks tired. 'You get anything?'

'The way you handled the restaurant was perfect,' Connie says. 'Saying that you were glad Stella died.'

The decoy nods and takes another mouthful of coffee.

On the table behind him, a picture of Stella has replaced the one of Claire.

PART FOUR

'It was reported that after his last stroke Baudelaire could no longer recognise his own reflection in a mirror, and bowed to it politely, as if to a stranger.'

Baudelaire, ed. Clark and Sykes

CHAPTER THIRTY-FOUR

'For many actors, the most important part of Stanislavski's teaching is what he called "affective memory". It means reaching into your own past, remembering some powerful emotion or event, and using it to create a character.'

Paul pauses, as if for questions, but no-one speaks. The students are standing around him in a semi-circle. Occasionally one of them will do a posture exercise, centring themselves as they listen.

'Now I want you each to close your eyes and think of a time when you experienced a very powerful emotion. Don't think of it in the abstract, though. I want you to remember exactly what you were doing when you felt that way and what action you were engaged in.'

He has them do the exercise half a dozen times, until he's satisfied they understand what he means.

'OK. Now perform the actions you were thinking about. Leon, you go first.'

Leon, a tall, lanky student from Carolina, blushes a little, then starts to rush around the rehearsal space frantically searching for something. After a few minutes Paul stops him. 'What are you doing, Leon?'

'I'm doing, uh – there was this time when I had

to get to the airport and I lost my car keys. I got into a real panic.'

'Why did you panic?'

'Because I had only, like, two minutes to find them or I'd miss my plane.'

'So what happened after two minutes?'

'What?'

'What happened after two minutes? You were looking for the keys for what, about five minutes just now. Why didn't you stop looking for them once it was too late? Why didn't you phone for a cab or ask a neighbour to take you?'

Leon, who has gone a deeper shade of red, mumbles, 'I thought—'

'Haven't you listened to a single fucking word I've said?' Paul shouts suddenly. 'Don't think, you moron. Don't ever think. Act.'

'Screw you,' Leon says.

There's a dangerous silence. 'What?'

'Screw you. And screw your fucking mind games. It's just a power trip, man. You've got your favourites, and you tell them they're wonderful. Like *her*.' He gestures at Claire. 'The rest of us might as well not exist.'

'I'd praise you, too, if you just put an iota of effort in,' Paul says. His voice is very calm now. 'But you don't. It's just another class to you, isn't it? Another bunch of grades to count towards your major. Towards a nice comfortable job.'

'I'll get a better job than yours, anyway,' the student jeers. 'If you're so hot, how come you aren't famous? It's like they say: those that can't do, teach.' He pulls on his sweat top. 'Fuck you, asshole. I'm outta here.'

When he's gone, Paul says, 'Good. A class like

this shouldn't have to carry passengers. Elouise, why don't you show us what you've prepared?'

The class goes on, a little stunned. Paul is so calm that Claire wonders if he didn't choose Leon with the express intention of pushing him into walking out. A ritual sacrifice, she thinks, to reinforce their collective sense of identity as a group.

When she leaves the rehearsal building she sees an unmarked car by the kerb. Frank leans against the trunk, waiting for her.

'Hey, Frank,' she says wearily.

'Hey, Claire.' He opens the rear door. 'Need a ride?'

'Do I have a choice?'

'You always have a choice.' The way he stands there, holding the car door impatiently, seems to contradict what he's saying.

'I know, I know,' she says, sliding into the back seat. 'I'm sorry I took the mike off last night.'

Frank grunts. 'That's City property, that surveillance stuff. We spent most of the evening going through the restaurant trash for it.'

'I said I'm sorry.'

'Why d'you do that, anyway?' he says. He glances at her in the rear-view mirror as he pulls out into the traffic.

She shrugs. 'I guess I'm fed up with this lack of privacy.'

'You giving up on us, Claire?'

There's a moment's silence, then she says, 'Christian said something odd last night.'

Frank grunts. 'That man says a lot of odd stuff.'

'He said I couldn't go to Europe with him because I'd never get back through Immigration.'

She traces a mark on the side window with her finger.

'That's fair enough,' Frank says. 'You wouldn't.'

'But how did he know that?'

'How'd he know what?'

'How did he know I haven't got an American passport? I've never told him.'

'Musta done.' Frank takes a hand off the wheel to gesture. 'Maybe you told him when you were talking about Raoul. You know, how Raoul said you were getting a New York accent.'

'I never said I had a British passport,' she says, shaking her head.

'Maybe he found it when he was snooping round your apartment, or maybe he just assumed.'

'Maybe,' she says. Then, looking at the traffic, 'How come you never see any motorbikes in New York?'

CHAPTER THIRTY-FIVE

'It was amazing,' she says, 'the way he goaded this guy Leon into losing his temper. It was like, poke you here, poke you there, poke you again just here, bang. Like watching someone who's really good at origami – you can't quite work out how it can be that easy.'

Christian, lying in bed beside her, grunts as he reads some academic book. She swings her legs onto the floor. 'I'm going to take a shower.'

'I'll join you in a minute,' he says, turning a page. She smiles.

The shower is in a tiled cubicle, set apart from the rest of the sleeping area. She turns the shower taps on so the temperature will settle. 'What's that you're reading?' she calls to him over the noise of the running water.

'It's a new biography of Baudelaire. They've asked me to give them a quote for the jacket.'

She's leaning into the bathroom mirror now, unhooking her earrings. 'A puff.'

'A what?'

'A puff. That's what publishers call them. Puffs. Ah, shit.' She's dropped an earring. Getting down on her knees, she gropes behind the column of the washbasin. 'Is it any good?'

'Average. There's some new stuff on his relationship with Poe. But overall . . .'

She can't hear him. His voice has vanished, as if
sucked away down a long tunnel. All her concen-
tration, suddenly, is on the thing she's just noticed
behind the pedestal: a tiny black wire, no thicker
than a strand of vermicelli, clinging to the back of
the porcelain. She touches it. Like vermicelli, it's
sticky to the touch. She gets one of her nails underneath it and gently prises it away.

It leads down to the edge of the carpet. She pulls
again. The little strand of black lifts itself from the
skirting, like a mooring rope on a beach lifting out
of the sand. She raises her arm higher, and then
higher still. When her arm is at full stretch she's
pulled ten feet or so of miniaturized cable clear of
its hiding place.

'. . . doesn't seem to grasp how unconventional
the Decadents really were,' Christian is saying.

'Sure,' she says.

She goes the other way. The thin black wire
snakes up around the back of the taps and through
a tiny hole. She follows it to where it disappears
behind the mirror.

For a moment she stares at her own reflection,
not quite believing, then she takes the mirror off
the wall and turns it over. Stuck to the underside,
where a tiny aperture has been scratched in the
silver, is a little chip.

In the van, Frank says, 'Oh, shit.'

The image of Claire's face sways crazily as she
takes the mirror off the wall. Their point of view
travels down past her knees into blackness.

* * *

Claire peels the tiny camera off the back of the mirror and examines it. Then she makes a loop of cable around her fingers and starts to wind it up. She pulls more wire from the edge of the carpet, and then more still. It leads round the corner of the shower cubicle. Behind a cupboard there's a tiny junction box, where another cable joins. She takes the path of the now doubled cable and pursues it on all fours.

Christian is still talking. Lost in his book, he doesn't see her following the wires into a recess. Books are piled in there, and she moves them.

Behind the casually piled up textbooks is a bigger junction, crouching there like a big black spider, its legs the dozen or so wires that spread in different directions around the apartment.

'Shit,' Durban says, more emphatically this time. 'Get hold of Connie. And call the backup. Tell them we've been—'

Suddenly, the images of Christian's apartment on their monitors simultaneously turn to snow.

She throws it on the bed in front of him. A plastic disc the size of a biscuit, trailing wires.

'What's this?' she asks him quietly. She sees him stiffen.

'You tell me,' he says over his glasses. 'I've never seen that before in my life.'

Slowly, ironically, she starts to clap. 'Bravo. We'll make an actor of you yet.'

'I'm sorry, I don't think I get this,' he begins. And now he's starting to look a little frightened, a little uneasy.

'No, Christian. You don't get it, do you? You

don't understand at all.' She can feel herself losing control, can feel the anger starting to explode. 'What did they tell you, you stupid fuckwit? That I was some kind of *psychopath*? That I might have killed your fucking *wife*?'

'Come and get us,' Christian calls to the ceiling. 'Come and get us, *now*.'

'They can't hear you,' she mocks. She throws another handful of cables onto the bed and imitates a sound technician's voice, 'Just give us one more for level, will you, Christian? You're not coming through very well.'

He rolls away from her, keeping the bed between them.

'Don't you understand?' she says disbelievingly. 'They think it has to be one of us. They just can't be sure which one. So they've bottled us up like two rats in a maze, and now they're watching to see which of us gets eaten first.'

She hears the lift whirring and knows they'll be here soon. Already there are shouts and the sound of banging doors. 'You stupid fuck,' she says incredulously. 'At least I told them I knew you didn't do it.' She starts to pound him with her fists. 'At least I fucking told them I knew you didn't do it.'

The entryphone is buzzing, on and on. 'Quickly,' he shouts, fending off her blows. 'Quickly. In here.'

The apartment door starts to thud as the men outside put the hydraulic ram to it. Claire backs away from him and sits down on the bed. 'Go on,' she says wearily, in her real voice. 'Let the bastards in.'

TRANSCRIPT NO. CR2449H (DUR-BAN, RODENBURG, VOGLER, OTHERS)

INTERIOR/EXTERIOR SOUNDS – some indistinguishable. Regular thumping sound identified as hydraulic ram. Door being opened.

VOICE #2 (VOGLER): For Christ's sake get in here.

VOICE #3 (DURBAN): You OK?

VOICE #1 (RODENBURG): Let me through.

VOICE (NO ID) Wait a—

VOICE #2: Let her go.

(PAUSE ON TAPE)

VOICE #3: What did she say to you in there?

(PAUSE ON TAPE)

VOICE #2: (indistinct) Nothing.

END OF TAPE.

CHAPTER THIRTY-SIX

The first thing she notices the next morning, waking in her own bed, is that a familiar warm shape is missing.

Augustus the cat has become accustomed to creeping onto her bed in the night, where he kneads his sharp claws against her back before curling up and going to sleep. This morning, there's no sign of him.

'Guess the cat's pissed off with me, too,' she murmurs. She gets up. To get to the shower she has to step over a mass of debris on the floor.

Last night, when she'd finally made it back to the apartment, she'd gone a little crazy. The TV lies on its side. Drawers have been pulled out and flung against the walls. The cheerful Swedish sofa has lost two of its legs, and now lurches sideways, like a crab.

Surveying the mess, she says, 'Can't say I blame him.'

Before she takes her shower, she pulls down the bathroom blind and switches off the lights.

That day, during Affective Memory, Paul stops the others and gets them to watch her. When she's done he says, 'What emotion was that, Claire? Anger?'

She nods.

'And the action?'

'I was hitting someone,' she says. 'It felt really good.'

After a few moments he says, 'Go home, Claire. Go home and get some rest.'

Walking down the sidewalk, she stops abruptly half a dozen times, turning round to see if there's anyone behind her. But they're good, these watchers, sliding out of her line of vision a split second before she turns.

She mutters to herself, 'I know you're there.'

She turns to a shop window, casually, as if she's simply looking at the display, scanning the reflections of the passers-by.

Nothing.

She goes into the shop, stands by a rack of CDs and picks one up. The plastic case is clear enough to use as a mirror and she angles it towards the door.

After a few moments a man comes in. Raincoat, plaid trousers. She knows she's seen him before. Quickly, she crouches down, as if she's refastening her trainers.

The movement triggers a sudden flash of memory. The time she met Victor in the cyber café. A man in a raincoat, watching them. *It's much more convincing if you turn the computer on, detective.*

She walks after him. The store is full of kids clustered around the listening posts, blocking the aisles, and she has to hurry to keep the brown raincoat in view. When he stops to scan the room, she increases her pace.

'Why don't you fuckers leave me alone?' she hisses, loud enough for other shoppers to hear. Heads turn in their direction.

Abruptly, the cop turns and heads for the exit. She goes after him. They're moving in parallel now, separated only by a rack of CDs. He breaks into a run and she does the same. 'You've got the wrong person,' she shouts at him. More people are looking now. The exit is at the end and he makes it just ahead of her. She follows him out. 'Come here, you *wanker.*' But there's a shrill beeping coming from behind her, an alarm of some sort, and just as she's about to grab at the arm of the raincoat, someone grabs her own arm from behind, a burly black hand fastening on to her wrist.

The store security guard. He gestures at the CD in her hand, the one she used as a mirror, and growls, 'We don't have many cash tills on the sidewalk, lady. Why don't you step back inside while we call the police?'

She tries to talk her way out of it, to no avail. The security guard simply points to a notice on the wall saying, 'WE ALWAYS PROSECUTE', and shrugs.

'Zero tolerance,' he says. 'They got the idea from us.'

She tries flirting and pleading and crying. None of those work, either. To her surprise, once she's started crying she finds it hard to stop.

The cop, when she finally turns up, is a uniformed woman so overweight Claire can't believe she can still walk the beat. Her name is Ryder, and she is gravely attentive as Claire explains what happened.

'This detective who was following you,' she says when Claire has finished. 'Do you know his name?'

'No.'

'How do you know he was a cop?'

'It's a long story.'

'Yeah?'

Claire sighs. 'There's this, er, surveillance operation. I've been helping the police.'

'So why did they follow you, Claire?'

'Oh, for Christ's sake,' Claire says, exasperated. 'It's only a twelve-dollar CD.'

Ryder's face is a mask. 'Why was the detective following you?'

She feels so tired, she just wants to go home and sleep and have all of this go away. 'Look,' she says, 'they think I killed someone.'

'Killed who, Claire?'

'If you phone Frank Durban at Homicide he'll explain.'

'Detective Durban, huh?'

'That's right.'

'Wait here.' She leaves Claire with the guard and goes in search of a phone and higher authority.

Claire waits. The CD is still on the table in front of her. It's a band she's never heard of.

'You're in luck,' Ryder says, returning at last. 'It's a borderline case. Charlie's supervisor has agreed to drop it after all.'

Claire stammers her thanks, but Ryder cuts her off. 'Forget it. You pay for that CD now and I'll give you a ride back to where you say you're staying.'

She insists on coming up.

'Nice place,' Ryder says, looking around. 'Big, for Manhattan. How much a month?'

Claire shrugs. 'I'm not sure. I don't pay for it.'

Ryder looks at the mess on the floor quizzically. 'Who's your landlord?'

'You people, I suppose.'

'The city?'

'The police. It's a police apartment.'

'No, really,' Ryder says. 'See, I'm looking to rent round here myself. How much would I be looking at?'

'It's part of the operation,' Claire says dully.

'Are you a sex worker, Claire?' Ryder asks. 'It's OK, you know. You can tell me.'

'No.' She can't get her head round all of this. 'Look, didn't you speak to Durban?'

'He wasn't there.'

'Oh.'

'Tell me about this operation, again?' Ryder suggests.

Claire takes a deep breath. 'This won't make any sense to you, but this whole apartment – I don't really live here, you see – is full of wires and microphones and closed-circuit cameras. They have these really, really small cameras that you can hardly see with the naked eye.' She stops, aware that she's gabbling.

'Would you excuse me, Claire?' Ryder walks into a corner and murmurs into her radio, her eyes on Claire. Then she listens. When the conversation is over she says, 'Claire, I'm getting one of my colleagues to come over. There's a few things here I want to follow up.'

* * *

The other cop's name is Murphy. He's younger and fitter than Ryder.

'I can see that this is news to you, but I've been involved in a surveillance operation,' she says yet again. 'This apartment is full of cameras. Your colleagues watch everything from an apartment downstairs.'

'Watch what, exactly?'

'Me and Christian Vogler.'

'This would be ... activities of an intimate nature we're talking about here?'

'Sex. Say it, for God's sake. Sex. Detective Durban asked me to have sex with Christian Vogler.'

'Do you take any medication, Claire?' Murphy asks carefully. 'Prozac, Lithium, insulin, anything like that?'

'No.' She's getting impatient now. 'Look, why don't you just call Frank Durban and ask him?'

'I did. Detective Durban is on leave,' Murphy says. 'He has been for some weeks.'

Once again she has a sense of vertigo, of standing in an elevator in which somebody has pressed the top button when she wasn't looking.

'Do you have a doctor in the city, Claire? A therapist, anyone like that?'

'I can prove it. Look, I know it sounds far-fetched, but I can prove it. Let me show you the apartment downstairs, the one where Durban's been hanging out.'

'OK,' Murphy says. 'Go right ahead.'

She leads the way down the service stairs to the floor below. 'Here, this is it.'

'You sure?'

'Absolutely.'

Murphy reaches past her and bangs on the door. They hear footsteps.

Claire nods at the door. 'This is going to be really funny,' she says.

The door is opened by a tiny Korean lady. 'Yes?'

'Police, Madam.' Murphy shows a badge. 'Is this your apartment?'

The woman nods and says in broken English, 'Apartment of my husband's company. Terlo company.'

'How long have you lived here?'

The woman looks confused, and he repeats, 'How long?'

Understanding dawns. 'Three year,' she nods.

'Wait,' Claire says. 'This isn't right. Ask her if they've been away.'

'Suppose you show us where in your apartment you think these cameras are,' Murphy says to her.

Silently they all go back upstairs. She takes hold of the edge of the wallpaper and rips it, looking for wires.

Nothing.

She tries to remember where the camera was that took the footage of Christian looking through her laundry.

'In the bedroom,' she says. 'There's a camera in the bedroom.'

She hears the female cop sigh.

'It should be right here,' she says, fetching a chair. 'Right here by the light hanging.'

But it isn't.

'OK,' she says at last. 'I know how to do this. There's a building out in Queens where the FBI people are staying.'

'FBI, huh?' She sees the look that Ryder gives her colleague. A look that says, do we really have to waste our time with this?

'Fine,' Murphy says, deadpan. 'Let's ride out to Queens.'

She knows, even before she gets there, what they're going to find.

The long, low building is empty, its doors locked. The billboard of a real-estate vendor covers one window.

Ryder peers through the window at a darkened office and shrugs. 'Hasn't been used in a while.'

'There's a lecture room in the basement,' Claire says desperately. 'They had Internet access and telephones. They were using electricity, for Christ's sake. It'll show up on the records.' She starts to cry. 'I'm sorry,' she says. 'I'll be all right in a minute.'

But she isn't. She isn't all right. For some reason she just can't seem to stop crying.

Murphy closes his notebook and pulls out a cell-phone. 'Listen,' he says gently, 'I'm going to arrange for you to see a doctor. I think that's best, don't you?'

CHAPTER THIRTY-SEVEN

After the funeral service for Rachel, the girl who died in the car crash, the Hopkins family and their staff are invited back to the house for the funeral tea. After politely accepting a soda, Glenn goes outside and waits by the hearse. He has a book, and he reads it quietly in the sun.

'Hi there.'

He looks up. Alicia Hopkins has come out of the house and is standing in front of him. Like him, she's dressed in black, but she's softened the severity of her funeral outfit with a light-blue cardigan.

'What are you reading, Glenn?' she asks. She comes and stands next to him to see, leaning, like him, against the warm hood of the car. Their shoulders brush. He has a sudden sense that she is standing slightly closer than she has to. 'Is that poetry?'

He turns it over and shows her the cover. '*The Collected Works of Charles Baudelaire*,' she reads aloud. 'I never read any of his stuff before. In school my favourite poet was Frost.'

He forces a grin. 'Baudelaire is nothing like Frost.'

'Read me one?'

'Well, uh, some of them aren't suitable for the occasion.'

'I won't be shocked,' she says, and just for a moment her eyes glint mischievously. 'You mustn't judge us all by Daddy's standards, you know.'

He smiles nervously. 'Why don't I try to find one that *is* suitable?' he suggests, thumbing the pages. 'Let's see, there's—'

'Did he write any love poems?' she interrupts. 'I like hearing love poems.'

Glenn thinks for a moment. 'There's this one,' he says, turning towards the back of the volume. 'It's called "Tranquillity".' He clears his throat and reads:

Let us now be tranquil, O my sad and restless soul.
You wanted evening: see, now it is here.
Dusk has engulfed us in its dark embrace,
which brings to this man peace, to this one fear.

Now, while the vile multitude strip bare
and squeal as Pleasure's whips strike home,
numbing their feelings of sorrow or despair,
come, take my hand: let us stand back and watch.

Let us stand back: above us in the sky
ghosts will watch with us in the fading light,
dressed in the costumes of a time gone by.

Let us stand back: the weakened sun
is slowly slipping out of sight:
Death, triumphant, sweeps in from the sea:
Listen my love, listen to the sweet approach of night.

'I like that,' she says when he's finished. 'It's weird, but I like it.'

He nods and smiles cautiously. 'He's pretty neat.'

She thinks for a moment. 'Do you find people react to what you do, Glenn?'

'What do you mean?'

'Like, when I'm at a party, someone will always go, "Hey, everybody, this is Alicia. She's a mortician." But they never go, Hey, this is Phil, he's a retailer, or a mechanic, or whatever.'

'People laugh at things to do with death because it frightens them.'

'That's so true,' she says. 'Maybe that's why I feel more relaxed with other morticians. Like in your poem: "Let us stand back and watch." How did that go again?'

Now, while the vile multitude strip bare
and squeal as Pleasure's whips strike home,
numbing their feelings of sorrow or despair,
come, take my hand: let us stand back and watch,

he reads again.

'Pleasure's whips sounds like the Beat Box on a Saturday night,' she says. 'Plenty of stripped-off multitudes in there.'

He doesn't respond.

'Maybe we should go and watch them sometime.'

'Maybe,' he says. After a moment, he picks up the book again and riffles through the pages.

'Is that a sketch?' she says suddenly.

'What?'

'There. Go back.' She turns a few pages back. Her hand brushes his. 'Did you do that? What is it?'

'It's just a drawing. It's a study of one . . . one of the poems.'

'It's good,' she says. 'I knew you were artistic.' She turns her head sideways. The drawing is a fragment of a nude, a female nude, reclining on a bed. 'Did you do life classes?' She giggles. 'Silly question. You don't need to do life classes. You're like Leonardo da Vinci, aren't you?'

'Why him?'

'Because he learned his anatomy from bodies, of course.'

She smiles at him and wanders back inside.

CHAPTER THIRTY-EIGHT

The psychiatrist to whom the police medic has referred her is called Dr Bannerman. He's young and slightly obese, with the bad skin of the chronically overworked. He spends a long time tapping Claire's reflexes and shining lights into her eyes. To her surprise and shame she begins to shake uncontrollably.

'Are you suffering from any physical stress or trauma that you know of?' he asks.

'I already told you. I've been involved in under-cover work.'

'Nothing like a car crash? Or a mugging?' He peers into her eyes once again with the little torch.

'Nothing,' she says through chattering teeth.

'Have you suffered from traumatic stress dis-order before?'

'Never. What do you mean, before?'

'Any nervous conditions? Epilepsy, hypo-glycaemic attacks, psychotic episodes?'

'I killed a doctor once.'

The light flicks off.

'Joke,' she adds. He doesn't smile.

'Any thoughts of self-mutilation or suicide?'

She looks at her hands. 'Not recently.'

'Have you taken any controlled substances or

non-prescription drugs in the last twelve months?'

'Some E, occasionally.'

He makes a note on his pad.

'Look,' she says, 'someone killed a woman called Stella Vogler. They used a trick to get me in front of this shrink, and then she subjected me to all these tests. I guess I didn't eliminate myself, because she tricked me again into signing a whole bunch of consent forms so that they could film me and use the films as testimony. They took me out of my apartment, they followed me with cameras night and day.' She stops, aware that she's getting overexcited.

'What tests?'

'Sorry?'

'You said she gave you some tests. What were they?'

'Oh.' She tries to remember. 'We just talked. About my parents mostly, and my job.'

'Weschler Memory Scale? Minnesota multiphasic personality inventory? Benton tests? Visual Reasoning? An EEG?'

'Um, she did suggest hypnosis. I said no.'

He makes another note.

'Do you believe me?'

'Of course,' he says.

'Really?' She's surprised. 'Thank God. You know, for a moment there it sounded pretty crazy, even to me.'

Still writing, he says, 'I once had a patient who believed he had a tree growing in his stomach. He thought he'd swallowed an apple core, you see, and that the seeds had germinated inside him. He was suffering from agonizing stomach cramps. Once we'd given him medication to relieve the stomach pains, he stopped worrying about the tree. He convinced himself it must have died and been excreted.'

'But he was still mad,' she says, not quite understanding the point of this.

'Was he?' Bannerman finishes writing his notes and tucks his pen away in his top pocket. 'We all inhabit our own reality, Claire. Like, let's see' – his eye falls on his computer – 'like a computer network. Different computers on the network run different software. Sometimes there are little glitches, compatibility problems if you like. Then they have to be fixed by tech support. Do you see what I'm saying?'

'Not really,' she says.

He glances at his watch. 'Let me put it this way. There are some little chemical imbalances in your system that need to be tweaked. Then you can be rebooted and you'll be right as rain again.'

'What do you mean, tweaked?'

'I'm going to admit you to the hospital for a few days, Claire. That way we can be sure that the regime we suggest is the best one. Sometimes these things take a little time to sort themselves out.'

CHAPTER THIRTY-NINE

Greenridge Hospital. A residential mental health facility twenty miles upstate. During the year she's spent in New York, Claire's only been out of Manhattan twice, once with Christian and once when she rode in from JFK airport. Nothing in her experience of America has prepared her for the squalor of its public-access health institutions.

The ward she's been admitted to is protected by electronic combination locks. In theory, she and the other patients are secure while they're assessed for risk of injury to others or themselves. In practice, they're prisoners. One man, a huge Negro whom the orderlies call Meathead, is actually cuffed to his bed for twenty hours out of every twenty-four, for reasons she never discovers. The other patients are mobile, after a fashion, though they shuffle up and down the polished corridors as if hobbled by invisible leg irons, muttering in an urban patois she doesn't understand.

It's very hot on the ward, and none of the windows open. Many of the male patients go bare-chested, and even the medical staff wear nothing under their thin blue overalls. At night, men and women are separated only by a corridor. On her first night, she hears the screams as a girl across the hall is attacked in her bed. The staff pull her assailant off her, but two hours later he's back in her cubicle again.

Dr Bannerman comes to Greenridge twice a week, for what he calls his clinics. These involve a brief, mumbled conversation as he updates his notes, followed by a flurry of activity as he writes a new sheaf of prescriptions. Claire's made the mistake of telling him that fear of the other patients is disturbing her sleep, so in addition to all her other drugs she's given sleeping pills, small gel-filled capsules that leave her groggy for half the following day. She's being 'stabilized', whatever that means, with what the doctor refers to as 'attack' levels of Pimozide, Proverin and Iclymitol, drugs that he assures her have no side-effects, but which she's convinced are blunting her thought processes and coating her once-quick synapses in a thick, gluey syrup of medication. They also make her constantly hungry. She seems to spend her whole day in the television room, waiting like some lethargic, bloated fledgling for the orderlies to come round with yet another tray of stodgy hospital food.

It seems ironic that Bannerman is so obsessed with medication, since it's clearly drug abuse that has fried most of his patients' brains in the first place. They compare prescriptions with all the savvy of the gourmet – 'You got methadone? Fucking A, all the man gave me were two fuckin' Tueys and a scrip for some Deth' – and tell anyone who'll listen about the higher reality they've experienced on angel dust or PCP or crack.

CHAPTER FORTY

Glenn Furnish finishes loading the autoclave, strips off his Nitrile overall and gloves and dumps them in the prep-room waste disposal. 'Good night, Harold,' he says politely, sticking his head into the office next door. 'I'm all done here. Unless you'd like for me to give you a hand with those burial licences?'

Harold waves him away. 'Go on, get out of here. You, too, Alicia,' he adds to his daughter. 'I can finish up here. You young folks probably got stuff you want to be doing.' Harold is not an overly observant man, but even he's noticed that his daughter seems quite interested in her co-worker. Perhaps if they get off work at the same time, Glenn will ask her out.

'I don't believe I'm doing much tonight,' Alicia says idly. But if she, too, is hoping that Glenn will suggest they do something together, she isn't in luck.

Claire's ward, Faraday, has an administrator's office with a computer. While the administrator's away on a supper break, she goes in there and takes a look. As she'd hoped, it's hooked up to the Net. She pulls up a search engine and looks for Dr Constance Leichtman.

More than a dozen matches come up. Claire was expecting links to sex offenders and serial killers, but what she gets, so far as she can tell, is a series of papers on social anthropology and the family structure of gorillas. Perhaps there are two Dr Leichtmans.

Instead, she goes into a site on Baudelaire and downloads a translation of *Les Fleurs du Mal*.

I have more memories than if I had lived a thousand years.

She's certain there's an answer somewhere in the poems, if only she could see it.

Glenn stops by the store on his way home. As it's the end of the day the staff are busy restocking the shelves, clearing up the perishable goods and returning them to the chiller rooms out back. He goes over to the fish counter and asks to examine a red snapper. Wordlessly, the assistant gloves his hand in a plastic food bag, picks up the fish and proffers it to the customer. The eye is milky, cauled in a soft opaque substance. Glenn sniffs delicately, then nods OK. He puts the fish in his basket and goes over to the fruit display. An assistant, an attractive young blonde, is bent over the counter, pulling out all the over-ripe fruit. Glenn admires the way her hair, pushed up under the regulation hygiene hat, has worked its way loose during the course of the day; two or three coils brush her long neck and the collar of her store uniform. 'Excuse me,' he says softly. The girl straightens up. Yes, she's as nice looking as he'd thought. There are fine blond hairs on her cheeks and her forehead, like the soft furry mould that grows on a preserve.

'Can I help you?' she says.

He points at the bin of apples she was rummaging in. 'I'd just like some of those,' he explains.

The girl says, 'Oh, I'm afraid these are going bad.'

'Really?'

'Yes. There must have been a rotten one in there. We're going to have to throw all of them away.'

'Don't do that,' Glenn murmurs. He has pulled an empty bag from the dispenser and starts to fill it from the bin. The apples are pock-marked with ginger-coloured areas of bruising. Here and there the bruises have split, and the broken skin is covered with a soft grey rind. 'I like them ripe,' he says. 'It's an acquired taste. Like burned toast.' From her name tag, he sees she's called Marianne. 'What time do you get off work, Marianne?'

She looks confused at the sudden change of tack, then defensive. 'I'm, uh, working late,' she says.

'Perhaps another time, then,' he says. He reaches past her into the grapes bin, scooping up a handful of the loose over-ripe ones that have fallen off the bunches. He puts them in his mouth all at once, like a handful of peanuts.

Marianne doesn't answer. He walks off, dragging his basket along the edge of the counter so it rattles.

Returning to her office, the administrator, Sheryl, finds Claire fast asleep in front of the computer screen. A pile of printouts have slipped from her hand to the floor. The administrator picks them up and frowns.

'You shouldn't be doing this, Claire,' she chides gently. Claire wakes up with a start.

'What?'

'This machine isn't for patients' use. This material may not be helpful to your state of mind. I'll have to give it to the doctor so he knows what you've been doing.'

For no reason that she can discern, Claire starts to cry again.

An hour after he spoke to her, in the staff car park round the back of the store, Glenn watches Marianne coming out of the staff exit. She goes to a small Japanese car. He watches her unlock it – with a key, he notes; there's no remote alarm – and pull her seatbelt on before she turns on the ignition.

He follows her to her house, a small post-war prefab in a run-down development about five minutes from the store. There are children's bikes and a baby walker in the yard. Marianne must be a few years older than she looks, or perhaps she just started breeding very young.

He's tempted to find an observation point and wait, but he doesn't really have the time. He decides to save it for another night.

'You've got to put all this behind you,' Bannerman is saying. He sounds uncomfortable. In his hand he has the sheaf of poems Claire had downloaded from the Internet. 'This is not, uh, appropriate reading for someone in your condition.'

'What is my condition?' she murmurs.

'How are you getting on with the Proverin?' he asks, ignoring the question.

She looks out of the window. 'Fine.'

'Ah!' For the first time in this afternoon's session the doctor shows real enthusiasm. 'As I thought, it must have been an abreaction between the Pimozide and the Iclymitol which was causing the nausea. Excellent progress.'

CHAPTER FORTY-ONE

Glenn uncorks a bottle of wine, sniffs at it delicately and eats the first apple, crushing the soft, rotten flesh between his palate and tongue. It tastes vaguely sherry-like. The apple falls apart in his hands as he eats it, and he has to lick his fingers and rinse them before sitting down at his laptop. While he waits for the modem to connect, he hums tunelessly and licks his fingers again.

> Welcome to Necropolis.
>
> This is a members-only adult website which—

Even before the page has finished loading, he's typed in his password and hit the Enter button. The menu page comes up. Again he hits the link he wants before the whole page has appeared.

There's another screen now, an innocuous-looking list of sites on related topics. He positions the mouse arrow over the lower right-hand quadrant of the screen, and moves it in a circle until it turns into a hand, indicating that he's found a hidden link. He clicks.

> You are in a dense grove of black
> poplar trees. They surround you in all
> directions, except one, the north.

Impatiently he types in, 'Charon'.

> Recognizing you as a denizen of this
> place, Cerberus lets you pass.
> You have three messages waiting.

Glenn scrolls down the list of messages. They are all from his customers – his patrons, as he likes to think of them. One thanking him for delivery of his last piece and letting him know that payment has been made by transfer to an Internet bank account, another making some textural observations, and a third which says simply:

> The Venus is unattainable at present.
> You missed your chance. Will you be
> able to move faster next time,
> Charon? I shall contact you as soon
> as I have news.
> Regards,
> Helios

Glenn deletes all the messages, logs off and erases all the history files from his computer, wiping the record of which sites he has just visited. Then he picks up his battered copy of *Les Fleurs du Mal*, and turns once again to a page so well thumbed its corners have turned to lace: Vogler's introduction. He reads:

It is the job of the translator, not merely to

transcribe from one language to another, but to *transfigure*, to liberate these dark captives from the dank and remote dungeons of history, and to assist their emergence, blinking and newborn, into the chilly, inhospitable air of the present. To be a translator is to be midwife to a bloody but triumphant rebirth.

The passage has been underlined once, in pencil. Beneath it, in the same pencil, Glenn Furnish has written a definition from the dictionary:

Transfigure: (vb. trans) 1) to alter the figure or appearance of; 2) to elevate or glorify, to transform from flesh to spirit.

He closes the book and carefully reaches for another apple. More rotten than the first, the soft, squishy sac drips its juices down his fingers as he transports it gingerly to his mouth. The skin, already shredding like a wet paper bag, is so soft that, when he puts his lips to it, he can simply suck and the pungent vinegary-sweet mush goes straight down his throat. When he has finished, he licks his fingers clean, then reaches for a pencil and his sketchbook.

CHAPTER FORTY-TWO

Meathead sits in the television room, reading a comic. During the past few days his restraints have been removed, although he's clearly on an even stronger drug regime than Claire is. He seems friendly, though, and she assumes that now he's free to roam about he's no more dangerous than any of the other patients.

There's a box of tattered, ripped-up books at the back of the room and she looks through it for something her glued-up mind can cope with. They're mostly pulp Westerns and kung-fu books. A couple of hospital romances were presumably donated by the nurses.

Meathead looks up. 'Hey, Claire. Whatcha got?'

She looks at the title page unenthusiastically. '*Raging Pleasure*. You?'

He grunts. '*Judge Dredd*.'

'Swap?'

Meathead looks contemptuous. 'I don't read books that don't have no pictures.'

She looks at the first page. The words seem to wriggle and squirm. After a while she puts the book down and looks at the television. Fifty-eight per cent of viewers think the woman should give her straying boyfriend one more chance.

*   *   *

'Claire, you have a visitor.'

She must have nodded off. She looks up, startled, at the sound of the orderly's voice. Next to her, Meathead has abandoned *Judge Dredd* and is staring dopily at the television. Behind him, staring down at her, is Christian.

They go to one of the consulting rooms. Christian seems shocked at the way she looks. She's put on weight, and her skin has erupted in greasy spots as a reaction to the drugs.

'Christ,' he says, 'you look terrible.'

'You really know how to charm a girl,' she mutters. She stumbles a little as she gets a chair. The medication is affecting her balance.

'I'm so sorry,' he says. 'Claire, I'm so sorry.'

She knows he isn't referring to his remark about her appearance. She makes a gesture. She wants to say that none of this is his fault, but the words are hard to find.

'If it's any consolation,' he says, 'they fooled me, too. Dr Leichtman and that detective.' He sits opposite her and takes one of her hands in his.

'I'm OK,' she says. 'Christian, really, I'm OK.'

He says, 'I've had lawyers working on this, Claire. Good lawyers. Finding out what was really going on.'

There's a spot on her forehead and she picks at it absently. 'I know all this,' she says. 'They told me that you were the suspect. They told you that *I* was. They lied to us both.'

He shakes his head. 'There was more to it than that, Claire. Much more.'

Her hand leaves the spot.

'Strictly speaking, Dr Leichtman isn't a forensic psychiatrist at all. She holds some kind of research position at Quantico. It's all pretty murky, but from what I can discover, her job was to find ways of studying killers.'

'You mean, before they'd been caught?'

'Sometimes even before they'd killed. Studying them in the wild, if you like. She lured her subjects into a series of Internet communities that she'd established for just that purpose. Like a series of glass-sided ant farms, with Connie watching everything that went on.'

'Necropolis,' she says.

He spreads his hands. 'It was a crazy idea. You can't police the Internet, much less control it. From what I can gather, instead of just observing killers, her communities were actually helping to create them. The FBI was overwhelmed by the sheer volume of work. It's been a mopping-up operation ever since.'

'I should have known she wasn't a shrink,' she says, half to herself. 'She never tried to drug me.'

'They sent you into Necropolis and deliberately dangled you in front of the killer, twitching the line every now and then to maintain his interest. At the same time, they seeded the Internet with enough information to enable him to find you. They already knew he uses the net to track his victims – the prostitute had a web page at an escort agency site and Stella left a trail when she went into Necropolis. There were other killings, too, from what I can discover, murders we never even knew about. An IT worker in Houston. A girl in Denmark who'd set up a webcam in her bathroom.

All by the same man.' He wonders how much of this she's taking in. 'Do you see, Claire? We were *bait*. Tethered goats, both of us, to lure the killer into Connie's trap. Everything else was just a pretext to keep us in the right place.'

Claire looks out of the window. A sudden gust of wind shakes the trees on the hospital lawns. A cooking smell drifts through the open door. It's nearly time for lunch. Her mouth waters.

'We'll sue the bastards, of course,' he says. 'It doesn't matter how many forms we signed. They'll pay up just to stop the story getting out.'

'What about Frank? Won't that screw up his career?'

'Hopefully.'

'I can't get my head round this,' she says. She starts to cry again, soundlessly.

'What have they done to you?' he says, his voice harsh with anger.

She dries her eyes on her sleeve. 'Just a chemical tweak, apparently. But I don't want to sue anyone, Christian. I want to get out.'

'Are you sure? Dr Bannerman—'

'I'm an actress. What do I want with Dr Bannerman's idea of sanity?'

'There's also the question of safety. Until they catch this guy, it could be dangerous out there.'

'At the last count,' she says wearily, 'there were three psychos, two schizophrenics, six manic-depressives and half a dozen crackheads in this place. Do you really think I'm in less danger out there? We'll just have to hope they catch him.'

He nods slowly. 'You're a gutsy woman, Claire.'

She digs her fingers into her stomach. 'About

fifteen pounds gutsier now than when I came in, unfortunately. And now you have to go. I'm already missing lunch.'

CHAPTER FORTY-THREE

Harold Hopkins has finished his supper and, as is his custom, he sits himself in his favourite arm-chair and reaches for the newspaper. It's his intention to end the day by reading. He turns first, as he always does, to the announcement of deaths, in case a fatality has occurred which he should know about, and reaches to the arm of his chair, where his spectacle case should be. To his annoy-ance, though, he recollects that he has left his reading glasses in the little office of the funeral parlour, when he was filling out those burial licences.

'I'm just going to the office, Ellen,' he calls. There's no reply. His wife has the radio on while she does the dishes.

Harold levers himself out of his chair and walks the short distance from his house to the funeral parlour. The key is on his chain, and it's dark, so he fumbles once or twice before he finally gets it into the lock.

Harold has never found the funeral parlour a spooky place at night. The dead, in his opinion, are the least spooky people of all, not least because they lose any mystique they might once have had when you are constantly purging and aspirating them. He thinks of them much as a child nurse might think of babies: messy, slightly wayward critters, always vomiting or defecating or generally causing trouble. Consequently, Harold doesn't turn on the main lights; he can see well enough by the light in the yard. He goes into the office to collect his reading spectacles, which are on his desk. As he turns to go, he notices, with a tut of annoyance, that someone has left the pump table light on in the prep room.

The pump table has a powerful but highly directional light attached to it, like the light on a dentist's chair. Harold guesses that someone must have left it on when they went home; an easy thing to do, since the directional beam is hard to spot from the side. He goes to turn it off. There are three cadavers in the prep room at present, about as many as the funeral parlour gets at any one time. One is from the retirement home, another is Peggy Watts' old mother, struck down by a heart attack at the age of eighty-two, while the third is a young girl, an assistant at the big store on the way into town. Marianne Collins, that was her name. The poor girl had been electrocuted in her own yard by a faulty mower lead.

As he reaches for the light, Harold hears a sound, a sort of scurrying noise. For a moment he wonders if it might be a scavenger come out of the woods, a rat or a feral cat. Then he hears it again, and this time he's pretty sure it's human.

The living, Harold Hopkins does get spooked by, particularly the living who have broken in where they shouldn't. He turns the pump light back on, reaches for the nearest heavy object – a putty gun – and edges through the room. Holding the steel putty gun upended, like a bottle, he makes his way through to the hall.

There's no one there. Maybe he was just imagining it. But, being a careful man, Harold turns to have one last check. And that's when he sees a leg – a man's leg – behind one of the caskets that are stored on their ends all along the hallway. He starts to say something, and then the casket is pushed and topples down on him. There was a time when Harold could have dodged a falling casket, but that time is long past. It catches him across the shoulders as he turns, sending him sprawling across the floor. He dimly hears the sound of running feet, then breaking glass, then nothing.

CHAPTER FORTY-FOUR

'Thing is,' says Dan Etheridge, 'nothing's been stolen and nothing's been broke. Apart from the window and the casket, of course.'

'That's right,' Harold agrees. He's tired now. The patrolman has come as quickly as he was able, but he lives on the far side of the valley, and then they had to make a careful inspection of the woods all around, and check the verges beside the road for tyre tracks, and see if anything had been taken. The broken glass he had heard was quickly explained: the intruder smashed the window beside the back door as he escaped.

'And that's what's puzzling me,' Dan says. 'Look, I can see where he busted out, but I can't see where he busted in. That's not to say he didn't, of course, only that I can't say with any exactness how.'

The wound on Harold's temple is hurting, and he takes out a folded handkerchief and holds it to the spot. 'Must have been the same place he got out, then,' he suggests.

'And then there's the question of what he was doing here,' Dan continues. 'Now, Harold, it's possible that this was a burglary and you disturbed him before he could find anything of value. That's one possibility.'

'What are the others?' Harold says, more to hurry the policeman up than because he can't think of any other possibilities himself. Indeed, one such possibility has been troubling Harold greatly ever since it occurred to him, half an hour ago.

'Well,' Dan says. 'You've got the body of a young woman here, an attractive young woman. I don't like to say this, Harold, but there are sick people out there. I think we've got to consider the possibility that someone was trying to interfere with her. Which means we should really get the funeral postponed and have her shipped to Longbay for them to run some forensic tests. See if they can find any physical evidence of that kind of thing.'

'Dan,' Harold says, 'you and I know that if we postpone the funeral for that reason it will be the end of my livelihood. No-one will ever entrust their dear departed to me again. If anything of that kind did happen to that poor girl – God rest her soul – this evening, it isn't going to change things for her. She's dead. But speculating about what might have happened will surely make things a whole lot worse for her family, as well as for me. Now, what say you and I take a look at her together, and if there's any physical evidence, any shred at all, that your speculation may be right, we'll ship her off to Longbay. But if we can't find anything, we'll just let the poor girl rest in peace.'

Dan Etheridge chews his moustache. 'I guess taking a look's not such a bad idea,' he says at last. 'Then we'll have a notion what we're dealing with.'

Together, the two men undress the body and inspect it carefully.

'I can't see anything untoward,' Harold says. 'I think we may have been lucky. Either I disturbed him, or else it really was a thief.'

'Hold up,' Dan says. 'Turn the light that way, will you? Over there.'

Harold turns the pump table light towards the corner of the room. 'What is it?'

Dan peers at something on the floor. It's a small black disc, a little bigger than a coin. 'I'd say it's a lens cap,' he says at last.

'Looks a little small to be a lens cap,' Harold says.

'From one of those digital cameras. My brother Ed has one. They take a smaller lens.' He looks around. 'You got any plastic gloves, Harold?'

'Sure.' Harold pulls a pair of Nitriles out of the dispenser. The policeman pulls one on and picks up the disc.

'Looks like he might just have been taking some photographs. Might have been a college kid doing it for a dare, for all we know. So we'll say no more for the moment, Harold. But I'd better hang on to this, in case it happens again.'

When Christian returns to the hospital two days later he brings someone with him, a doctor, whom Claire understands works for Christian in some way. This man, who is called Dr Felix, asks her some questions in a thin, high voice, and takes her over to the window so that he can examine her in the light. Then, his lips set, he tells the orderly at the door that he wishes to see Dr Bannerman. The orderly mumbles something about Dr Bannerman not being on call, and she sees Dr Felix's lips set even thinner. He talks to the orderly for a long time in a low voice. Soon Bannerman turns up, visibly flustered, and Dr Felix takes him aside. Dr Bannerman hasn't changed into his hospital uniform and Claire can see that he's breaking into a sweat. Then Dr Felix returns and tells Christian quietly, 'We can go. It's all taken care of.'

'It was nice of you to come,' Claire says. 'Will you come back?'

'Would you give us a minute?' Christian says to Dr Felix.

'Of course,' the doctor replies, with the graciousness of a man who knows that every minute he gives them is being handsomely paid for.

When they're alone, Christian says gently, 'You're coming with us, Claire. Dr Bannerman has agreed that you're not in need of his services after all. You'll stay with me until you're better. That way the police will only have one address to watch – if that's all right by you.'

'Of course it is.'

'Good. We'll talk some more in a few days, when you've got these drugs out of your system.'

CHAPTER FORTY-FIVE

Glenn Furnish leans over Ellen Vortenssen and looks into the girl's deep blue eyes. Tenderly, almost reverently, he squeezes a drop of superglue into the exact centre of her iris. Then he thumbs the eyelid shut, holding it for a moment for the glue to take effect.

It's two days since the pregnant teenager was cut down from the beam of an outhouse behind her parents' farm, and her eyes have turned milky now, a film of decomposition as pale as cataracts over the bloodshot corneas.

Bloodshot, because the fall had not been long enough to break the girl's neck. Attempting to hang herself, she had actually suffocated instead. Blood vessels all around her eyes and behind the delicate skin of her cheek have burst, giving her the appearance of a sixty-year-old derelict.

With her eyes sealed, she looks better already. Almost, Glenn thinks, as if she has just come in from riding her horse on a cold winter morning. A little flushed. But soon, when he has got to work with his SkinTone, there'll be no sign even of that.

Glenn leans over her once more to hold the other eye closed. And – he can't help himself – seeing the girl's lips, pale and drained as a statue's, just below his own, he delicately touches his mouth to hers, taking her dry bottom lip between his own wet lips, pulling it into his mouth and inhaling the gamey, ripe scent —

'Hey, Glenn.'

He jumps back, startled. He had forgotten that he wasn't alone, that this was not his private time, but an ordinary working day in the prep room. Alicia is standing at the door.

He stares at her, waiting for her to scream, to make the first move. He already knows that he will have to kill her.

Then she smiles. 'I won't tell if you don't.'

'You aren't . . . upset?' he says.

'Fuck, no,' she says. 'You think when I was younger I never took the chance to take a good look at some of the young guys who came in here? I guess all us morgue rats are the same.'

'I guess,' he says uneasily.

'Besides, you know what they say about working with the dead,' she says, coming closer to him.

'What do they say?'

'That it makes you horny,' she whispers. She giggles. 'Nature's way of making sure we keep the species going. Whenever we see a corpse, we want to get laid.' She reaches for his hand. 'Dad's at a funeral.'

'I know.'

Her fingers run down his hand, stroking his fingers, brushing the front of his pants. What she finds there makes her grin even wider. 'Can we go to your place?'

Glenn's mind is racing. 'OK,' he says, 'I'd like that very much.'

* * *

282

Alicia looks at the photographs on Glenn's wall and says, 'Wow.'

There are six prints, each blown up to two foot by three. They show the red snapper Glenn bought from the supermarket. He took one photograph each day for a week, capturing the colour changes as the scales turned first violet, then black. By the end the fish had been little more than bones in a pile of mouldy, iridescent jelly.

'They're beautiful,' she says. 'Weird, but beautiful.'

Coming to stand behind her, he nods. 'Rembrandt used to say that the best fruit for a still life is fruit that's about to rot.'

'Like, it's decaying, but you stop the decay with your photographs. That's neat.'

'Yes,' he says, surprised that she has understood his art so quickly. Just for a moment he wonders if it might be possible for this girl and him . . . but no, there is too much behind him, too many ghosts, for that. 'It's part of a . . . project,' he adds.

For a moment they stand there, each thinking their own thoughts. 'Where's the bedroom?' she says at last. 'Is it this way?'

'Uh-huh.' He follows her, as he knows she intends.

'Oh, that's neat, too,' she says. She's looking at the Insect-O-Cutor on the wall above the bed, a glowing neon circle mounted directly above the pillow. The blinds are drawn and the room is filled with pale-blue light from the tube. 'Like, found art, right?'

'Right,' he says. She bounces onto the bed and turns to look up at him. He can see by her eyes that she's excited. She reaches for the clasp of his belt.

He stands there and watches her, as if through a movie camera. She is freeing his penis, making the noises they make in movies, holding it in her fist as if she's holding a knife to stab herself with. She is wetting the head with saliva, running it around her lips like a tube of lipsalve. She's lapping at the tip, licking it long and slow, taking her eyes off it occasionally to look up at his. She is pushing her fingers underneath his sac, palming his balls, rolling them in her fingers, not realizing that they are bombs which, when they go off, will destroy her and the world with her. She is wrapping her lips around the head of his cock, pouting at him, not understanding that she is wrapping her lips around the barrel of a gun. He feels her trying to suck the power from him, suck the bullets out of the gun and the explosive from the bombs, and for a moment he wilts in her, but only until he puts his hands around her neck. She looks a little doubtful, but she doesn't stop. He presses his thumbs against the front of her throat, feeling for the delicate cartilages of the larynx, the springy thyroid and the harder knob of the cricoid underneath. He squeezes, and she tries to pull away, but standing above her like this he is the one with the power. For a moment she tries to make a sound, but the pressure on her windpipe is too great. He reaches down with his free hand to the bed, to the belt she pulled from his trousers just a few minutes before. Looping it around her neck, he puts the buckle underneath her ear and tightens it, pulling upwards with all his strength. She starts to rise with it, but he pushes her down with his other hand on her shoulders. Her tongue, protruding from her mouth with the pressure on her larynx, pushes his penis out of her mouth. He barely notices. He hadn't wanted to come yet, anyway. Not just yet.

CHAPTER FORTY-SIX

'OK,' Rob Fleming says. 'I might have something for you here, Frank.'

Durban nods.

The computer crimes technician indicates the screen in front of them. 'As you know, the lawyers haven't had much success with getting picture-man.com pulled.'

'Tell me about it,' Frank growls. 'How many hits has it taken so far?'

Fleming checks something on the computer screen. 'Over half a million. Anyway, I asked myself, what other ways are there of getting a website off the air? And then I thought, what about hacking it?'

Positano, watching from the side of the room, stirs uneasily. 'Hacking it?'

'Sure. Only last week some college kids got onto the Pentagon site and deliberately crashed it. And that's the Pentagon; they've got a full-time team working on counter-hacking measures. Pictureman.com's just a souped-up homepage.'

'Is hacking legal?' Positano asks.

'It's a grey area, just like sticking up a site like this in the first place.'

'And?' Durban says. 'Can you do it?'

'Bear with me. First, I opened an account with the server myself, to see what sort of site-builder software it provides. As I thought, it allows the designer of the site access privileges, in case he wants to update the site, change the typeface or whatever. After that, it was just a matter of getting hold of the relevant codes. I didn't even have to go to the software manufacturers; all the information was out there on a hacker's bulletin board. See?' He types something on his keyboard, and the web-page on the screen is filled with his gibberish. He clicks with his mouse and it disappears again.

'Great,' says Durban. 'What are you waiting for? It's a no-brainer, Rob. Get this guy off the air.'

'Well,' Rob says, 'that's what I was going to do. But then I had this other idea.'

Durban looks at him. 'What's on your mind?'

'You ever heard of mirror sites, Frank?'

Durban shrugs. 'Can't say I have.'

'They're websites that look identical to another website and even appear to have the same address; they're just being run by a different server. People set them up when their existing site gets clogged with traffic.'

'Go on,' Durban says.

'Well, it's just that, if I were to set up a mirror site to this one and hide the real one, we could rig it so that, when the killer comes along to update his site, look at the number of rubberneckers he's been hit by, whatever, we'll know about it.'

'Jesus,' Durban says. 'You mean, just by watching, you could tell when the killer's online? And maybe trace the phone connection?'

'Screw watching,' Fleming says. 'We could get the website to send us an e-mail.' He laughs. 'They call it the worldwide web, don't they? We're gonna be the spider in that web.'

For a week Christian nurses her, despite her protestations. He brings her delicacies from the Italian store across the street, runs baths filled with sweet-smelling Parisian oils for her, and swaddles her afterwards in vast soft towels. He has a gym room, and she starts to exercise in it, slowly losing the weight she gained in the hospital, toning her body while he watches in the double wall of mirrors that reflect a thousand Claires, a thousand Christian Voglers. He trims her hair while it's still wet from the shower, brings her clothes he's picked out for her in Barneys and Donna Karan, cooks her meals of fresh produce from the Union Square Farmer's Market and Dean & DeLuca.

Twice a day, Dr Felix visits. He tells them she's making an excellent recovery.

On the seventh night after her return from Greenridge, Christian takes her to Liberty Island on the ferry. They stand like tourists beneath the hollow lady, watching the lights of Manhattan dancing on the silver-black water.

'Claire,' he says, 'there's something I need to know.'

She waits.

'How much of it was acting?' he says softly. 'All of it? Some of it?'

She stares across the water. 'Connie was very clever,' she says at last. 'There was just enough of my real self in the cover story to make all those crazy things she made us do seem plausible. Even when I was certain you hadn't done it, I didn't want it to end.'

'Me neither.'

'What about your wife?'

'Stella was the reason I agreed to help them, initially. She wasn't the reason I agreed to go on. I thought if I walked out I'd lose you altogether.'

'I understand,' she murmurs.

'Do you think . . . could we ever start this again, from the beginning? Or has there been too much water under the bridge?'

She gazes across at the elegant tracery of Brooklyn Bridge. 'Some bridges can span an awful lot of water.'

'I love you, Claire. I want to be with you.'

'And me with you.'

'Whatever happens,' he says, 'I've given you my heart. Will you accept my hand as well?'

'Christian. My God . . . are you saying what I think you're saying?'

'Marry me,' he says simply, and after the briefest of pauses she answers, 'Of course.'

He spends the whole night, almost, inside her. At times they barely move, rocking together, murmuring. Eventually he falls asleep, still inside her, without coming, and she understands that it is this, and not the physical climax, that he really craves: to be whole again, to complete the circle; to be joined to her by his penis, as a baby is joined to its mother by the cord.

PART FIVE

'Through the unknown we find the new.'
Le Voyage, Baudelaire

CHAPTER FORTY-SEVEN

'Harold, I am so sorry,' Dan Etheridge says awkwardly. 'Please accept my condolences. And Martha sends hers too.'

Harold nods bleakly. All those years of uttering condolences himself, the grave formula of sympathy and regret. Now he understands how empty, how meaningless they are.

'We've had the report back from the autopsy,' Dan says slowly. 'Just so's you know, it was pretty much what we expected. When folks hang themselves, there's a distinctive mark underneath the ear, and in this case the buckle . . .' His voice tails off. 'It happens, sometimes, with kids. Kind of like a craze. One of them will do it, and then another will copy her, and before you know where you are there's a whole epidemic going on.'

'Yes,' Harold says. He looks out of the window, towards the woods where his daughter's body was found, hanging from a tree, after a week-long search.

'I don't know whether you'll want to handle the . . . arrangements yourself,' Dan says. 'Harold, I think I should warn you. Her body – out in the woods like that – some animals must have got to her while she was hanging there. It might be best to ask another firm to take care of her.'

The young assistant, Glenn, who has been standing quietly behind his employer, speaks for the first time. 'Harold?' he says gently. 'Harold, I'd be honoured to see what I can do for her. I would very much like to do my best for Alicia.'

Harold feels he has lost the power to make any decisions at all. 'If you think you can do it,' he says.

Dan Etheridge lets his gaze travel down the soberly attired young man. For the first time he notices that Glenn Furnish's trousers have no belt.

Furnish hums tunelessly as he hooks the aspirator pump up to Alicia's body. One tube in, another tube out, as if the aspirator were some mechanical steel heart, an alternative circulation that, once connected, will make the dead girl sit up and walk again.

Glenn smiles at the memory of those days, the days they spent together. Him and Alicia. A tranquil time. His smile broadens. For the piece he intends to call *Tranquillity* he had arranged the girl in front of a television screen on which a porno tape was showing an orgy scene.

Now, while the vile multitude strip bare
and squeal as Pleasure's whips strike home,
numbing their feelings of sorrow or despair,
come, take my hand: let us stand back and watch.

He had experimented with various objects inserted into her vagina. Finally, in a reference to her insight into his work, he had decided on a rotten fish. 'Death, triumphant, sweeps in from the sea.' His patrons, he knew, would appreciate the irony of that.

Glenn intends to price *Tranquillity* at $10,000.

While the aspirator pump shakes and gargles, and Glenn gets on with repairing the damage done by scavengers, he starts to turn over in his mind the possibilities of another idea.

After all, he has the bodies of two young women here. An opportunity like that only happens rarely.

Soon, Glenn knows, it's going to be time for him to move on. He has time for just one more piece before he has to go.

He read somewhere that Michelangelo had said the statue was already captive in the marble; the artist's job was merely to release it. Intrigued, Glenn looked up the series of sculptures known as the *Captives* and studied them for hours, entranced by the grimaces on the faces of the artist's subjects as they struggled to free themselves from their cauls of stone. He knew the power Michelangelo must have felt, the godlike power, as he stood over his creations and knew that he, and he alone, had the power to release them.

When Glenn was in Italy he made a special pilgrimage to see them, queuing outside the Accadèmia with all the other American tourists at opening time. The others, of course, had been after a glimpse of the sculptor's graceful, serene *David*, not the stunted, writhing effigies of the *Captives*. Cameras raised, they had advanced down the long colonnade of statuary, clicking away at the *David*, strategically placed at the end of the gallery. Glenn had been amazed. How could anyone simply walk past the *Captives*, ignoring those stark, tortured forms?

One day Glenn will do something as great as the *Captives*. Not in marble, of course, but in his own medium, the medium of the age in which he lives: flesh. His artworks preserved as bytes, electronic slices of information flowing from computer to computer through the infosphere.

Not yet, though. Not yet. For the moment, Glenn needs his patrons' money, just as Michelangelo needed the Medicis' gold. Just one more piece here, and then it's on to the city and his next commission.

Dan Etheridge methodically goes through the sheaf of faxes that have come in from the FBI, Interpol, the NYPD and other police departments. In the usual course of things, Dan doesn't exactly ignore these notices – nothing is ever thrown away, and each fax is added carefully to the stack behind the spare printer cartridges – but neither does he actually pay them much mind. Out here, law enforcement is usually more a matter of keeping drunk drivers off the roads than keeping a lookout for criminals on the most-wanted list.

Now, however, something is bothering Dan. The young assistant Harold has taken on is getting good reports from almost everyone who's had dealings with him. But on the other hand, there have been rather more deaths than usual since he turned up. Particularly of young women. Then there was the break-in at Harold's funeral parlour. And, finally, the matter of the belt.

The belt Alicia hanged herself with was a man's belt. Nothing particularly odd about that – plenty of girls preferred a bigger belt, and she'd been wearing Gap jeans with big, man-sized loops – but, put with all the other things, it's making the policeman uneasy.

Suddenly, as he sorts through the pile of Federal Alerts and BOLOs – Be On Lookout notices – he sees one that makes him stop and whistle through his teeth.

He gets into his car and heads out to Harold's place.

CHAPTER FORTY-EIGHT

There aren't many people to tell, only Bessie and a few of her friends from the acting group. She hasn't seen Bessie in months. To her surprise, her former roommate is now ensconced in a condo on the Upper East Side, surrounded by Hollywood scripts stamped with the logos of ICM and William Morris. The phone calls that interrupt them are not for auditions but screen tests. Sometime during the interim, her friend has been transformed from an energetic Sheep into a rising star.

'*Married?*' Bessie shrieks, aghast. 'Fuck, girl, you've only known this guy a few weeks.'

'It's months now, Bessie. Long enough.'

'For half of which time you thought he'd axed his wife. And what about the age difference?'

'Christian isn't old. He's just older than I am.'

'Well,' Bessie says, 'I sure hope the sex is terrific. Because otherwise I can't see what the hell you're doing this for.'

Claire doesn't answer.

'That good, huh?'

'That good.'

'Do I get to be best girl? Matron of honour, or whatever they call it?'

'Not unless you're prepared to fly to Paris.

We're going to get married there.'

The other girl's eyes narrow. 'Is he rich?'

'I . . . I guess so. We don't discuss it.'

'That's not why . . . ?'

'Bessie!'

'And he has American citizenship, right? So you get a green card *and* a gold card. What does he do for a living again?'

'He's an academic.'

'Fabulously wealthy, fabulous in bed and smart, too. Sure it wasn't you who bumped off the first wife? Don't answer that, in this country you have the right to take the Fifth Amendment. When's the big day?'

'As soon as term ends. Christian's got lectures, and I want to finish my acting classes.'

When Etheridge gets to the Crossways, he drives round the back of the funeral parlour and knocks on Harold's door. Harold answers the knock himself. Dan notices how tired the mortician looks. Harold's taking it hard, he reflects.

'How are you, Harold,' he says politely.

'The Lord will see us through,' the other man replies. Dan sees that he has a Bible in his hand.

'Harold, I'm sorry to disturb you. It was Mr Furnish I'd like a word with, if he's around.'

'Glenn? He's finished for the day. Finished with . . . with . . .' the old man almost breaks down, but recovers and says, 'He's finished with Alicia. Says he's made her look real peaceful. I was just reading the book before I go to spend some time with her.'

'Sure,' Dan says. 'Do you have his address?'

'Must have. It'll be in the office, on the Rolodex. I'll—'

'Don't worry,' Dan says quickly. 'I didn't mean to disturb you, Harold. I'll find it for myself.'

'You'll need the key,' the mortician says, fishing in his waistcoat pocket. 'Here. Glenn locked it when he went. Said we couldn't be too careful, with Alicia and all.'

Etheridge takes the key and goes to the door of the funeral parlour. The office is on his right, and he can see the Rolodex on top of the filing cabinet, but something makes him go and take a quick look in the prep room first.

He walks in and flicks on the lights. The big fluorescents come on overhead, one by one, flickering and filling the room with light. Illuminating the grotesque tableau on the floor.

Etheridge wants to pull the girls' bodies apart, wants to drag them away from each other, but he knows he can't. Not before they've been photographed.

Photographed. Dan remembers the lens cap he found on the floor, and guesses that the crime search people won't be the first to record this scene.

He runs outside, pausing only to grab the Rolodex. Then he locks the funeral parlour door behind him and goes to the house.

'Harold,' he asks when Harold finally comes to the door. 'Is there another key like this?' He holds up the key he's used to lock the parlour door.

'No, that's the only—'

'Good. Harold, I've locked it. Things aren't right, and I don't want you going in there, you hear? Just stay away for a while. Some other cops may come by to take a look. I'll call you later.' Dan is already running to the car as he says this. He doesn't hear Harold's reply over the noise of the engine.

Glenn downloads his latest pictures and calls up his messages. There are a stack of them. He ignores most of them and opens one from Helios. As he reads it, he nods thoughtfully.

> Venus is alive and well and waiting for you in NYC. I have in mind something simple and quite sentimental.
> Something like 'The Death of Lovers'.
> Best wishes
> Helios

Glenn goes to the bookshelf, pulls out his copy of *Les Fleurs du Mal*, and finds 'The Death of Lovers':

> There is a bed, with pale sweet-smelling sheets;
> cushions soft as earth within a tomb;
> exotic flowers on the window ledge,
> to block the daylight from this quiet room.

> And, like two logs that smoulder in a grate,
> which, knocked together, suddenly relight –
> catching and roaring in a burst of flame –
> so our hearts, pressed together now, ignite.

> A cold mysterious fire engulfs us both,
> a sudden flash of incandescent white;
> a flame that burns and does not burn
> but fills the mirrors with its ghostly light.

When in some future age these doors are broached,
they shall find only this: an empty bed,
some charred and blackened bones; a film of ash,
the mirrors broken, and the fire long dead.

He nods slowly. It would be easy enough to do, of course. The charred bodies and the broken mirrors. But that would be a very literal interpretation.

Glenn Furnish prides himself on approaching his subject matter a little more obliquely.

He goes to his own homepage and updates it with a brief mention of his recent pieces. He considers posting some of the *Tranquillity* pictures, then decides not to. It might affect their commercial value. He contents himself with uploading some more of the *Martyr* series. He looks at the hit counter and frowns. The hits from visitors are tailing off. Maybe it's time to mount a spectacular.

His next call is to a tourist site, where he downloads a street map. The connection is slow, and the map takes a little while to come through. While he's waiting, he sits on his bed, crosslegged, and stares at the glowing circle of the Insect-O-Cutor. His eyes glaze over and the violet tube loses focus. Then a housefly flies into it and the crack of the electric current jerks him awake. Carefully, he unplugs the fly killer and lays it on the bed, together with his suitcase. The tin tray is full of dead flies, and he pours them into his palm. They weigh no more than corn chaff. Experimentally, he pours a few into his mouth and crunches them up. They have a faintly bitter taste, not altogether unpleasant.

A sudden noise from the computer reminds him

that there isn't much time. He saves the map to his hard drive, then puts the laptop into the suitcase.

Rob Fleming is writing a birthday card to his niece in Ottowa when the ping of his e-mail alert tells him he's got mail. Seeing what it is, he quickly grabs the phone and dials a number.

'Joan? The fly's entered the web.'

A few moments later, a computer at AT&T starts to locate the origin of the phone call by means of which the webmaster of pictureman.com is entering his kingdom.

He's only online for a few minutes, then, abruptly, he disconnects.

'Hell, that was quick,' Rob mutters. 'Is that enough to trace him?'

'Should be,' his contact says at the other end of the phone. He hears the clatter as she types some commands into her computer. After a few moments she says, 'Yep, we got that one. Got a pen?'

Rob gets straight onto the other line. 'Frank? We've got an address. It's upstate from you. About two hundred miles.'

The Rolodex gives Furnish's address as 86 Gordons Drive, but as soon as Dan turns into the street he recalls that number 86 is a boarding house. Sure enough, the landlady tells him Furnish moved out weeks ago, as soon as his first pay cheque came in.

'Did he give a forwarding address?'

'He didn't, no.'

Damn, thinks Etheridge, but then the landlady

303

adds, 'I know where he went, though. He's taken the old Kessler property in Craven Road; the realtor is a friend of mine.'

Etheridge thanks her and hits the road again. He's already called the city cops and told them to search the funeral parlour. He hears them talking to each other on their radios as their cars bring them closer.

The Kessler property is a clapboard house, small but pretty. Etheridge notes that there are no close neighbours. There's no car in the driveway, but Dan draws his firearm for the first time in several years as he approaches the door.

The door swings open to his touch. The air smells fetid, an aroma of rotting fish mixed with something sweeter. Dan pulls out a handkerchief and puts it to his nose. Then he edges inside.

There's no-one there. Only a few pictures stacked against the wall beside the front door, as if Glenn Furnish had been packing and had suddenly decided to travel light.

Half an hour later Frank is back on the line. 'Rob, I'm here with Mike Positano. We're going to the speakerphone, OK?'

'Fine.'

A second later Rob Fleming hears the detective's voice again. 'The local guys have already called that address in, Rob. Seems the bird has flown. We're going to keep some people back here in the city in the hope you'll be able to trace him the next time he stops.'

'You'll be in the right place, then,' Rob says.

'What do you mean?'

'After he left pictureman.com, we followed him

to a map site. He downloaded a street map of New York City.'

As Glenn drives south in the gathering dusk, he gradually becomes aware of hollowed-out pumpkins flickering in windows and groups of children assembling in ghost suits and fright masks. He laughs aloud. Of course; Hallowe'en. He couldn't have picked a more appropriate date.

His eye is caught by an older child, a teenage girl to judge from the shape of her body, dressed in a costume on which a skeleton has been painted in glowing, luminous paint. It's a standard Hallowe'en outfit, and Glenn barely glimpses it as he drives past, but something about it lingers in his mind.

For perhaps twenty miles he turns the image over in his mind. He tries to push it away but, like a fly buzzing around a piece of meat, it keeps coming back to nag at him. Eventually, seeing a store with a sign advertising Hallowe'en costumes, he makes an abrupt turning off the highway.

They wait. For hours they wait.

Forensic Crime Search takes Furnish's rented house and the funeral parlour apart. Lieutenant Lowell flies out by helicopter to supervise.

At nine, Frank sends out for sushi. At midnight, he heads to a hotel to take a shower and get some rest.

He's under water when he hears the phone ring. Cursing, he runs for it, still flecked with suds. The receiver is slippery in his hand, and it takes a moment to get it to his ear.

It's Fleming. The technician sounds excited.

'You're not going to believe this. The bastard's just used his laptop in a motel.'

'Where?'

'Westchester. The Marin Road Motel. And Frank? Just for good measure, we've got his credit card details. He paid for his room in advance, with Visa.'

Frank thinks. 'That doesn't make sense,' he objects. 'He must suspect by now that we're after him.'

'Right. But this isn't his card. It's registered to a Harold J. Hopkins. Want me to report it stolen?'

'No. It's better for us if he's using it. Tell Positano and Weeks I'll meet them in the station house in fifteen minutes.'

A few minutes later he's in the car, one hand on the wheel, the other pressing shower water out of his ear, when his cellphone rings. This time it's Positano.

'Everything's ready this end. One thing you should know. The same credit card's just been used again. He's booked himself a hooker.'

'Shit. Are we sure about this?'

'One hundred per cent. The transaction has just been processed by the A1 Escort Agency.'

'Phone them. Tell them not to send her out.'

'We have. We're too late, Frank. She's already gone.'

He thinks for a moment. Weeks' voice says in his ear, 'Want me to phone the motel? The desk clerk could maybe intercept her and stop her going in.'

'No. No, don't do that. If it's him, we can't risk the desk clerk acting suspiciously. Get the team into the cars. I'll wait for you by the ramp into the tunnel.'

CHAPTER FORTY-NINE

The man in the motel room unpacks his case carefully, taking out all the things he has brought with him and double-checking them before putting them back in the case and pushing it under the bed. He glances at the clock in the headboard. A little after nine. She's late, but not by much. He feels the excitement welling up in him, an unruly emotion, and forces it away. He must remain calm. Control is everything.

When the knock comes at the door, he crosses quickly to unfasten the chain. 'Who is it?' he says quietly.

'Corinne. From A1.'

He lets her in, standing back so that she can go past him into the room. She's not bad looking for a whore, a little trashy, to be sure, but the package is good. Beneath her raincoat she's wearing cut-offs and a little T-shirt with a V-shaped neck. Blond hair, five foot five inches high, just as it said on the A1 Agency's website. He smiles with relief.

Misunderstanding, she smiles back at him. 'Hi, I'm Corinne, and I'm from A1 Escorts. I'm very pleased to be here. Why don't you tell me your name and what you have in mind for us this evening?' she says mechanically.

'I'm Harold,' he says.

'Well, Harold, you've already paid an introduction fee, but maybe before we get to know each other you'd like to hear about some of the extras I can offer you.'

'Thank you,' he says. 'I'd like to hear that very much.'

'Full sex is two hundred. Without a condom is three. Oral sex, also with a condom, is one hundred and fifty. Massage is fifty.'

'And what if I want something . . . more specific?' he says.

'Well, that would depend on what you had in mind. So why don't you share it with me and we'll see what we can do.' He seems to hesitate, and she prompts, 'I'm a pretty adventurous person, Harold. Nothing's off limits for a good-looking guy like you.'

'This is something quite . . . unusual,' he says, and the smile flickers momentarily, revealing not doubt but cold, naked greed.

'Good,' she says. 'Why don't we get comfortable and you can tell me about it?'

They're in luck. The commuter traffic has cleared now, and the convoy of cop cars makes it onto the freeway in fifteen minutes, their massed sirens cutting a swathe through drivers eager to demonstrate their sobriety by pulling promptly out of the way. As they leave the city it starts to rain, great sheets of water that melt the windscreen and turn the surface of the road to soup. Durban peers past the wipers at the tail lights of the car ahead, struggling to keep them in focus, and swears under his breath as they take an exit ramp too fast.

Next to him, Positano grabs at the doorstrap as the back end slides precariously on the slippery road.

When the phone goes again, Frank tucks it between his shoulder and his ear so he can keep both hands on the wheel. 'Yep?'

'Weeks. I've just been talking to Ellis – he did a stint in Vice? Apparently, standard operating procedure is that the escort will phone her booking agent as soon as she gets to the room. Which means the agent will warn her we've been making inquiries.'

'Fuck. OK, get on to the local cops. Get them to lean on the agent, quickly. Tell him that if the girl realizes something's wrong she'll put herself at risk. Make it clear we're already in position, the girl won't come to any harm.'

There's a short silence. He wonders if Weeks is about to quarrel with his decision. But all he says is, 'Fine,' before the connection's broken.

If the girl in that hotel room dies, Frank knows they're going to have a lot of explaining to do.

'I just have to authorize this,' Corinne says. She swipes his card through a hand-operated credit card machine which she takes from her bag, then she gets on the phone to Visa. He hadn't anticipated this. He isn't sure whether the card number's going to be good for another such scrutiny.

'Hopkins, Mr H. J. Hopkins,' she says into the phone. 'Two thousand dollars.'

While she waits, tapping her long fingernail on the card, she says to him, 'Do you wanna get us some drinks from room service, Harold?'

He doesn't want anyone coming to the room.

'Sorry,' he says politely, 'I'm in AA.' She shrugs. The operator must have come back on the line, because she says into the handset, 'Oh eight nine two zee. Thanks.' She writes it on the credit slip and hangs up.

Then, 'Just one more call.'

More waiting.

'Judy? I'm here. No, I'll be a while. Tell him I'll call him tomorrow. Yeah, pretty good. An all-nighter. I'll call you tomorrow, OK?'

Corinne puts down the phone.

'Right,' she says, getting to her feet. 'That's all taken care of. Would you like to sit and chat a while, or would you prefer to get started?'

'I think I'd like to start,' he says.

'OK.' She pulls off her T-shirt. Underneath she's wearing a push-up bra. 'Where is it?'

Silently, he pulls the case from under the bed and opens it. The Hallowe'en costume is folded up on top. The skeleton, picked out in luminous paint, glows a little. He puts it on the bed.

Corinne flicks her hair up and turns around. 'Would you unhook me, please?'

He feels the dampness from the rain on her skin as he undoes her bra. She turns back around, holding her bra against her breasts with one arm, then lets them spill in front of him. She glances at the costume and giggles.

'This is going to be great,' she whispers.

They turn off the sirens and headlights about a mile from the motel. Someone's radioed ahead: a cop car is waiting at the intersection. It leads them at a more careful pace to the side of the building.

They jump out, leaving the car doors open. No point in alerting their quarry with the sound of slamming metal.

The local cop has a word with the clerk on the desk and comes out again. 'Room twelve. The one at the end. He asked for it specially.'

They've already broken the rifles out of the trunk of the lead car. Frank draws his sidearm, using it to wave the others into position.

The girl is on the bed now, encased in the costume. It's made for a child, so it's tight on her, but that doesn't matter. There are two tiny air holes, one under each nostril, but they're too small to bother him, to spoil the moment. He grips her arms, feeling her bony flesh through the thin plastic. As he eases himself into her, a small sound escapes his own mouth, a moan of satisfaction, and it coincides exactly with the double crash from the doorway, the first as the flimsy lock gives way and the second, a moment later, as the force of the blow sends the door slamming back against the wall. He looks up, his eyes narrowing as the room fills with uniforms and guns. For just a second he's balanced on her, then he goes sprawling to the floor as Corinne sits up, tears the rubber mask from her face and spits, 'What the fuck is going on?'

CHAPTER FIFTY

Christian picks up the phone. 'Yes?'

He listens, then says, 'Thank you. Well done. We shall certainly celebrate.'

'What is it?' Claire asks.

'The police have just captured someone. They're pretty sure it's him.' Carefully, he replaces the handset in its cradle. 'We're free, Claire. That's it. No more protection, no more bodyguards, no more cops hanging around. It's over now.'

They bring Glenn Furnish back to the city that night for processing. At the NYPD's headquarters in New Jersey, his clothes are taken away for fibre analysis and he's given a white paper jumpsuit to wear. First, though, he's given a physical examination as thorough as those given to rape victims. Hairs are taken from his head, his chest and his groin; scrapings are made under his fingertips; DNA material is swabbed from the roof of his mouth, and a sample of blood is syringed from the crook of his arm.

When the medic has finished taking bloods, the puncture mark leaks a few drops. The medic's about to swab the wound when the young man forestalls her by putting it to his mouth and sucking it.

'I read somewhere that when a shark is bleeding,' he says conversationally, 'it can drive itself crazy trying to feed on itself.'

The doctor says nothing. She's seen a lot of people pass through this examination suite, but she's never seen anyone so relaxed.

At precisely 8.30 a.m., Furnish asks to make a phone call. He's taken to a holding cell and left alone with the phone. He dials a number he memorized a long time ago. A woman's voice answers. 'Chance, Truman and partners. Good morning.'

'Mr Truman, please.'

Despite the early hour, he gets Truman's secretary. Or maybe it's an intern, picking up the phone.

'Is he there?'

'Mr Truman is in conference. May I—'

'Tell him it's Charon,' Glenn interrupts. 'He owns some of my, uh, artwork. I think he'll want to speak with me.'

Two minutes later a man's voice comes on the line. 'Truman.'

'Listen,' Glenn says. He tells the voice at the other end everything that's happened to him.

There's a pause. 'And you're sure that's all the police have got?'

'Certain.'

'OK,' Truman says. 'I'll be there in an hour or so. In the meantime, I'm faxing a letter of contract for you to sign, appointing me as your attorney. My firm bills eight thousand a day.'

'That's more than I was expecting.'

'It's a standard rate, Mr Furnish.'

For the first time this morning, Glenn feels a flash of irritation. He, the artist, the one who takes the risks, probably makes less money in a year than this corporate scumbag. 'What about a discount?' he says.

Truman's voice is cool. 'Why would we give you a discount, Mr Furnish?'

'I think you know why.'

'And I think you'd better just forget that line of thinking altogether. I don't know who referred you. As far as I'm concerned, you're just a client who needs my services. If you don't accept that, then I'll put the phone down right now and you can find yourself another lawyer. Is that clear?'

'Uh, OK,' Glenn says. He decides he can always blackmail Truman later, if he needs to. 'Fax the letter through and I'll sign it.'

'On that previous subject,' Truman says, 'I take it the police don't have access to a list of your, ah, customers?'

'No. There is one, but it's safe. Fax me the letter, Truman. I want to get out of here.'

Durban and Positano take the first shift in the interview room. Behind the two-way mirror, the observation area is crowded with other cops who have worked the case. Glenn Furnish looks calm. Occasionally he scratches under the white paper jumpsuit.

'Well, Glenn,' Frank says when the tapes are running, 'it's taken us a while, but we got there.'

The pause lengthens. Eventually the man in the jumpsuit says, 'What does that mean? Got where?'

The lawyer puts a restraining hand on his arm. 'What's your question, detective?'

The lawyer is well-dressed, urbane and disinterested. Frank ignores him. 'You've had a good run, Glenn. A whole bunch of women are dead. But you know what? I bet a part of you is pretty glad we finally caught up with you. Stopped you hurting any more innocent ladies.'

Again the lawyer interrupts. 'Your question—'

'But maybe you didn't see them as ladies,' Durban muses. 'Maybe you thought those whores deserved everything they got.'

Glenn Furnish smiles. 'You've got this wrong,' he says. 'I'm not the guy you want.'

Truman says, 'My client mistakenly picked up his boss's credit card instead of his own. He presumes that's why he's here.'

Frank laughs. 'What about multiple murder?'

'What about it?'

Frank takes some pictures out of a thin brown folder and pushes them across the table. 'This is your work, Glenn, isn't it?'

The lawyer picks up the photos first and looks at them. He passes them along to his client, who glances at the topmost one and hands them back. 'I worked on those bodies, yes. I'm a qualified mortuary technician. Who arranged them like that?'

'You tell me.'

'Whoever it was, he must have used a lot of lubricant. Who'd have thought Alicia's little wrist could have got all the way in there?'

Durban stares at him.

'In any case,' the lawyer adds, 'no crime has been committed here, that I can see. Except perhaps the felony of trespass by whoever did this.'

'That's where you're wrong,' Frank says. 'First,

forensic re-examination of Alicia Hopkins' body suggests that she may not have died by her own hand. She could have been strangled with a belt similar to one that your client has been seen wearing. Second, if any photographs were taken by whoever did this,' he taps the folder, 'and they were downloaded from, say, a digital camera onto a laptop, then material that would be likely to deprave or corrupt has been stored in a retrieval system, which is also a felony.'

Glenn Furnish yawns ostentatiously.

'Let's take a step back,' Positano says. 'Glenn, are you aware of a website with the address pictureman.com?'

'Yeah,' he says dismissively.

'I don't see the relevance—' begins the lawyer.

Positano presses on: 'Have you ever visited that website, Glenn?'

'Maybe.'

'As far as I'm aware it isn't a crime,' says the lawyer, 'to visit a website, no matter what its content.'

'*Did* you visit it, Glenn?'

Encouraged by his lawyer's comments, the young man shrugs. 'Yeah, OK, I've been there.'

'Did you access it from your home address yesterday at four fifteen p.m.?'

'I guess so.'

'In what capacity?'

Glenn gazes at him. He's guessed where this is leading now, how they traced it back to him.

'Did you enter the access code for the site administrator?'

He shrugs.

'You're smart, Glenn. You know about Internet

stuff. That means you know that if we traced you, we've got everything we need to identify you as the killer. And don't forget, we've got your laptop. Our people are going through the hard drive now.'

Glenn leans back in his chair. 'I guess it's time to come clean,' he says. His lawyer glances at him quickly, a warning glance, but Glenn ignores him. 'I set up pictureman.com. I am the webmaster. But it's all bullshit, man.'

'Go on.'

'I haven't killed anyone. I just got off on pretending I was the killer. Kind of like a *hommage* to a pretty cool guy.'

'Uh-uh, Glenn. The name pictureman.com first came to our attention when it was written on the body of one of the killer's victims.'

'Then I guess the killer must have liked it, too.'

'Where did you get the pictures?'

Glenn shrugs. 'Some dude on the Internet. You can find all sorts of stuff if you know where to ask.'

'Are you a necrophiliac, Glenn?'

The young man leans back even further and speaks directly to the ceiling. 'I'm prepared to explore my dark side,' he says languidly.

The lawyer, Truman, leans across the table. 'Do you people actually have any charges? Or any evidence of any crimes committed by my client? Because if this is just a fishing expedition, I'm going to advise Mr Furnish not to answer any more questions.'

'This isn't right,' Connie says in the observation room. 'This guy is way too calm.'

'Wait till the techies are done with his laptop,'

someone says in the darkness. 'That's when he'll start to crumble.'

'But he knows you've got the laptop,' Connie says. 'He must know time's running out. Why isn't he getting nervous?'

The answer to her question is over in computer crimes, where Rob Fleming is prising the secrets from Glenn's computer. In a dust-free air-conditioned room as sterile and bright as an autopsy lab, the laptop is being dissected piece by piece.

'This is a lot easier on a laptop than on a desktop computer,' Fleming is saying. 'These laptops are pretty modular; everything just clicks out.' Carefully, he lifts the hard drive out and places it in a laptop of an identical make and model, then boots the machine. 'We'll copy it before we go in, just in case it's password protected.'

'Would that be a problem?' Weeks asks.

'Not really. It would just slow us down. If the information's on there, we can get at it.'

A few minutes later he says: 'Right. Let's see what we've got.' He types a command on the screen.

'Is that DOS you're using?' Weeks asks.

'That's right. Most people put their energies into hiding stuff from Windows. They forget that Windows isn't the computer's real operating system. It's just the pretty stuff on the surface. If you want to talk to the BIOS, you've got to do it the old-fashioned way.' While he's talking white text is appearing on the screen, line by line. 'This looks pretty straightforward, though.'

'We're particularly interested in picture files or movies.'

'There's only one. A picture file. Want me to bring it up?'

'Sure.'

After a few moments, the hard drive whirrs softly and a picture appears on the screen.

It's a cartoon, a crude computer graphic of a skull on a black background. A joker's painted smile has been superimposed onto the skull's mouth. Underneath it, some words in Gothic script say:

𝕶𝖎𝖘𝖘 𝖒𝖊 𝖖𝖚𝖎𝖈𝖐

'Shit,' Weeks says. 'You sure this is all?'

'That's all,' Fleming confirms. 'There's virtually nothing else on here. No documents, no organizer, no address book. Just an Internet browser and a word-processing program.'

'Could this son of a bitch have switched the hard drive?'

Fleming nods. 'That's certainly possible. It wouldn't take more than a few minutes on a machine like this. And, so long as you kept it dry, you could store the other hard drive almost any-where. Even underground, if you wrapped it in plastic.'

'Fuck,' Durban says when Weeks phones him with the news. 'OK, here's what we do. We'll charge the bastard with credit card theft, get a high bail set and then start digging up every location we can link him to, starting with the area around the house he was renting.'

CHAPTER FIFTY-ONE

'Everything we have been doing together up to now has been focused on developing your abilities as actors. Now it's time to bring those techniques to the service of a play.'

Claire, standing at the back of the group, closes her eyes in order to concentrate on what Paul's saying.

'So, what is a play? It's a story. But what sort of story? Our improvisations are stories, after all. The difference is that, in improvisation, we accept whatever is offered to us. In a play, one character may not necessarily accept what another one wants, resulting in conflict.'

Claire opens her eyes. Paul is looking directly at her. Then his gaze moves on, circling the group. Just for a moment, she thinks she caught a glint of coldness, an anger directed at her. But it was such a quick look, it's impossible to be sure.

'Stanislavski described the essence of a play, the goal of its primary character, as the play's "superobjective". Often the superobjective remains hidden from the audience until the last curtain is about to fall. But *you* must always know it. Only then can you define how the individual scene, or as Stanislavski put it, the "through action", fits into the theme.'

'What about the writer?' someone asks. 'Don't the words define the play?'

'Screw the writer.' There's a laugh, but he goes on seriously: 'For the words to have meaning, they must have truth. Your truth.'

Nobody has any more questions.

'Right. The play we're going to do is *Hamlet*. Chris, you're the prince. Keith, the King. Ellen, Gertrude. Claire, you're Ophelia.'

Again the cold look. And why Ophelia? Given Paul's insistence on reliving one's own experiences through Affective Memory, the part of a suicidal madwoman is hardly one she'd have chosen. Leon, the student who walked out, had been right: there were a lot of mind games here. She wonders if Paul's casting is some kind of punishment, and if so, what on earth she's being punished for.

A dozen or so men are brought up from the holding cells into the largest of the seven New Jersey courtrooms. The area they're shown into is enclosed by glass and walled off from the rest of the court, although there's a slit at head height for the defendants to speak to their attorneys.

A lawyer gets up from the attorneys' tables and walks to the glass booth. 'Mr Felstead?' he asks, scanning the faces expectantly.

One of the defendants goes over to the opening. 'Are you Brook?'

The lawyer puts his hand through the opening. 'Michael Brook, that's right. How are you?'

'I didn't get much sleep. The cells were kind of noisy.'

'Of course,' Brook says. 'Look, we should have

you out in no time. The question is, are you going to enter a plea today or leave it until later? It's really up to you, but it might have an impact on the bail.'

'In what way?'

'Well, I spoke to the prosecutor. Your wife is definitely going to press the assault charge, but so long as you agree to be bound not to go near her, I don't see how they can refuse bail. It might be that if you plead not guilty the judge will set bail a little bit lower on the basis of presumed innocence. But I wouldn't count on it.'

'OK. Not guilty. Just get me out of here.'

New Jersey municipal judge Harvey Chu works his way through a long list of arraignments. He checks his list. 'Peter Felstead,' he says.

The lawyer, Brook, approaches the judge's desk, as does the prosecutor. Because of the muttering and whispering, it's virtually impossible to hear what they're saying from the glassed-off area. Eventually the judge looks up and says, 'Ten thousand dollars' in a bored voice.

Brook returns to the defendant. 'OK, Mr Felstead. We should have you out of here in half an hour or so. Then we'll go to my office and sort out this bail bond.'

'Thanks, man. I just have to swing by my own office to let them know something's come up.'

They've broken for lunch and resumed again before Judge Chu nears the end of the arraignments. 'Furnish,' he calls wearily. He looks up. A man in a white jumpsuit is the only one left in the holding area.

Positano, sitting behind the attorneys' tables, whispers to the prosecutor, 'Where's Furnish?'

She glances back at the holding area. 'There.'

The detective feels his chest tighten. 'That's not Furnish.'

'Are you sure?'

'Of course I'm sure.'

'One minute, your honour,' the prosecutor says to the judge. She makes her way back to the holding area.

'Who are you?' she says to the remaining defendant.

'Felstead. Peter Felstead.' The man stares at them defiantly. 'Is something wrong?'

Ellen Saunders and her new friend Jake Fincher have had a really great lunch. They had to stand in line for a table at Flint's, sure, but frankly they were lucky to get a table at all. The place is heaving, as it always is on a weekday, though the two of them have been so busy talking they've hardly noticed the slightly chaotic service and the long wait between courses.

Finally Ellen looks at her watch and says, 'Oh my God, Jake. I'd no idea it was so late. We'd better get the check.'

'Fine. But this is my treat.'

'Let's go Dutch, then. I insist.' But when the check comes, Jake settles the argument by pulling out his credit card and pushing hers away. He holds out the plate with his card and the bill on it, waiting for a waiter to take it.

'I hope you enjoyed your meal, sir.' A waiter has appeared next to him, not the one who brought the bill, but Jake's in a hurry now. 'It was fine,' he assures the waiter.

'Sure you wouldn't like some coffee?'

'No. We have to get back.'

The waiter nods and takes the plate with the card on it. Five minutes later, an exasperated Jake beckons to a passing waitress.

'Are you ready to pay?'

'What do you mean, ready? I've been waiting to sign my slip for five minutes now.' As the waitress goes off to sort it out, he mutters to Ellen, 'And *she* can forget about a tip.'

After a moment the waitress returns. 'Which waitress did you give it to?'

'It wasn't a waitress. It was a man.' Jake scans the tables, but he can't see the man who took his card anywhere.

'Gone?' Frank stares at the other detective. 'What do you mean, gone?'

'He switched with another prisoner. Some ass-hole who was still half-drunk from the night before. Furnish seems to have convinced him it would be a good joke to play on his ex-wife.'

'What about the lawyers? They must have known.'

'The drunk's lawyer had never met him before; he had legal insurance and dialled the helpline from custody. But Truman should have spotted that his client wasn't in the holding bay. He's happy to be rid of this one. Too happy, if you ask me.'

'Doesn't like the smell of it?'

Positano snorts. 'Since when did that put a lawyer off a case? Usually, the bigger the headlines the more they want it. No, if you ask me, Furnish had something on Truman.'

'Check it out. Anything else?'

'We asked to be copied on all police call-outs within a ten-mile radius of the courthouse. About twenty minutes ago someone phoned in a credit card theft. Weeks is down there now. It sure as hell sounds like Furnish. Not that he's probably even called that. There's no trace of that name at the places he said he worked. Records are phoning all the mortuary schools to see if we can find out who he really is.'

Weeks calls in from the restaurant. 'It's him all right. Cool as you like. The victim can't even remember the card number, only that it's Amex.'

Frank groans. 'Don't tell me. Gold?'

'Yup. He thinks his credit limit – sorry, the amount he's shown Amex he can afford to pay – is about fifty thou.'

'Great. OK, get back here. I'll get Rob to phone American Express straight away.'

Twenty minutes later, the stolen card has been traced to a cyber café off Second Avenue. The patrol car that races there, its sirens screaming, reports that the user of the computer in question downloaded a virus after concluding his on-line purchases. By the time the cops reach the machine the bug is already munching every last byte of information on the hard drive.

Of the man who has been using the computer, there is no sign.

CHAPTER FIFTY-TWO

The cameras are back.

Claire paces up and down the apartment, a muscle in her jaw working dangerously. Christian sits in one of his big leather armchairs, his face expressionless.

The police technicians ignore them. They've brought their own ladders. Tiny wires hang from corner to corner of the high loft ceiling. As one technician glues the wires carefully to the join of ceiling and wall, another follows behind with a can of paint.

One of the technicians is a Korean woman. The same one who pretended the police apartment belonged to her husband's company.

Durban, watching from his post by the door, says, 'Listen, Claire. There's still time to replace you both with cops.'

'No offence, Frank, but that's going to be about as convincing as a Hasidic pope.'

Frank shrugs. 'Your choice.'

'Not in there,' Claire snaps at one of the technicians as he starts to walk into the bedroom. 'You're not putting those things in there.'

'It's only a panic button,' Frank says soothingly.

'I thought you said he couldn't get past you.'

'He can't. We've got observation points at both ends of the street. We've got an armed response unit stationed in the caretaker's apartment. We've got surveillance teams who'll be following wherever you go. The panic buttons are simply added reassurance.'

'What makes you so sure he'll come for us, anyway? Why wouldn't he just go somewhere safe and hide?'

'We're not certain what he'll do. That's why we have to cover—'

'He'll come for you.'

The voice belongs to the woman who has just appeared in the doorway – diminutive, elegantly dressed, a pack of Merit and a lighter in her hand.

'Hello, Dr Leichtman,' Claire says coolly.

'Hello, Claire. I was sorry to hear you've been . . . unwell.'

'Save it, Connie.'

Connie shrugs and walks a little further into the apartment, inspecting the technicians' work. 'He'll come,' she says. 'I guarantee it.'

'You sound pretty sure of that,' Frank says.

Connie goes to the laptop on the desk. She brings up a search engine.

Despite herself, Claire watches over her shoulder. Connie types in, 'Blond+Baudelaire+camera+address' before hitting Enter.

The first name on the list of results is Claire's.

'Click on the link,' Connie says.

Claire takes the mouse and clicks. Her own face fills the screen.

'Your homepage, Claire. You're getting quite a few hits now, as a matter of fact.'

'Unfortunate terminology,' Frank mutters.

There's a large blank area at the bottom of the page. Claire taps it with her finger. 'What's this?'

Connie looks up at the wires being pasted to the ceiling. 'Webcam. It's not operational at the moment, of course.'

Claire turns on her heel and walks away. Connie calls after her, 'If you were a famous actress you'd have hundreds of sites devoted to you, Claire. Most of them with faked-up pornographic images attached. If you really intend to be successful one day, you'd better get used to it.'

Frank touches her arm. 'Leave it, Connie. What's the point in the search engine stuff? Why does that make you so sure he'll come for Claire?'

'Because he can, Frank. Because we've made it easy for him. Quite literally, Claire's at the top of his list. A killer doesn't stop killing just because he's had a lucky escape. For him, it's a compulsion, not a choice. Even if he suspects a trap, he'll still come.'

When all the cops and Connie have finally gone, the apartment is silent. They look at each other, unsure how to begin.

'Just like old times,' Claire says.

He reaches out and touches her neck. 'Not quite. Your real accent is much nicer. And then, you have this.' He turns her hand to look at the ring on her finger. 'When this is over, we'll move from here and start over, somewhere where there aren't any memories. Perhaps somewhere out of the city.'

'That would be nice.'

'A big house by the sea.'

'Perfect.'

'I'll talk to a realtor tomorrow. It'll be something to take our minds off all this.'

She says, 'Christian?'

'Yes?'

'There's something I need to know.'

'What?'

'Did *you* ever go to Necropolis?'

A long pause. 'Yes,' he admits. 'When Stella and I . . . when we began to drift apart, I thought there might be someone else. I started going through her e-mails. Spying on her, I suppose.' He looks at the floor. 'I'm not proud of it, Claire. But I loved her, you see. Or I thought I did.'

'It's all right,' she says. 'I understand.'

'I found a message in her inbox with a password for an Internet site I'd never heard of. I was curious. I used the password to get into the site myself. I wasn't altogether surprised at what I found there. There had always been a part of her that responded to that kind of thing. That was the problem, I suppose. I couldn't fulfil those needs of hers.'

'But you spoke to people, when you were there? People who might have assumed you were her?'

'Yes. I was trying to find out what she'd been doing.'

'Do you remember talking to someone about Baudelaire?'

He shrugs. 'It's possible.'

'Please, Christian. Try to remember.'

'Well, vaguely, yes, I do recall something of that sort. But it was just a casual conversation, nothing more.' He looks at her sharply. 'Why do you ask?'

'I'm not sure yet. It's just something that's been

bothering me about all this. Something I don't quite understand. And I think I know where to go to find the answer.'

CHAPTER FIFTY-THREE

They sit at Christian's antique desk, a writing table hundreds of years old, and prepare to go on a journey that would have mystified any of the desk's previous owners.

They sign onto Necropolis, then locate the door that will lead them to its hidden underworld. As Christian moves the mouse cursor around on a blank area of the page, it suddenly turns into a hand, indicating that he's found a hyperlink. He clicks. Text fills the screen.

> You are in a dense grove of black
> poplar trees. They surround you in all
> directions, except one, the north.
> They sway slightly in the cold north
> breeze that is wafting towards you,
> like the icy air which escapes from a
> large underground space. There is a
> path through the poplars, heading
> north, and you follow it towards a
> set of black gates. Beside the gates
> sits an enormous three-headed dog.
> The dog sniffs you and growls
> threateningly.

'He wants our password,' Christian mutters. He types something. A few seconds later the screen says:

> Recognizing you as a denizen of this place, Cerberus lets you pass.

'We go north,' Christian says. He types:

> >> Go north

After a moment the computer responds with a new paragraph of text.

> You are in the Asphodel Fields, the first region of the underworld. There are some gods here, sleeping, but it's mostly filled with the diaphanous, insubstantial figures of the dead. They twitter like bats, continually rustling and shaking in the cold breeze that comes from the north, where a large Palace towers over the meadows of Erebus. To the west, a white cypress shades the dark river of Lethe, where the common ghosts flock down to drink, as timid as river birds. To the east, across meadows filled with white daffodils, lies the silver-topped Pool of Memory and the entrance to Elysium.

'North again.'

> >>Go north

As you enter the Palace of
Persephone, the coat check girl, a
Fury called Tisiphone, asks if she can
take your garments. Ahead is the ruin
of a once-imposing Staircase, now
splattered with the droppings of
ravens, who have entered through the
ruined ceiling. To the east is the Hall.
The twenty-foot-high doors are closed,
but you can hear the sound of laughter and strange, discordant music. To
the west lies the entrance to the
Cellars.

'When you meet someone, you can type in a
command that brings up their description. Or you
can speak to them,' he explains. He types:

>>Look Tisiphone

Tisiphone
You see a hip Italian chick with dark
eyes and a long, straight nose. She's
wearing heavy Timberlands and a pair
of baggy dark blue cargo pants. She
has a much-customized skateboard
under one arm. Dreadlocks and beads
are woven into her curly hair. She has
an Indian mark painted onto the
centre of her forehead.

'Want to take over?'
'Sure.'
It feels strange to her at first, navigating by
words, like trying to find your way blindfold,

using only your fingertips. She flexes her fingers over the keyboard, unsure what to write.

'Try going into the Hall.'

'OK.' She types:

>>Go east

You are in a cavernous room, decorated with painful friezes by Piranesi and Goya. Flaming brands burn in the iron wall-holders, tipped with inky smoke. At the far end of the Hall is an enormous throne. Many gods are clustered round the throne. To the east is the Library. It's quiet in there. West is the Music Room. From the noise and laughter there seems to be a party going on.

'Type "@who" to find out who else is here.'

>>@who

Morpheus is here.
Chronos is here.
Pluto is here.
Minthe is here.
Persephone is here.
    Persephone says, 'Did you have a nice sleep, dear? You were snoring for ages.'

'In terms of the MUSE, to be absent is to be asleep,' Christian explains. 'We've taken Stella's old character, Blanche. So to all these players, it looks as if Blanche has just woken up.'

'What do I say to her?'

'Nothing, unless you want to. She won't be offended if you don't chat. Type "Look Pictures" to see your surroundings.'

>>Look Pictures

Slowly, a picture scrolls down. It's an engraving, a seventeenth-century depiction of a prisoner being mutilated by his captors.

'Piranesi. This is just atmosphere,' Christian says matter-of-factly. 'The real porn is in the art gallery.'

'What's going on in the music room?'

'A gang bang, probably. Half a dozen players and a corpse. I don't recommend it.'

'How do I locate a particular player?'

'Type "Find"'

>>Find Charon

Charon is in the library, asleep.

'How do I get to the library again?'

'You don't have to follow the directions. Just type "go library" and you'll be there.'

>>Go Library

You are in a well-appointed library, stocked with texts both ancient and new. There is a pleasant smell of slowly curing leather. A few armchairs are dotted around and, for those who become inflamed by their reading, a

leather-bound Couch big enough for
two.

>Look Charon

You see a pleasantly smiling young
man whose mild demeanour is belied
by his dark, cruel eyes. His jeans and
T-shirt are covered in stains, running
the gamut of hues from fresh
vermilion to deep port-coloured
streaks of more ancient blood. None
of the blood is his. He resembles an
art student who wipes his brushes
directly onto his clothes.

'That's him, all right. The artist. But why's he in
the library?'
'Who knows? Characters can choose to sleep anywhere they like.'

By Charon's left hand is a stack of
unread Messages. In his right hand,
the fingers stained with chemicals, he
holds an artist's Sketchbook.

'Can we read the messages?'
'No. Only he can do that. We can see who
they're from, but, of course, that doesn't help us.'
'What about the sketchbook?'
'Try it. He wouldn't have built it into his
character description unless there was some point
to it.'

>>Look Sketchbook

> You see a small vellum-bound note-
> book full of thumbnail sketches.
> Charon will show it to you when he is
> awake. Leave him a Message, telling
> him what sort of art you like.

'Damn.' She pauses, her fingers over the keyboard.

'You're right, though. There must be something unusual about it for him to keep it hidden. Presumably the thumbnail sketches are his samples.'

'Isn't there any way I can find out what's in the book?'

'Maybe if you were a programmer. But even then, not necessarily. Some objects can only be controlled by their originators.'

'How could I find out where else Charon goes? Where he keeps his stuff?'

'You can't, really. This place is vast. Every new character adds their own rooms to the basic design. Some of the rooms don't even have doors. The only way to find them is to type the "go to" command. For which, obviously, you have to know where it is you want to get to.'

She thinks and types:

>>Go to Charon's Studio

Invalid command

>> Go to Artist's Studio

Invalid command

'Damn.' She thinks. 'What else?'

337

'He says his fingers are stained with chemicals,' Christian says. 'Could that be a reference to photography?'

'Of course. Charon wouldn't need a studio in the conventional sense.' She types:

>>Go to Darkroom

After a few moments the computer replies:

You are in complete blackness. You cannot see anything to the north, south, east or west.

'Ha!'

>>Go north

You stumble awkwardly into a table. Reaching out, you find your hand sinking into the decomposing remains of a once-female corpse. Warmth closes around your hand. It is the warmth of rotting compost.

>>Go east

You stumble over piles of books, discarded clothing and loose bones. Putting out a hand to save yourself, you feel something soft and wet. It is a bowl of fruit, slowly fermenting in its own juice.

'Try listing the books,' Christian says.

>>List books

Anatomy of Melancholy / Robert
Burton
Captives / Michelangelo
Der Anatom / Gabriel von Max
Entombment of Christ / Rembrandt
Fleurs du Mal / Baudelaire
Humani Corporis Fabrica / Vesalius

>>Look *Fleurs du Mal*

You cannot look at anything. It is dark.

'Damn!'
'Try finding a light switch. Or lighting a match.'

>>Switch Light

By the eerie glow of the red developing light, you see a small leather-
bound volume. The leather is very
soft. As you turn it over, you see the
reason for this. Towards the bottom
of the front cover, exactly in the
centre, is the belly button of a young
woman. The skin has been cured so
expertly that you can still make out the
rosette of blond hairs that encircle the
navel, like the tonsure of a novice
monk. Below, at the bottom of the
volume, a thicker line of blond hairs
indicates where the pubis once began.
     The navel, and the hairs around it,
resemble a flower. Other than that,

there is no indication of the book's title.

>>Open Book

You cannot open the book. There is a small padlock in the shape of a serpent swallowing its own tail.

>>Unlock Padlock

You need to have the key to unlock the padlock.

'Damn!' she explodes. Then: 'It doesn't matter. I think I know what's in the book.'

'What?'

'When I was in hospital, I tried to swap reading material with someone. Know what he said? He told me he only read books with pictures.'

'I'm not with you,' Christian says, shaking his head.

'Do you have a copy of *Les Fleurs du Mal*?'

He hands her a copy from the shelf, and she flicks through until she finds the page she wants. 'Remember this one?'

'Of course. "*The Martyr*". "Amongst rich piles of fabrics, flasks of wine . . ." '

She takes up, reading from the page:

> Amongst rich piles of fabrics, flasks of wine,
> the precious marble, and the glowing fire,
> the sickly perfumes of pale hothouse flowers,
> that live a day, and then expire:

a naked woman, sensuously sprawled,
her limbs spread wide to curious eyes,
her secret places shameless and exposed,
a glimpse of pink between the plump white thighs.

Only a candle, burning bright,
its still flame undisturbed by breath,
betrays this lover's dreamless sleep,
the cold compliancy of death.

Only a crimson swathe of blood,
encircling the severed head,
reveals that she is perfect now,
as all are perfect that are dead.

Tell me, cold beauty: did your intimate in death
– whose lusts you could not, living, sate –
on your inert, voluptuous corpse
his monstrous passion consummate?

And did he, all his passion spent,
take in his hands your icy head,
and press a warm and breathing mouth
against those lips no longer red?

No matter where that man goes now,
he cannot hope to hide or flee:
for he has tasted of death's fruit,
and loved for all eternity.

She closes the book. 'It's a beautiful poem. If you
ignore what it's about.'
He shrugs. 'Beauty from evil, that was his

philosophy. But it was only an idea he was playing with, he never really—'

'When I was working with Connie,' she interrupts, 'there was a murder. A black prostitute. The killer cut off her head; just like the woman in the poem, in fact. Then he took pictures – the pictures that found their way onto the Internet.'

Christian looks thoughtful.

'Stella – I'm sorry, Christian – Stella was disembowelled, wasn't she? The killer took her spleen.'

'Oh, no. Don't tell me you think—'

'Spleen. That's the title of another poem, isn't it?'

He says hoarsely, 'You're saying that it's my fault. That I inspired him in some way with my translations of the poems.'

'In the old days, connoisseur's editions of poetry would sometimes have plates, right?' she persists.

'Yes. There's a very famous edition of *Les Fleurs* illustrated by Doré. It's worth a fortune now. I have a facsimile somewhere.' He indicates the shelves of books with his hand.

'That's what he's doing,' she says. 'Don't you see? He's creating a sort of virtual edition of *Les Fleurs du Mal*. His photographs are the illustrations to the poems.'

'My God.' Christian closes his eyes, appalled. 'Then I *am* to blame. It's my translations which have made him do these things.' He puts his head in his hands and rocks. 'Stella, Stella. What did I do to you?' he mutters.

She wants to tell him that he isn't responsible for what this monster does, any more than the people who translated the Bible were responsible for the

Spanish Inquisition. That sick people find sickness to feed on wherever they look. But she knows that this isn't the time.

'How do I get out of this?' she says gently indicating the lines of text on the screen.

'Just type "Sleep",' he mutters.

>> Sleep

Morpheus, God of Sleep, brings you a glass of cold, clear water from the icy river of Lethe. You drink it. The mineral, slightly sulphuric taste stays in your mouth long after you have returned to the world above.
You will come back very soon.

In a rented apartment on the Lower East Side – rented via the Internet, from the computer in the cyber café – Glenn Furnish hooks up to a laptop, purchased in a similar fashion and delivered the same day to the apartment. As the modem whistles and stutters, he dips a knife into the pool of ripe Roquefort that spreads across a dinner plate on the table beside him, and licks the blade meditatively. A bottle of wine older than Glenn himself is open next to the cheese. He sniffs the cork, passing it back and forth under his nose in the way a smoker might sniff an unlit cigar, inhaling the smell of must and damp, cobweb-filled cellars.

Glenn enters Necropolis' underworld not as Charon, but in the guise of one of his other characters, Bran, Celtic god of forests. He has been keeping Bran in reserve for just such an emergency.

If you typed the command for a description of him you would read only:

> You see a stockily built man dressed in black and without a head. He carries a bag slung over his shoulder, in which the errant extremity is presumably located.

Bran slips into the library by a roundabout route and watches the sleeping Charon for a while. He types:

> >>@who Charon/last

and the computer replies:

> Blanche was here.

Glenn sits very still, thinking. Blanche cannot have been in the library just now, because Blanche was the name of the translator's first wife, and she's dead. He types:

> >>Go to Darkroom

and then:

> >>@who Darkroom/last

> Blanche was here.

Bran picks up the virtual edition of *Les Fleurs du Mal* from the table where Claire left it, unlocks it and flicks through its pages slowly, stopping to admire some of his work from time to time. So nearly finished. He will have to move all this, now that his hiding place has been discovered. Luckily, in this virtual world, creating a new space for oneself is no more arduous than imagining it.

In the real world, Glenn sits lost in thought, the wine cork forgotten between his fingers.

CHAPTER FIFTY-FOUR

The decadence of nineteenth-century Paris. An underworld modelled on the ancient Greeks'. A brief stopover in twenty-first century Manhattan. And finally, fourteenth-century Denmark, as imagined by a seventeenth-century English playwright.

Not surprisingly, Claire's finding it hard to get her head round the part of Ophelia right now.

' "There's rosemary, that's for remembrance. Pray, love, remember: and there is pansies, that's for thoughts," ' she says, miming the gesture of handing them out.

'No!' Paul roars from the side of the rehearsal room. 'Claire, this is terrible. You're not giving me the truth.'

What's the truth? she wonders. Ophelia handing out herbs seems to her about as remote from reality as it's possible to get.

'Do your Affective Memory,' he snaps. 'Try to ground this in something.'

Obediently, she closes her eyes and thinks back to the hospital. She tries to imagine what Bannerman's patients would have made of a scrip for twenty milligrams of pansies.

'What's funny?' Paul demands icily.

'When I was in the hospital, they weren't very big on herbs,' she says. 'Methadone and Primozide were more their thing.'

'Then swap them. You don't think Shakespeare would have used Methadone and Pimozide in this speech if they'd been invented? Try it.'

She pauses, then, 'There's Tuenol, that's for remembrance. Pray, love, remember: and there is Prozac, that's for thoughts.' She mimes pouring a jar of pills into the hand of the actor playing Laertes. Unexpectedly, she shivers.

'Better,' Paul snarls. He glares at her. 'Don't hold out on me, Claire. Don't start pretending just because it feels safer.'

He struts off to harass another group.

Glenn stares at the webcam image on his laptop. The Venus walks from left to right, oblivious to his gaze. She is holding what looks like folded linen. He clicks on the link marked 'bedroom' and sure enough, a moment later he sees her enter and float the sheet over the big double bed.

An autumn storm darkens the sky outside, and Glenn reaches out to switch on a table lamp. Then, his hand still on the lamp, he switches it off again.

On the screen of the laptop, a shaft of sunlight is falling through the window of Claire Rodenburg's bedroom.

He goes to the window of his rented apartment and looks south, towards Manhattan. Rain flecks the glass. It's so murky he can barely make out the skyscrapers. But he can see enough to be sure there's no sun there either.

He goes back to the screen, and clicks on it.

There's a copy of the *New York Times* on the floor of Claire's bedroom, its headline pixellated.

Glenn goes in closer. For a long time he stares at the image, like a man waiting for a Magic Eye poster to slowly swim into focus.

The only other person she needs to tell about her engagement is her old employer, Henry. She takes a cab to the Lower East Side, tailed all the way by an unmarked Lincoln, and goes up to the fourth floor in the dilapidated grille elevator.

In the corridor she notices the fresh paint and renovated industrial-chic light fittings. But the real surprise is Henry's office itself. The 1950s furniture and bentwood hatstand are gone. Henry's office, now expanded to include the suite next door, has been redone in cream and red. Gleaming chrome-legged worktables bear a cluster of bright pastel-coloured iMacs.

Henry's feet are still up on the desk, but the soles that face her as she walks in bear the brightly coloured logo of a fashionable workwear label. And instead of the half-mast tie, he's wearing a T-shirt under his suit.

'Hey, Claire,' he says, with evident pleasure, as he swings his feet off the table and gets up to greet her. 'How are you doing?'

'I'm fine,' she says. She looks around. 'And this place looks great.'

'Neat, huh?' He jerks his thumb at the computers. 'We do most of our work online now. Sure as hell beats sitting in bars all day.'

She laughs. '*You've* started using computers?'

'Well, not personally,' he admits. 'I have a bunch of college kids who come in and do the hard work.

Wanna drink?' He goes to a metal locker and pulls out a bottle.

'And this is all being paid for by missing pets?' she wonders.

He shakes his head. 'Missing persons, mostly. Kids who run away from home, fathers who default on their maintenance, middle-aged men who suddenly realize that girl they kissed in high school was really the love of their life. Information is a boom market now.' He leans forward and winks. 'Matter of fact, I could find out what our customers need to know with a couple of phone calls. But the computers look pretty, and I know a bandwagon when I see one. Now,' he hands her a glass, 'tell me all your news.'

'You're not going to believe this, Henry, but . . .' She tells him about Christian and her.

He listens, nodding thoughtfully. 'Tell me something,' he says when she's finished. 'Would you like Christian checked out? Kind of as a wedding present? I could run a few enquiries on him, see if he's susceptible to playing around, all the old stuff.'

'Henry!' she scolds. 'If I didn't trust him, I wouldn't be marrying him. Besides, he's been checked out. Remember? I made a pass at him and he turned me down flat. How many men could you say that of?'

'Yeah,' Henry says. 'That's true.' He looks thoughtful.

'What is it, Henry?'

The feet swing up onto the desk again. 'That whole decoy thing we did on him. What was that about, do you suppose?'

She shrugs. 'We were seeing if he had a wandering eye.'

'Not exactly.'

'What do you mean, not exactly?'

'In most cases, yes, that was how it worked. But some of the work we got' – he's avoiding her eyes now – 'was referred by a firm of lawyers. Divorce lawyers. These are tough guys, Claire. They like to fight as dirty as they can for their clients.'

'What are you getting at, Henry?'

'Well, most women who employed us wanted their husbands to be faithful, obviously. But the ones who were referred by the law firm, they wanted the opposite. They wanted the husbands to hit on you big time, and on tape, to give them more leverage in their negotiations.' He spreads his hands. 'What can I say, Claire? It's a dirty world.'

'Why didn't you tell me this at the time?'

'Hell,' he says, 'I wasn't sure how you'd take it. You seemed kind of innocent back then. A romantic. I figured the less you knew about all that, the better.'

She sighs. Yet another thing someone had decided she didn't need to know. 'You were probably right. So Stella, she was one of these divorce referrals?'

He nods. 'She was about to walk out on him. Christian didn't know that, of course. But the point I'm making is, the marriage was falling apart. And I'm figuring, maybe before you tie the knot yourself, you might like to know why. I can call my contact at the lawyers and get Stella's depositions sent over. That way, at least you'll know what you're getting yourself into.' He reaches out a hand for the phone.

'No,' she says.

He raises an eyebrow. 'Sure?'

'I'm sure,' she says. 'Look, Henry, I appreciate the offer, but I already knew that it wasn't working out for Stella and Christian. It happens, right? And I'm not saying it was all her fault, but let's face it, what kind of woman lets her lawyers pull a stunt like that? Christian's never said a word against her, but reading between the lines, she was a pretty neurotic individual. I think she simply couldn't handle the fact that he was devoted to her. Anyway, Christian deserves a second chance. Everyone does.'

'Suit yourself,' he says, shrugging. 'Looks like I'll have to buy the happy couple a toaster instead. But if you change your mind, let me know, right? It would only take a couple of calls.'

Glenn Furnish sits very still. He has been sitting without moving in the little Miata for over an hour now, his gaze fixed on the door of the office block he has followed the girl to.

Eventually, he sees Claire walk out. He watches as she walks past an unmarked Lincoln further down the street. He sees her raise her arm to stop a passing cab. As the cab pulls away, the Lincoln follows it.

Glenn sits still a moment longer, thinking hard. Then he reaches under the dash and takes out the keys.

Henry drains the last drops of bourbon from his glass and sets it carefully on the desk. As he does, there's a knock at the door.

'We're closed,' he calls.

'It's the janitor,' a voice says. 'There's been a report of a flood on the floor above you. I just need to check for water damage.'

Henry chuckles. 'There's no water coming in here. It wouldn't dare.'

'All the same, Mr Mallory. If I could just check.'

'All right, all right.' He opens the door. The janitor is a young man. He looks at Henry's thin frame and says, 'Boy, am I glad you're not obese.'

'I'm sorry, kid?'

It's the last line Henry Mallory ever delivers. Apart, that is, from the brief speech he makes later, when Glenn finally takes off the gag and permits him to talk.

CHAPTER FIFTY-FIVE

The realtor is late, and Claire glances at her watch more than once as she waits outside the house. A little way along the road, Positano and Weeks are a reassuring presence in the unmarked Lincoln. She glances their way. Weeks is flicking through the pages of *Playboy*. Positano is staring blankly at her, his mouth moving. Every so often Weeks nods without looking up from his magazine.

She looks again at the outside of the house. It is, as Christian promised, a vast white clapboard construction – vast, anyway, compared with what she's used to in the city. Here in Westchester, fifty miles upstate, it seems pretty homely by comparison with some of its bigger neighbours. She notices that some of the houses along this road have little placards stuck into their front lawns. Each one says 'Armed Response'.

A car turns the corner into the road. It pulls up alongside her and a woman's face peers through the side window. 'Miss Rodenburg?'

'Yes. Mrs Loncraine?'

'Sorry, I was held up in traffic.' Claire sees Positano lean forward as the realtor gets out of the car, then relax again as he sees that everything's fine.

'No problem. I like the look of the place, any-way.'

'Wait until you see inside. It's wonderful.' She unlocks the door and holds it open for Claire. The hall's as big as Christian's whole apartment, with a double staircase rising up through three storeys at the back.

'Your fiancé's not with you?' the realtor asks as Claire looks around.

She means, am I wasting my time? Claire thinks. 'No, he had to stay in the city. But he saw the pictures on your web page. And, if I like it, he'll come and have a look this afternoon.'

'Properties like this are very rare,' the realtor says smugly. 'Very rare indeed. This one's just come on the market, and I promise you it'll be sold within a week.' They walk through into a kitchen the size of a basketball court. The fridge alone is larger than any kitchen Claire's ever had.

'Very nice,' she says.

'Wait till you see the upstairs.'

She troops obediently up the stairs behind Mrs Loncraine. Suddenly the other woman stops.

'Oh,' she says.

'What is it?'

'I thought the house was going to be empty,' she says. 'But I think there's somebody here. Hello? Hello?'

'Hello,' a man's voice calls. Claire hears the sound of a shower being turned off. 'Don't mind me,' the voice calls. 'I'm decent.'

Another car turns into the tree-lined street. In the Lincoln, Positano sees it in the rear-view and nudges his partner. 'Company.'

Together they watch the car as it cruises slowly up the street and parks behind them. Two men get out. They're both wearing uniforms. They walk importantly up to the Lincoln, one on each side, unstrapping the flaps of their gun holsters. The one next to Positano taps on the window.

'Yes?' he says, pressing the button.

'Could you tell me what you're doing here, sir?'

'No,' Positano says. He flips his badge at him. 'Suppose you tell me what *you're* doing here.'

'Williams Response. We, uh, had a report of a car acting suspiciously. Thought we'd better check it out.'

'OK, you've checked it. Now back off.'

'No problem, officer,' the security guard says, saluting ironically. 'It's just another hour's overtime to me, know what I mean?' The two guards stroll back to their car and depart.

'This is the master bedroom,' the man says. 'As you can see, it has a wonderful view of the woods. Oh, and the treehouse. My wife built that.'

'Your wife built that herself?' Mrs Loncraine makes a face at Claire behind the man's back.

'Yes. She likes to sleep in there when it's a full moon.'

The realtor laughs uncertainly. The man takes hold of the belt of his bathrobe and sashays up and down the room, swinging it like a dancer with a feather boa. He turns and stops suddenly, staring at Mrs Loncraine. 'My,' he says to her, 'you have such lovely skin colour. Is it real?'

The city controller comes through on the car radio. 'Everything OK with you guys?'

Weeks picks up the mike. 'Apart from nearly getting shot up by some freaking security guards. Anything your end?'

'Plenty. They just found the body of Henry Mallory, the investigator Claire worked with. We don't know if it's connected yet, but take care, all right?'

'Right,' Weeks grunts. He clips the mike back on its holder.

'What did he mean, an hour's overtime?' Positano says.

'Who?'

'That security jerk. He said it's just another hour's overtime.'

'I guess that's how long it takes him to get back to his office or whatever.'

'Yeah, that's what I'm wondering.'

'Why?'

'Well, if he took half an hour to get out here, we couldn't have been the car he was called out to, right? We haven't been here that long.'

Weeks nods slowly.

Positano gets out of the car and pulls his jacket off the back seat. 'I'm going to take a look. Wanna come?'

Weeks picks up *Playboy*. 'Nah.'

The body of the realtor flies through the air, propelled by Glenn Furnish's foot in the small of her back. She falls three storeys before she hits the floor of the cavernous hallway.

'Well,' Glenn says, 'think of it as a feature.'

Next to him, Claire screams. She screams deliberately, carefully. A lot of thought goes into Claire's scream, as well as many years of training in projection, breath control, using the diaphragm and voice.

Calmly, Glenn pulls a roll of duct tape from his pocket and measures off a strip as long as his arm.

Positano, unable to open the locked front door, peers through the security shutters. What he sees on the hall floor has him running back to the car, cursing.

Glenn has a car round the back of the house and he lowers her carefully into the trunk. It smells strange, an unfamiliar vinegary smell. She lies in darkness and feels the car bumping over rough ground. After a while she feels stonier ground beneath them, not a road, but some kind of farm track. He's driving through the woods, she guesses, in the opposite direction to the police at the front of the house.

After about ten minutes the car stops and the trunk is opened. Glenn looks down at her. In his hands he has a length of cloth.

'I'm going to blindfold you,' he says calmly. 'Please don't be alarmed.'

When the blindfold is in place, he lifts her into another vehicle. This time the trunk she has to lie in is small, like that of a sports car. But it smells of new wood and polish, like a crate, and the engine note is more like a tractor or a van than a car.

They meet in a hastily convened operations room at the NYPD. Frank, quiet and watchful, his dark face giving nothing away. Christian, his green eyes incandescent with anger, his face white with worry, loudly threatening lawsuits if every cop in the city isn't pulled off other duties to find her, if every helicopter and tracker dog this side of the Rockies isn't mobilized at once. Connie outwardly calm, her fingers rolling the forbidden cigarette, unlit, to and fro between her fingers. Saying nothing, but thinking hard.

The roadblock has caused a long tailback on the entry ramp to the Thruway. Glenn waits calmly, the engine idling, as the queue of cars creeps forward. There's just the one cop, his motorcycle parked behind him, looking at each driver carefully, asking for papers, peering into the well of the seats and checking in the trunks.

When at last it's Glenn's turn he winds down his window. The cop apologizes for making him wait.

'That's OK, officer,' Glenn says politely. He nods his head, to indicate what's behind him. 'This gentleman's not in a hurry, so neither am I.'

The cop looks at the coffin in the back of the hearse. 'Guess not,' he says. He checks the papers, which seem to be in order, then nods Glenn on. 'Have a good day, Mr Samuels.'

The hearse glides slowly on its way.

After an hour's driving she feels the vehicle slowing. It stops, then backs up. Glenn gets out. She hears the scrape of doors being opened. He gets back in, and they reverse through them.

Air on her face tells her the box she's in has been opened. It isn't fresh air, exactly; it smells the way the car trunk had smelled, the same formaldehyde smell, but stronger.

She feels herself being manhandled onto a trolley of some kind. Her wrists are untied so that she can lie flat on her back, and her arms are buckled into some kind of restraint. A sudden brilliant light makes her dark-adapted eyes water, even through the blindfold. Then a sharp pain in the crook of her arm, like an incision, makes her cry out.

Fingers tug at the knot of her blindfold. She can see, but the light above her is dazzling, and the face leaning over her is little more than a silhouette. He reaches for the gag, and takes that off too.

'Listen,' she says, as soon as the gag is removed. 'You don't have to do this. Killing me won't help you, it'll just feed your need to go on killing. You're strong enough to stop yourself. I could help you, but not if you kill me.'

'Of course,' he says, 'you're an *actress*. You want to scream and beg and cry, but you're pretending to be calm instead. And you've been trained, haven't you? You know what to say to me. You know how to fake it.'

'I'm not pretending, Glenn. Not now. Before, when I was helping the police, I was pretending. Not any more.'

'It's what you do,' he says. 'Women. That's what your clothes and make-up and pretty smiles are for, isn't it? You pretend. It doesn't matter. I am the truth. My pieces are true because I am true.'

He speaks calmly, almost conversationally, so that it's a moment before she realizes that she has no idea what he's talking about. 'Where am I?' she asks.

Instead of answering, he flips the light around to show her, sweeping it slowly around the room like a spotlight.

She appears to be in some kind of disused hospital. An operating theatre, perhaps, or an anaesthetic room. There are three or four trolleys, each with some kind of machinery connected to it, alongside big metal sinks, and huge directional lamps, like the one she's under now, some of them cracked. Pipes and cables jut from the walls where equipment has been ripped away. Dirt and slabs of plaster have been pushed into the corners, clearing a space around the trolley on which she is now strapped.

'It's not the cleanest,' he says, following her gaze. 'But don't worry, I've disinfected. Everything works.'

'Was this a hospital?'

He laughs. 'Not exactly. No-one who came here was cured.'

He sets a small camera up on a tripod at her feet. At the back of the camera is a lead, which he plugs into a laptop computer on the next trolley.

'Let me explain,' he says. 'This is a digital camera, Claire. It's hooked up to this computer, which in turn is hooked up to a couple of websites. If someone clicks on the website, they'll see what the camera sees. You, in other words. Live.' He smiles mirthlessly. 'In a manner of speaking.'

She feels blood hammering in her head. 'What do you mean? What is all this?'

His fingers brush across the keys of his computer. 'That was my press release going out,' he says calmly. 'It's gone to all the world's major news services, as well as newsgroups and bulletin boards. Are you OK for make-up? I know you'll want to look your best.'

By noon, the atmosphere in the ops room is sombre. Then the message comes through on the radio that there are video feeds of Claire on the news wires.

'Great,' Christian says. 'This is his first mistake. We'll be able to see where he is now.'

'Hold on,' the voice on the telephone warns. 'According to his press release, it's more complicated than that.'

'You see, when I became aware that this was to be my finale I decided to attempt something a little different.'

He is painting her face now, standing behind her and applying foundation to her cheekbones. 'The tube in your wrist is called a trocar, Claire. It leads to an aspirator pump. When the machine is turned on, it will pump the blood out of your body and replace it with embalming fluid. At some point during that process, your heart will arrest and you will die.'

'What are you waiting for, then?' she says. 'Why not do it now?'

He laughs. 'Well, that's the clever part, you see.'

In the operation room Connie, Durban and Weeks sit hunched over a computer, staring at the text on the screen.

When a thousand people have logged on to this webcam, it will automatically trigger a switch. You will then have the pleasure of watching the subject die in front of your eyes. Any attempt by the authorities to close the camera down will have a similar effect. Click here to access the camera, but only if

you want to be one of the thousand
individuals who will become active participants in this unique artwork.

This web event is entitled *To The
Reader*, after the famous poem by
Baudelaire that inspired it. Click
<u>here</u> if you would like to read the
poem.

Furnish paces up and down the prep room, gesturing with the book as he recites:

> There are some men who like to bite and kiss
> the sucked-out breasts of anorexic sluts,
> extracting every precious drop of bliss,
> like squeezing an old orange of its juice.
>
> For others, it's like woodworm in the brain:
> they're eaten through with unfulfilled desires,
> while others still pump death into a vein,
> or suck it deep into their poisoned lungs.
>
> And if you're of the moralizing faction
> for whom pornography, and pyromania, and rape
> give no apparent satisfaction,
> I say, you simply haven't got the guts.
>
> And yet, in this menagerie of the perverse –
> libertines, addicts, fantasists and prudes –
> there is still one exhibit even worse,
> a creature more depraved than all of these.
>
> He does not have the loudest cry,
> his cage is often quiet and still,

yet he destroys creation with a sigh,
or crunches in his yawning jaws the world.

He weeps with boredom – and dreams of death.
He smokes his hookah – and smiles with every
   breath.
Who is this monster? My friend, you know him,
   too.
My brother – my double – hypocrite reader! – it is
   you.

He sighs reverently and closes the book.

'It won't work,' she says.

'Won't it?' He glances at his computer. 'We've got over two hundred participants already. You really think there aren't a thousand people in the world who, given the opportunity to become murderers in the secrecy of their own homes or offices, won't take it? Forty per cent of all Internet traffic is hardcore pornography. Of those millions, aren't there just a thousand who, in their darkest, unrealized dreams, really want to be like me?' He gestures at the digital camera. 'But please, why not put your point of view directly to our guests? We're wired for sound as well as pictures. They can hear you fine. Tell them why you shouldn't die. Perhaps they'll decide you're right and go away.'

She stares at the little glass iris in the middle of the camera, as dark and unresponsive as the barrel of a gun. 'Listen to me, all of you,' she says. She's enough of an actress to keep from breaking down, but her voice shakes a little as she says, 'I'm not just some picture on your computer screen. I am a real person. For breakfast I had Cheerios and milk. I read the newspaper, the same as you did. I got annoyed with the rain, just like you sometimes do. I could be anybody you know, one of your relatives perhaps, or your next girlfriend. By staying on this site you are going to kill me. It won't be like some computer file wiping itself, it will be messy and painful and real. Think how you will feel about yourself after that happens. And log off now. Please.'

'Very good,' he murmurs. He goes over to the screen. 'And effective, too. Forty-six people have logged off as a result of your appeal.' He pauses. 'However, they are more than compensated for by the three hundred and twenty three who didn't.'

CHAPTER FIFTY-SIX

'We need to access this camera,' Connie says, staring at the press release. 'We need to see what's going on in there.'

'What happens if nine hundred and ninety nine sick fuckers have already done just that?' Frank demands. 'How are we going to explain that it was the NYPD who killed her?'

'One more viewer is unlikely to make the difference.'

'That's what every creep who's already watching is telling himself. Not to mention all the news desks who have hooked up in the so-called public interest and the guys who are taping it at home in the hope of making a few bucks.'

'There's a risk in adding to his audience, granted. But we need to balance that against the potential gain to our rescue. Access the site.'

After a moment, Frank nods at Rob Fleming. Fleming clicks on the link, and they see a grainy image of Claire, trussed to a trolley.

'What's that she's on? Some kind of gurney?' Frank mutters.

'It's a morgue trolley,' Connie says slowly. 'He's taken her to a mortuary. That means we can trace her, Frank. He can't be more than an hour's drive from where she was lifted.'

Frank turns to the computer crimes technician. 'Rob? Any way of listing all the morticians within fifty miles of Westchester?'

'Sure. There are a dozen sites that will give you a list.' Fleming's hands clatter across the keys. 'Found one,' he says. 'I'll print it out.'

'How many addresses?'

'About ninety.'

'Ninety?' Frank looks despondent. 'We'll never check out that many in time.'

Connie says, 'Do you have any *old* telephone directories?'

He shrugs. 'I guess. Why?'

'He'll need somewhere that's gone out of business. Quite recently, so the premises haven't been sold on yet. If you could find a directory from a year or so ago, and cross-check it against Rob's list, then any names that were on the old list, but not the new one, might have closed down in the interim. Do you see?'

Frank's already striding out of the room, looking for telephone books.

There are two. One in New Jersey and one in Tannersville, up in the Catskill mountains.

'We'd better split up,' Frank says. 'I'll take the city one first, then come on up if he isn't there.'

'I'll go with Mike,' Connie says.

Frank shoots her a look. 'You think Tannersville's the one?'

'He likes rural communities, Frank. Isolation. If I was a gambler, that's the one I'd put my money on.'

'Right now,' Frank mutters, 'we're all gamblers.'

Fleming stays behind to try to organize a news blackout. To begin with, the major news stations agree to leave the story alone. But when it becomes clear that it's already travelling across the Internet like a fire sweeping across a dry prairie, they instantly break their promises and the story. As one of the editors says to Rob, with only a hint of regret, once the genie's out of the bottle, it can't be pushed back in.

Rob phones Frank to tell him.

'Shit,' Frank says. 'Well, is there any way we can keep track of how many people are hitting the site? At least that way we'll know when we're out of time.'

'There is, but only if I stay on the site myself.'

'Do it.'

Frank gets to the disused mortuary in New Jersey slightly ahead of the SWAT team. The doors are boarded up, and he kicks them in while the armed snipers are still dispersing around the building.

A wino, sleeping off a bottle of Thunderbird in the derelict building, gets the shock of his life.

Frank phones through to Positano.

'Mike? There's nothing here. Looks like it's Tannersville after all. Take it easy, will you? We're half an hour or so behind you.'

In the prep room, Glenn Furnish croons as he works on Claire's make-up. Occasionally he holds a mirror up for her so she can see his handiwork. She no longer recognizes the person he shows her. Her skin has been toned an ugly, artificial pink. Highlights of rouge in her cheeks make her look like a doll. Her eyelashes stick out straight and stiff as spider's legs.

'They'll get bored,' she says. A strange coldness is numbing her arm from the needle in her forearm. Some of the fluid is already seeping into her from the ancient machine. 'They'll think it's a hoax.'

He shakes his head impatiently. 'They've seen the other pictures. They know I don't hoax my customers.' He stands back. 'Perfect, even if I say so myself. Let's see how the numbers are stacking up, shall we?' He checks the computer. 'Five hundred and eighty three. Welcome, friends. Thank you for your patience. We just have to fill a few more seats, and then the freak show will begin.'

Once they're off the Thruway, the road up into the hills narrows considerably, twisting and turning as it negotiates the foothills of Hunter Mountain. Unable to overtake on the blind corners, the police cars are forced to slow to a more normal pace.

They're not using the radios, in case he's got a scanner tuned to the police frequency. In the lead car, Positano's cellphone rings.

It's Frank. 'Hey, Mike. You got an ETA yet?'

''Bout twenty minutes. We're pushing it as much as we can.'

'OK. I'm right behind you. Listen, Rob hasn't had any luck getting that website off air, but he thinks it might be possible to spam it.'

'Spam it? What's that?'

'If a large number of people all try to hit the site at the same time, it'll crash the software.'

'I thought people hitting the site was what he needed to start the device?'

'Yeah, but it won't be able to cope with more than a few dozen at a time. Rob thinks that if he can get a couple of thousand, the site will just freeze up.'

Positano thinks. 'Won't he kill her anyway?'

'Maybe. Let me speak to Dr Leichtman for a minute.'

Positano hands the phone across. Connie listens, then says, 'Possibly, but he'll waste valuable time trying to fix the problem first. Do it, Frank. It's the best option we've got.'

'Seven hundred and ninety,' Glenn says. He inhales deeply. His nervous, jerky energy has been replaced by a purposeful calm.

Claire's seen that kind of focused energy before, in actors, as pre-performance nerves are gradually replaced by a sense of the inevitable approach of curtain-up.

'OK, Rob. Go ahead and try it,' Frank repeats into his phone.

'Right. I'm going to send a press release and an e-mail simultaneously. We'll ask everyone who wants to help, first to send the e-mail on to five other people, and second, to access the site at exactly six p.m. Eastern Time.'

Frank looks at his watch. 'That's forty minutes away.'

'It has to be six, Frank. That way we get overlap with the West Coast and Europe.'

'OK. Do it. I just hope you're right.'

The police cars pull up a quarter of a mile from the derelict mortuary, their sirens off.

As the guns and armour are being issued, Connie joins the line. Seeing her, Positano comes across.

'You're to stay by the radio,' he says quietly. 'Orders from Frank.'

'Why? I might be able—'

'If there's going to be shooting, you have to stay back. Sorry, but that's the way it is.'

'You ever done Hostage and Negotiation, Mike?'

The detective shakes his head.

'What about these other guys?'

'Them neither.'

'You might need me, then.'

He puts a hand on her shoulder. 'If any kind of negotiation starts up, we'll call for you. But right now, the plan doesn't call for any talking.'

At the rear of the derelict building is a hearse. Positano feels the hood.

'Still warm,' he says quietly. 'He's here all right.'

Silently, the armed policemen begin to creep into position.

Glenn looks at the screen. 'Nine hundred and fifteen participants,' he says gloatingly. 'Not long now, Claire. Not very long at all. Nine hundred and sixteen. Nine hundred and twenty.' He closes his eyes. 'I can feel it coming. Like a wave. Get ready.'

Twenty to six.

As Fleming's e-mail snakes from computer to computer, it subdivides and subdivides again, like a cell after the instant of conception, doubling and redoubling of its own accord. Its components flow from computer to computer, criss-crossing the Atlantic as tiny pulses of light, bouncing from satellite to satellite in the form of radio waves, streams of ethereal dots and dashes that, once reassembled, turn themselves back into words, thoughts and ideas – an appeal for help.

Inside the prep room, Glenn reaches over and turns a switch on the pump. As it chugs into life, she cannot prevent herself from crying out.

'Don't worry,' he says. 'Just making sure it's all primed and ready to go.' His fingers check her restraints. 'And now I shall say my farewells. This piece doesn't require my presence, so I'll leave you.' For an instant his eyes, as clear and untroubled as a child's, gaze down on her. Then he turns the laptop towards her, so that she can see her own face on the screen. 'I'll be watching,' he says.

Then he leaves the room.

She hadn't considered that he might leave her to die without him.

She waits. Silence.

She starts to yell at them, at the unseen watchers lurking behind the camera, at the faceless, digitized, anonymous lusts she can feel sniffing at her; nosing her tentatively, like a pack of dogs gradually creeping towards their prey, ready to scurry back at any moment.

The second hand hoists noiselessly upwards on Positano's watch, like the police siege ladders being hoisted noiselessly against the walls of the old building.

'Now,' he says.

* * *

Claire screams.

The screen of the laptop goes white.

> Internet Explorer is unable to display this page. It may have moved to a different location, or the computer you are connecting to may be busy. Please try connecting later.

From somewhere outside, she hears the sound of breaking glass.

Connie, waiting by the cars, hears someone crashing through the undergrowth. All around her, police radios are crackling into life. She looks up.

Glenn Furnish is standing there, twenty yards away, watching her.

Slowly she raises her gun.

His face betrays no expression, other than mild surprise. Her finger tightens on the trigger.

Behind him there's a shout, and the sound of people coming after him. He turns and crashes off down the hill. For a second, perhaps two, she has him in her sights.

She lowers the gun.

Furnish careers down the hillside, out of control. The ground is uneven, and his pursuers can't get a decent shot, handicapped by their guns and body armour. He's getting away from them by the time he reaches the road. He sprints across it and half jumps, half slides down to the next bend, just as Frank comes around it at the head of the second cavalcade of police cars. There's an impact, and for

372

a moment Furnish is spread across the windscreen as the car fishtails out of control and slides down the hillside sideways. Then Frank draws his gun and shoots him twice through the glass. The glass turns first crazy like a cobweb, and then red, before the whole screen collapses in on him and the young man falls through onto Frank's lap. His lips form a word, and he whispers something, or tries to, but Frank's second bullet has punctured his lung, and his voice has no pressure behind it to speak the words: just an empty hiss, like air escaping from a balloon.

CHAPTER FIFTY-SEVEN

Five days later, Claire flies to France with Christian.

Within hours of Furnish's death, journalists were camping on Christian's doorstep. The NYPD offered them a safe house for as long as they needed it, but it seemed just as easy to bring the wedding forward and escape. They chose the dress together, Christian apparently unbothered by the superstition that to see it before the wedding day would bring bad luck. She guesses that, on the contrary, he's in the grip of a more personal hex: that, if she were to get hold of the pictures from his previous wedding, she would find that Stella had worn just such a dress to speak her ill-fated vows.

There is a distance between herself and Christian now. Not that he isn't solicitous about her well-being – on the contrary, he clearly still feels racked with guilt that he wasn't with her when the killer struck – but a part of her has withdrawn from him, replaying the events of that strange afternoon on an endless loop of film, so much more vivid and intense than what is happening here and now. She still has a ringing in her ears from the stun grenades the police used as they stormed the

its headquarters down here, and some of the galleries used to be mushroom farms. But it was in the eighteenth century that they had the bright idea of freeing up building land by moving the cemeteries down.' He shines his light at the roof. Some words have been carved into the rockface. '*Arrêtez! C'est ici l'empire de la mort,*' he reads aloud. 'Here is the kingdom of the dead.' He steps forward. 'Ready?'

'I guess,' she says doubtfully.

She directs her torch all around her. At first she thinks she's in quite a narrow space. Then she realizes that the gallery they've stepped into is actually huge. What she had taken for walls are actually piles of human skulls, and other bones, black with age, that rise as far as her torch can reach.

'These are the remains of six million Parisians, probably more than there are in the city above us. Everyone from Rabelais to Robespierre.'

Slowly, they walk through empty limestone chambers as high as churches. Some are lit by openings high above them, through which the evening sunshine falls.

At last Christian stops. 'Here,' he says, gesturing.

They are at the top of some steps which have been carved into the rock. Below them is a vast, clear pool of water.

'The workers who quarried here needed to bathe. So they simply dug down to the water table. Look.' He leads the way, scoops up a handful of water and lets it pour through his fingers. 'It's purer than Evian and twice as old.' He puts the torch down and holds out his hand to her. 'Shall we bathe?'

'Won't it be cold?'

'Almost freezing.' He starts to unbutton her clothes. 'There's a towel in my backpack. As well as some essentials.' He takes out a silver candelabra and three candles, a half-bottle of Château Yquem and glasses, a sliver of foie gras and a fresh baguette. 'Pleasure and pain.'

'In that case . . .' She steps out of her clothes, and he does the same. The candles throw a yellow glow over the cavern, their flickering fingers gouging the rocky walls. Even before she gets into the pool it's cold. Her skin dimples with goose bumps. She gasps as she extends a foot into the pool.

'Come,' he says, and steps into the water. It reaches up to his thighs. 'A baptism,' he says softly. 'And a rebirth. Here, in the empire of the dead, we are still alive.' He reaches for her, lifting her to him with strong arms. Despite the cold, he's erect. Her legs touch the icy water and involuntarily she raises them up, clasping them around his hips.

'Put me inside you,' he whispers. She reaches down and angles him so that he can push into her. She's cold and tense, and she winces as he pulls her all the way onto him.

He makes love to her gently, and she wraps one arm around his neck to take some weight and let him use his hands to guide her movements. She starts to moan, and in the complete silence it's as startling as the sound of a stranger. 'Now,' he says, 'trust me.'

In one fluid motion he bends at the waist, letting her fall backwards into the water, his hands holding her under the surface as easily as they had supported her above it. The shock of the freezing water drives the air from her lungs and she swallows some, chokes on it and tries to come back up to breathe. But his hands are still holding her down. Through the water she can see his face, see how carefully he's watching her, and then his hands are round her neck, and even if she wanted to she couldn't breathe, couldn't swallow yet more water. The hammering in her lungs and the hammering in her sex are somehow connected, are somehow joining together, each thrust of his cock pounding behind her ears, her eyes, lighting up the limestone cavern with fiery Catherine wheels, sky rockets and lightning bolts of pain.

Afterwards, he rocks her in his arms, caresses her and wipes the bloody snot off her face gently with his hand.

'Thank you,' he whispers. 'Thank you for going there with me.'

She isn't sure whether he means this place, or the dark catacombs in his head.

Yet if he intended, quite literally, to lay her ghosts to rest, it seems to have succeeded. The shock of the freezing water and the violence of his need have cleared some of the cobwebs from her brain, and slowly she starts to come to life again. He takes her to the haunts he knows best – the tiny cobbled streets of the African Quarter, where they eat couscous in crowded bars, full of noise and the stench of cheap French cigarettes, drinking rough wine from unmarked carafes. There are hookahs bubbling in the café windows, their mouthpieces tipped with silver foil in a token gesture at twentieth-century hygiene, and he shows her how to smoke them, pulling the hot smoke through a bath of spirits to smooth the taste. It's thick as the smoke of a cheroot, a powerful surge of nicotine and alcohol that, after just a couple of pulls, leaves her dizzy and lightheaded.

'Wait here,' Christian says, and he goes to the zinc counter at the back of the room to have a muttered conversation with the proprietor. When he returns, it's with an unmarked bottle in his hand.

'Absinthe,' he says, pouring her a shot of lurid green liquid. 'Just to complete the decadent experience. It contains a mild hallucinogen made from wormwood. You know what Oscar Wilde said about this stuff? "After the first glass you see the world as you wish it was. After the second, you see things as they are not. And after the third glass you see things as they really are." ' He takes a spoonful of sugar from the bowl on the table, dips it into the green liquid and holds it over the flame of the candle. As the sugar starts to bubble and caramelize, he stirs it into the absinthe.

'If we're getting married tomorrow,' she says, lifting her glass, 'shouldn't we be trying to avoid hangovers?'

'Unlike Baudelaire, we have access to ibuprofen. *Salut!*'

'*Salut,*' she says. 'I love you.'

They take the bottle back to the hotel. She can remember nothing about the rest of the day, just a vague recollection of pulsing colours, rollercoaster vertigo and Christian reciting Verlaine and Rimbaud while her brain expands seamlessly, like helium.

*　*　*

The next morning they go to the American Embassy to pick up their paperwork. They spend over three hours negotiating the elegant labyrinth of French bureaucracy, then just three or four minutes at the town hall being married by a representative of the *maire*, the mayor. Married by the *maire* – the words seem to go round and round in her brain. Maybe she's still a little high. The service is all in French, of course, and occasionally she loses her way, so that Christian has to prompt her when it's time to say her vows.

The *maire* is looking at her expectantly, and she realizes that something else is required of her: her hand. Christian reaches for it, produces a ring from his breast pocket and slides it down her finger. Not a conventional wedding ring, but an antique signet ring of heavy white gold, bearing the same family markings as the torc around her neck and the ring on Christian's finger.

The *maire* speaks more words. Her French isn't really good enough to follow this, either, though she catches the odd word. She can tell by the cadences when he's winding up. She looks at her hand, twisting the ring from side to side.

Then Christian is kissing her and the *maire* is all smiles. More paperwork, and then they're outside, and Christian is hailing a cab, bustling her back to the hotel for more sex.

He sees her looking at the ring. 'Do you like it?'

'It's heavy,' she admits.

'It's very precious to me,' he says. 'As are you.'

In a dream, she allows herself to be carried over the threshold of her room, laid on the bed and fucked in all her finery. There is a candlestick beside their bed, and somehow it doesn't seem at all strange that Christian should break off making love to light the candle and rub some ointment into her right thigh, high up on the inside; heat up her new wedding ring in the yellow cuticle of the flame and press the glowing metal against her now-numbed skin, so that she will always be marked there by his family crest.

Afterwards he sleeps. Quietly, she slips out of bed and, wincing, pulls on some loose-fitting clothes. She takes her passport and a little money.

She walks stiffly down to the concierge on the front desk and asks for directions to the nearest police station.

'Is there a problem?' the concierge wonders. 'Has madame perhaps suffered a theft?'

'The nearest police station,' she repeats. The concierge, shrugging, tells her how to get to a gendarmerie a few minutes' walk from the hotel. Although, as she limps away, it occurs to him that, in Madame Vogler's case, it might take rather longer than that. *Eh bien.* She's just got married. Perhaps her husband was a little too energetic with his nuptials. He smiles to himself, picturing the scene.

And when the lady's husband comes down twenty minutes later, the concierge sees no reason not to tell him where his wife has gone.

CHAPTER FIFTY-EIGHT

She demands a detective, and the man who comes to see her after what seems like an age is both impossibly good-looking and impossibly well dressed, his dark green shirt and lighter tie hanging on him elegantly. He looks, she thinks, more like a young doctor than a cop.

'So, tell me what I may do for you' – he looks down at his notes – 'Mrs Vogler.' His English, thank God, is good.

'I've just found out that my husband is a murderer,' she says.

'I see,' he says impassively. 'Who has he murdered?'

'His last wife. Her name was Stella.'

'Do you have any proof?'

She slides the ring off her finger and puts it on the table between them. The policeman picks it up. 'A ring?'

'His first wife was murdered in New York. When her body was found there was no jewellery on it. I saw her wearing this ring myself, earlier the same evening.'

He raises one eyebrow. 'You knew his first wife?'

'I met her only once. But I noticed the ring.'

'It's . . . *distinctif*,' he agrees, turning it over in his hand. 'For a man, *ne c'est pas*?'

'It's a signet ring. It's been in his family for a long time. Look,' she takes off the torc and shows him. 'It's the same design.'

Another man, also impossibly well dressed, comes in and whispers in the first policeman's ear. The first policeman looks up. 'Your husband is outside.'

'You must arrest him. Then you can talk to the detectives in New York. Detective Durban and Detective Positano. Weeks, Lowell. Tell them I've got the ring. Tell them he branded me with it. They'll understand.'

'He . . . branded you?' The policeman looks puzzled. 'I'm sorry, my English . . .'

'Hot. Burn. Szzzz.' She mimes the sizzle of a hot brand on flesh.

'Wait here,' he says.

She waits. She waits for an hour. The wound on her thigh grows a blister, a thin red dome of scalded flesh. She tries not to touch it.

Eventually the policeman returns. He sits down opposite her and blows his lips out. He smiles at her; he has nice eyes.

'So,' he says, 'I have talked to your husband.'

'Have you arrested him?'

He holds up a hand. 'Wait a minute. He tells me you were recently in a hospital in America. Is that right?'

'That's right.'

'You were prescribed some drugs, I think. Some *médication*.'

She nods.

'Are you still taking your drugs?'

She shakes her head hopelessly. 'I didn't need them,' she says. 'It was all a mistake.'

'Your husband is very worried about you, I think,' he says gently. 'He is going to arrange for you to see a doctor at the hotel.'

'No,' she says. 'You can't do that. He'll kill me.'

The policeman smiles. 'This is your wedding day,' he says gently. 'It is a big day. A big strain, yes? And you have been drinking absinthe. Your husband has told me this. Absinthe is not a legal drink in France today. Too many people were . . .' He makes a gesture to indicate a disease of the mind. 'Go home, Mrs Vogler. Your husband will look after you.'

She stands up. 'He did this,' she says. She drops her trousers to show him her thigh.

'Your husband says you burned yourself deliberately, with a cigarette,' he says calmly. 'He will buy some cream at the pharmacy. Please, madame. Cover yourself up.'

Meekly, she allows herself to be taken from the police station, to be escorted into a taxi. He strokes her hair, crooning to her. 'My precious, my precious. What were you thinking of?'

On the way back, he stops the taxi to make some purchases from a pharmacy and the garage next to it. When he gets back into the taxi he has a large bag in his hands.

At the hotel, he locks the door of their room and runs a bath for her. She waits, numbly, for it to fill. 'Come here,' he calls gently. She goes into the bathroom. He is stirring the water with his hand. Not too hot, not too cold.

Obediently, she undresses and steps into the water. Though the water is cool, the blister on her thigh stings. She lies down and he washes her, tenderly, as he washed her the first time they made love, soaping her hair and rinsing it. When he has finished, he brings her the bottle of absinthe.

'Drink this.'

She takes a long gulp.

'It will take away the pain,' he says. She doesn't know if he means the pain in her thigh, or the pain of what is coming next.

'I didn't get it quite right, did I?' she says. 'I thought it was Stella who'd had enough, that she was tired being adored by you. But it was you, not her, who wanted an end to it. Like Baudelaire, who found it easier to worship a goddess than to love a woman. Did she phone the apartment from her hotel? Is that how you knew where she was that night? You've already told me you were going through her e-mails.'

He looks at her with an expression of infinite regret. 'It was more than that,' he says quietly. 'It was someone I met. A stranger, a girl in a bar. She read to me, one of my own translations, and her voice . . . It was a perfect moment, a revelation, complete and unrepeatable. That was when I saw that it was over with Stella.'

'You killed her. You went to that hotel room and you killed her.'

'Yes,' he says. 'Yes, I killed her. And then she was perfect again.'

The room next door is very crowded. There's the assault team from the CRS – the French special force – in full riot gear, nursing their tear-gas guns and stun grenades. There's Connie Leichtman and other observers from the FBI. There's the surveillance team provided by the French authorities, including the policeman who stood in for the *maire*. And there's Frank, feeling naked without a gun of his own, pressed up against the wall, a pair of headphones clamped to his head.

The captain of the CRS is also wearing head-phones, but the captain's English isn't good, and it's Frank he's looking to for a signal. He raises an eyebrow.

Frank holds up his hand, palm outwards. Wait.

'Not perfect,' she says. 'Passive. She wasn't Stella any more, not after the things you did to her. She was just a body. Just flesh.'

'Don't spoil this,' he croons. 'Don't let's argue, Claire.'

'You were one of his customers,' she says flatly. 'Charon's. That virtual edition of *Les Fleurs du Mal* was for you.'

'A fitting tribute to the poems.' He picks up a book from where it lies on the floor. 'Read one,' he says. 'Read one out loud for me, like you did that first time.'

She looks at the page he has marked and, in a flat toneless voice, she begins to read.

I have more memories than if I had lived a
    thousand years.
An old cabinet stuffed with dead ideas –
bundles of abandoned verses, old receipts and
    bills,

dusty locks of hair, and long-forgotten wills –
is not more full of secrets than my aching head.

It's a sarcophagus, an immense grave where the
     dead,
those bodies I have loved, are tumbled willy-nilly,
prodded and nudged incessantly
by morbid reveries, like worms:
It's a house of shuttered, closed-up rooms
where closets full of wedding clothes
are slowly pulled to lace by moths.

She lets the book fall from her fingers into the water. Christian is weeping. He weeps as he opens a canister of petrol and lets the liquid flow into the bath. It floats on the water, a greasy, iridescent slick. Rainbows lap at her skin. He sets a box of matches on the side of the bath.

'I won't hurt you,' he says. He laces his fingers around her neck. 'No pain. I promise.'

'Now,' Frank screams. '*Allez, allez.*' The captain turns and shouts to his men. For a fraction of a second, nothing happens. Then—

The room explodes. It fills with serge-blue uniforms and men in riot gear and shouting in two languages at once.

Christian turns and takes a step backwards. One of the CRS immediately looses a tear-gas round, and the room fills with acrid smoke, from which only the policemen in their riot masks are protected.

Claire, pulled from the lethal bath by Connie and Frank, cowers on the floor, wet and naked, her bruised throat choking on the fumes. Stinging tears come quickly to her eyes.

Or perhaps – who knows? – they were there already.

CHAPTER FIFTY-NINE

La Martine, just outside Lyon, has a long and chequered history. Originally a lunatic asylum, it was used by the Gestapo during the war as an interrogation centre. Now a prison, it houses some of Europe's most high-security prisoners, including, by an ironic twist of fate, some of those same Nazis whose victims were once tortured there. Perhaps because of its proximity to Interpol headquarters, it has become the nearest thing there is to a prison of the world.

Dr Constance Leichtman arrives there one frosty morning in early December, as so many have done before her, to conduct an interrogation. She's shown into a small pastel-coloured room where, once upon a time, the questioners used lengths of rubber hose, baths full of shit and piss, truncheons and thumbscrews. She's brought a pen and paper, a small recording device and a pack of cigarettes.

Christian Vogler is brought in. He's wearing the prison uniform, loose-fitting jeans and a denim jacket. In one hand, he carries a pack of Gauloises and a lighter.

'I brought you some more cigarettes,' she says. 'I'd heard you were smoking now.'

'Everyone smokes in here,' he says. 'It isn't like America.' He sits down opposite her.

'Are they treating you well?'

He shrugs. 'It's tolerable.'

She lights a cigarette herself, then holds out the flame to his. 'I've got a proposition, Christian.'

'Yes?'

'They'll have to decide in which country you're to stand trial. It could be America, it could be here. Here is better for you, I think. Remember Jeffrey Dahmer, murdered by another convict? They're rather more civilized here. I'll bet they can't even bring themselves to serve you terrible coffee.'

He waits for her to continue.

'I could arrange for you to stay here, perhaps. While I study you.'

He blows a slug of ash from the end of his cigarette onto the floor. 'Study me?'

'Your relationship with Charon. I want to know how it worked. Who fed off who? Did you see yourselves as artist and patron, or as fellow artists working in different media? Would your own desires have remained unrealized if it hadn't been for the images he created? There's a lot of material here, Christian. If you give it to me, if you're seen to be co-operating, it might help.'

He thinks for a while. 'I have some questions, too.'

'Then, as a fellow academic, I will try to answer them.'

'About Claire mostly.' He looks away from her. In the windowless room the smoke gathers in thick, soft layers, like skeins of wool. 'How much of it was real?'

'Ah.'

He waits.

'She's a remarkable person, Christian. Finding her was the key. Right at the beginning of all this, I spent several days with her. I had to make sure she hadn't been involved in Stella's death herself, of course, but I also wanted to see how strong she was. That was when I realized the extent of her talents – and of her courage.'

She looks around for an ashtray. There isn't one, so she flicks ash onto the floor. 'She was studying a kind of Method acting, you know. She was very committed to that approach, the idea that an actor must inhabit a fictional character with absolute authenticity. She agreed to put herself in my hands without reservation. I told her the part she would have to play, but other than that, she had no idea what was going to happen.'

'And what was that part?'

'I told her she had to fall in love with you.'

He seems to sigh, though it might just have been a long release of smoke. 'What about the hospital? The drugs she took? The disorders the doctors said she was suffering from?'

'We needed you to be convinced that she was no longer working for us. As I said, she was prepared to inhabit the role with absolute authenticity. She'd been in something similar in England, you see, so I knew she could carry it off.'

He nods, thoughtfully. 'You followed us to France, of course.'

'Yes. After the scare Charon gave us, we couldn't take any more risks.'

'I did wonder why all the taxi drivers were being so friendly,' he murmurs. 'And what about the marriage?'

'You're not married, Christian. The ceremony you went through had no legal standing. Not that Claire knew that, either, at the time. She had to trust us completely.'

'As you say, a remarkable actress.' He glances at her. 'As are you.'

'I'm no actress, Christian.'

'Not in the real world, perhaps. But in the virtual one . . . You're one of the players, aren't you? One of the characters down there in Necropolis.'

'Care to guess which one?'

'I've been giving it some thought. You're Helios, aren't you? The Greek god of light. Dr Leichtman.'

She nods.

'An unusual way of conducting a scientific study, if you don't mind me saying. It's hardly common for the scientist to be one of the rats as well. I suppose you were in communication with Charon, weren't you? Telling him what to do. When to kill. Jerking his strings.' He sits back and crosses his arms. 'A part of you must be quite upset he's dead. Creatures like that are rather magnificent, aren't they?'

Connie pauses before she says, 'The Internet is a powerful new weapon for us, Christian. All the data you could ever need, if you can just get hold of it.' She exhales smoke from the corners of her mouth, sabre-toothed. 'And now we have even more data. Nearly a thousand people accessed Charon's website to participate in his little snuff show. All of them will be logged, traced, followed up and assessed. The ones who seem as if they might develop into killers themselves will be invited into the hidden parts of Necropolis, where we can keep a closer eye on them.'

'Poor bastards,' he says. 'But I notice that you didn't answer my question.'

'No,' she says. 'And now it's your turn to answer some of mine. Let me set up this microphone and we can get started.'

They remain inside the little cell all day. Within a couple of hours, her cigarettes are finished, and she starts reaching across the table to share his.

Her friend hasn't showed.

That's what you'd think if you saw her, waiting on her own at the bar of the Royalton, trying to make her Virgin Mary last all evening: just another young professional waiting for her date. Perhaps a little prettier than most. A little more confident. A little more daringly dressed. She hasn't come straight from the office, that's for sure.

The bar is packed, and when a table finally becomes free, she goes and sits at it, putting her drink on the table and her bag on the other seat, to keep it unoccupied.

'Excuse me?'

She looks up. There's a man standing in front of her.

'This is my table. I just went to the restroom.' He points. 'I left my drink to keep my place.'

Around them, one or two heads have turned curiously in their direction. But there's going to be no confrontation, no overspill of New York stress. The woman is grinning.

'Hey, Frank. What kept you?'

'Hey, Claire.' He picks the bag off the chair and hands it to her so he can sit down. 'Just paperwork. Jesus, I thought our system was bureaucratic, but the French . . . Which reminds me.' He takes a large manila envelope out of his jacket and slides it across the table. 'Those papers you wanted. It's all there. Just send it to Immigration, they'll do the rest.'

'Thanks.' She drops the envelope into her bag.

'So.' Frank looks around. 'What do I have to do to get a beer around here?'

She shakes her head. 'Uh-uh. Curtain's up in ten minutes. And I absolutely refuse to be late. These tickets are like gold dust.'

He sighs. 'This is the guy who had you audition for his next project, right?'

'The same.'

'Then I guess we'd better go and check him out.' He doesn't get up yet, though. 'I assume you got the part?'

She makes a rocking movement with her hand. 'Maybe. Maybe not. I'll know in a couple of weeks.'

He laughs. 'Come on. I know you better than that, Claire. I bet you were terrific.'

'I wasn't bad,' she says. 'No, I wasn't bad.'

And she smiles, and after a moment he smiles, too, because they both know the truth is a little different from that.

'In that case,' he says, getting to his feet, 'after you, Miss Rodenburg.'

THE END

ACKNOWLEDGEMENTS

Many people helped with the research for this book. In particular, I wish to thank the distinguished pathologists and morticians around the world who responded to e-mail enquiries from a total stranger with grace and forbearance. The late Professor Chao of Singapore's Institute of Science and Forensic Medicine was a mine of useful information, as were the many helpful voices on www.funeral.net.

This book would not have been written were it not for two very different accounts of the decoy operation that followed the murder of Rachel Nickell on Wimbledon Common in 1997: *The Jigsaw Man*, by Paul Britton, and *Who Really Killed Rachel?* by Colin Stagg and David Kessler. I hope that all those involved will forgive my using a real-life tragedy as the germ of my fiction. I am also indebted to several books on acting and stagecraft, particularly the writings of Keith Johnstone and Patsy Rodenburg.

Many friends read this book in its early drafts. I especially want to thank Michael Ward, Clark Morgan and Paul Philips for advice on all things

American; Natasha Taylor and Anthea Willey for invaluable help with Baudelaire's *Les Fleurs du Mal*; Mandy Wheeler for advice on acting; Clive Tanqueray for his enthusiasm; the inhabitants of VirtualChicago for insights into MUDs, MUSEs, netsex and netiquette; Brian Innes for his forensic expertise; Ian Wylie and Siân Griffiths for their support; and, most of all, my agents Caradoc King and Sam North at AP Watt for their seemingly limitless ability to pretend that there was nothing they would rather do than read *The Decoy* one more time.

This book is dedicated to Michael Durban, who will never read this, but thanks anyway.

THE POISON TREE
by Tony Strong

In the wake of a failed marriage and a misguided love affair, feisty academic Terry Williams moves to Oxford to resume her abandoned doctorate in detective fiction. But her new home, a terraced house on quiet Osney Island, was previously the scene of a savage sexual murder, and Terry soon finds the past returning to invade the present with horrific consequences.

A traumatized stray cat which eats its own babies, a famous neighbour involved in a hushed-up sexual scandal, and the discovery of a series of pornographic letters all serve to involve Terry in a mystery more brutal and more elusive than any tackled by the fictional detectives she studies.

'A debut to die for'
The Times

A Bantam Paperback
0553 50542 4

THE DEATH PIT
by Tony Strong

When young academic Terry Williams goes to a remote corner of the Scottish Highlands, she's simply intending to edit the letters of Catherine McCulloch, tortured and burnt as a witch in the seventeenth century. But then the body of a young woman is found on a local farm, dumped in the death pit amidst a pile of rotting pigs. She is Donna Fairhead, one of a nearby community of Wiccans – modern-day witches.

As forensic excavation of the death pit throws up yet more horrors, Terry's work on the letters reveals that there may have been more to Catherine's death than anyone had ever imagined. And as the present-day death toll mounts, Terry realizes that the identity of the killer may also be part of a three-centuries-old mystery, a mystery whose next victim might well be herself. . .

'Excellent . . . the ending chills'
Sunday Times

A Bantam Paperback
0553 50543 2

A SELECTION OF CRIME AND MYSTERY
NOVELS AVAILABLE FROM BANTAM BOOKS

THE PRICES SHOWN BELOW WERE CORRECT AT THE TIME OF GOING TO PRESS. HOWEVER
TRANSWORLD PUBLISHERS RESERVE THE RIGHT TO SHOW NEW RETAIL PRICES ON COVERS
WHICH MAY DIFFER FROM THOSE PREVIOUSLY ADVERTISED IN THE TEXT OR ELSEWHERE.

81184 3	THE DEAD OF WINTER	*Lisa Appignanesi*	£5.99
81187 8	SANCTUARY	*Lisa Appignanesi*	£5.99
81244 0	DARKNESS PEERING	*Alice Blanchard*	£5.99
50540 8	KILLING FLOOR	*Lee Child*	£5.99
50541 6	DIE TRYING	*Lee Child*	£5.99
04393 6	TRIPWIRE	*Lee Child*	£5.99
81188 6	THE VISITOR	*Lee Child*	£5.99
17510 6	A GREAT DELIVERANCE	*Elizabeth George*	£5.99
40168 8	A SUITABLE VENGEANCE	*Elizabeth George*	£6.99
40237 4	FOR THE SAKE OF ELENA	*Elizabeth George*	£5.99
40846 1	IN THE PRESENCE OF THE ENEMY	*Elizabeth George*	£5.99
40238 2	MISSING JOSEPH	*Elizabeth George*	£6.99
17511 4	PAYMENT IN BLOOD	*Elizabeth George*	£5.99
40845 3	PLAYING FOR THE ASHES	*Elizabeth George*	£6.99
40167 X	WELL-SCHOOLED IN MURDER	*Elizabeth George*	£5.99
81265 3	BIRDMAN	*Mo Hayder*	£5.99
50385 5	A DRINK BEFORE THE WAR	*Dennis Lehane*	£5.99
50584 X	DARKNESS, TAKE MY HAND	*Dennis Lehane*	£5.99
81220 3	GONE, BABY, GONE	*Dennis Lehane*	£5.99
50585 8	SACRED	*Dennis Lehane*	£5.99
81221 1	PRAYERS FOR RAIN	*Dennis Lehane*	£5.99
81222 X	MYSTIC RIVER	*Dennis Lehane*	£5.99
50694 3	GARNETHILL	*Denise Mina*	£5.99
81327 7	EXILE	*Denise Mina*	£5.99
50586 6	FAREWELL TO THE FLESH	*Gemma O'Connor*	£5.99
50587 4	TIME TO REMEMBER	*Gemma O'Connor*	£5.99
81263 7	SINS OF OMISSION	*Gemma O'Connor*	£5.99
81262 9	FALLS THE SHADOW	*Gemma O'Connor*	£5.99
81258 0	WALKING ON WATER	*Gemma O'Connor*	£5.99
81211 4	LOVE IS A RACKET	*John Ridley*	£5.99
81215 7	EVERYBODY SMOKES IN HELL	*John Ridley*	£5.99
50542 4	THE POISON TREE	*Tony Strong*	£5.99
50543 2	THE DEATH PIT	*Tony Strong*	£5.99

All Transworld titles are available by post from:
Bookpost, PO Box 29, Douglas, Isle of Man, IM99 1BQ
Credit cards accepted. Please telephone 01624 836000,
fax 01624 837033, Internet http://www.bookpost.co.uk
or e-mail: bookshop@enterprise.net for details.
Free postage and packing in the UK. Overseas customers: allow
£1 per book (paperbacks) and £3 per book (hardbacks).